Praise for Josephine Carr's
The Dewey Decimal System of Love

"Don't let a celibate librarian fool you—Alison Sheffield sizzles with sexuality. She is a refreshingly original, hilarious character who will have you up until the wee hours laughing and cheering. If you like sex and books (though perhaps not in that order), *The Dewey Decimal System of Love* is your number."

—Sarah Strohmeyer, author of *Bubbles Betrothed*

"A deliciously delightful debut with a dollop of devilishness you'll adore. It's a sweet, savory story about a lovelorn librarian who decides to reinvent herself in the pursuit of happiness. The heroine is witty, wise, and self-aware, and I want her to be my new best friend. Everybody who has ever cuddled up in the library with a wonderful book is going to want to put on some great music and be carried away by this delightful read."

—Nancy Martin, author of *Cross Your Heart and Hope to Die*

"A luscious one-sitting read. Deliciously funny and screamingly real—I didn't want it to end! Josephine Carr is an auto-buy. Don't. Miss. This. Book."

—Stephanie Bond, author of *Whole Lotta Trouble*

"A romantic comedy with a hint of mystery that confronts celibacy with laughter."

—Amanda Brown, author of *Legally Blonde* and *Family Trust*

"Carr has a knack for quirky characters." —*Kirkus Reviews*

continued . . .

"Carr's tale sparkles with sharp, clever, and occasionally earthy humor, and sassy, unconventional Ally is a terrific protagonist. . . . Much of the pleasure in this wonderfully amusing novel comes from Carr's realistic depiction of the everyday pleasures and occasional downsides to working in a library; her wonderfully quirky, all too real characters, and her delightfully acerbic prose."

—*Booklist*

"A strange and uniquely comic work . . . a most bizarre, unpredictable, and thoroughly delightful mess that keeps the pages turning and the laughs coming." —*The Tampa Tribune*

"Carr's quirky characters, screwball sense of humor, and right-on descriptions are marvelous, making the journey to the satisfying ending well worth the trip. . . . Hilarious. . . . The zingy, thoroughly modern tone and the exceptionally appealing heroine should catch the attention of readers who like their romances lively, smart, and funny." —*Library Journal*

OTHER BOOKS BY JOSEPHINE CARR

The Dewey Decimal System of Love

MY VERY OWN MURDER

Josephine Carr

New American Library

New American Library
Published by New American Library, a division of
Penguin Group (USA) Inc., 375 Hudson Street,
New York, New York 10014, USA
Penguin Group (Canada), 90 Eglinton Avenue East, Suite 700, Toronto,
Ontario, Canada M4P 2Y3 (a division of Pearson Penguin Canada Inc.)
Penguin Books Ltd., 80 Strand, London WC2R 0RL, England
Penguin Ireland, 25 St. Stephen's Green, Dublin 2,
Ireland (a division of Penguin Books Ltd.)
Penguin Group (Australia), 250 Camberwell Road, Camberwell, Victoria 3124,
Australia (a division of Pearson Australia Group Pty. Ltd.)
Penguin Books India Pvt. Ltd., 11 Community Centre, Panchsheel Park,
New Delhi - 110 017, India
Penguin Group (NZ), cnr Airborne and Rosedale Roads, Albany,
Auckland 1310, New Zealand (a division of Pearson New Zealand Ltd.)
Penguin Books (South Africa) (Pty.) Ltd., 24 Sturdee Avenue,
Rosebank, Johannesburg 2196, South Africa

Penguin Books Ltd., Registered Offices: 80 Strand, London WC2R 0RL, England

First published by New American Library, a division of Penguin Group (USA) Inc.

First Printing, September 2005
10 9 8 7 6 5 4 3 2 1

LIBRARY OF CONGRESS CATALOGING IN PUBLICATION DATA:

Carr, Josephine.
My very own murder / Josephine Carr.
p. cm.
ISBN 0-451-21646-6
1. Women detectives—Washington (D.C.)—Fiction. 2. Washington (D.C.)—Fiction.
3. Middle aged women—Fiction. 4. Apartment houses—Fiction. 5. Women domestics—Fiction.
6. Divorced women—Fiction. 7. Parities—Fiction. I. Title.
PS3553.A76323M9 2005
813'.54—dc22 2005008399

Printed in the United States of America

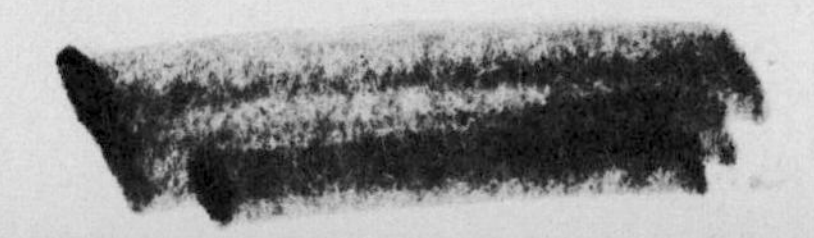

For Elliot,
my forever friend

Acknowledgments

To my entire family, spread wide like the fingers of two hands, I send my gratitude and love. I am thankful for the friendship and support of my children's father, Elliot, and I offer special thanks to our kids, Rachel and Daniel. You guys make me laugh and think . . . what more could a mother ask for?

I appreciate the enthusiasm of my agent, Stephanie Kip Rostan, and the great publishing team at NAL, including Ellen Edwards and Serena Jones.

Much of this novel was written at Politics & Prose Bookstore in Washington, D.C. Here's to the café staff for providing good coffee and turning up the heat when needed!

Finally, please note: This novel is fiction. Any resemblance to me, or to members of my family, is a figment of your own overactive imagination.

As a requirement of the newly divorced, only-just-fifty-year-old woman, I was supposed to be miserable, yet brave. After all, women of my age and situation knew they would either die alone or remarry a man twenty years their senior. Which is to say, seventy years and, possibly, older. Nothing wrong with a seventy-year-old man, other than bandy legs and no hair. I mean, no hair anywhere. Anywhere. But, no, to the disappointment of my friends and family, particularly my ex-husband, I was not miserable. Therefore, I had no requirement to be brave, either.

My divorce became final four months ago, about the time I left the family home. Soon after, my youngest child, Laura, began her freshman year at Juilliard and my son, her older brother, Andrew, started his final year at Swarthmore. Let's call this the happily-ever-after divorce story, because who ever said you *needed* someone to get old with? Since I had children who loved me, now all I really had to worry about was sex, and to be frank, you could always *buy* sex. It was a commodity. Besides, I had many reasons to smile.

To begin, I was comfortably well-off, though I confess that this wasn't due to my own hard work. My grandmother had left our small family about $5 million. Not enough to set up a foundation, when divided by five, so we each got a significant sum. And my share from the divorce settlement guaranteed a solid future financially. I used to have a career called motherhood. I was good at it, but retirement had come early, compared to the trajectory of other career paths.

After all, I was only fifty years old and well educated. A lot to offer yet. I was sure that I had just embarked on a fulfilling journey from marriage and motherhood to . . . question mark. I didn't know what would come next, which could have been slightly anxiety-provoking except that I refused to let it be. Also, I had to admit that dwelling in the no-man's land of No Man seemed infinitely superior to my role as a wife. For someone whose identity had been partially defined by the term *wife,* I'd been remarkably bad at the job. I was relieved at not having to act the part any longer.

I loathed going out to lunch, but on Saturday I lunched with one of my husband's best friends, Jonathan, at a small Lebanese restaurant on Connecticut Avenue in northwest Washington, D.C.

"You might consider volunteering," he said.

"Or I could shoot myself." I stared at him, wondering why I'd ever imagined having lunch with Jonathan would be a good idea. Maybe I'd been flattered by his invitation because his wife, Abigail, was out of town, visiting family. Maybe he was interested in me.

His bushy gray eyebrows shot up, and he burst out laughing. "What's wrong with volunteer work?"

"It's tedious."

"You're supposed to give back to society, as a sign of your thankfulness for all that you've received," he lectured.

"I thought about giving away all my money."

He blinked. "That's not what I meant."

"I know it's not what you meant." I grabbed my iced tea and took a hefty gulp. If I gave away all my money, I wouldn't be able to afford fancy lunches, and even though I didn't particularly relish the ladies-who-lunch tradition, I preferred that my options remain open. So I changed my mind. I looked at Jonathan as though he were a stranger. I decided, at that moment, what I needed to do: sleep with every man I possibly could.

"Would you like to go to bed with me?" I asked, hoping that he had no plans for the rest of the afternoon. He had a potbelly, but I've never been picky about a man's physical appearance.

Jonathan blinked again. "Your ex-husband, Peter, would kill me. Otherwise I couldn't possibly refuse."

"Peter slept with Abigail." Peter *had* slept with Abigail, but this was supposed to be a secret.

Jonathan's face turned from florid to virginal white. Pure as snow. I thought he might keel over and land in the pea soup. Instead he threw back his head and guffawed. "Good one," he yelled.

Abigail wasn't exactly a femme fatale. He figured I was joking. I wasn't, of course, but I decided to accept the judgment and get through lunch quickly.

My vast apartment at the Kennedy, several blocks up from the restaurant on Connecticut Avenue, welcomed me home quietly. I wandered to the bay window overlooking the fall colors of Rock Creek Park and the zoo. I gazed out so long without blinking that my eyes filled with tears. The heavy lunch, and Jonathan himself, had left me vaguely nauseated and out of sorts.

Perhaps it had been a mistake to choose one of the largest apartments at the Kennedy. I often felt like I was the kitchen catchall drawer where keys, stubby pencils, rubber bands, paper clips, hairscrunchies, and mismatched earrings accumulated. Though, unlike that drawer, my apartment was organized and pristine. I tried to mess it up sometimes, to suggest that a lot of living was going on. Only that morning, I'd dared to leave my bed unmade. And the down cushions on the couch in the library were flattened from where I'd sat the night before watching television. Still, I bopped around the apartment like a wildly bouncing pinball, sending out little dinging noises.

During the previous two years, I'd volunteered like a madwoman, something I hadn't bothered to mention to Jonathan.

He'd probably been set up for the lunch by Peter as a spy mission. My ex-husband wanted me to remarry quickly, because it would alleviate his guilt at having been faithless during our marriage. I knew, though he didn't, that the guilt was all mine. Deep down, I hadn't expected fidelity.

In the kitchen, I sipped a glass of diet soda without ice and continued to stare out its single window at another wing of the apartment building. Basically, the view was a nonview, but I still felt glued to the spot, unable to move.

I wanted sex, and more sex, and additional sex after that. But I didn't know how to go about it. I could purchase sexual services, but I saw that as a viable option only for later in life, when I no longer had anything whatsoever to offer by way of pleasure to my partner. I wasn't there yet, and, anyway, I was still considering signing up for an online dating service. I could probably achieve sex and more sex by using the Internet. My gorge rose, despite the soda. What I didn't want were all the complications a sex life would bring to me. Sex, despite my best efforts, always seemed to lead to love. And love was the course in life that I'd failed dismally.

I'd been through intensive therapy for years. I was happy. I didn't miss Peter at all. I didn't miss the kids, either. I had no pets, and I was thrilled not to have them. I had nothing whatsoever to do, and the truth—oh, dear God—the truth was that I liked it this way. I'd taken to staying in my nightgown much of the day. You might imagine this depressed woman wafting around her grand apartment, pale and puffy and miserable. But no, no, no.

I had a series of gorgeous white nightgowns. I did waft, but with a sort of incoherent joy. I loved to catch sight of myself in the ornate gold mirrors, my long brown hair in a loose braid, the nightgown billowing against my body and showing the drifts of breast and bottom. I felt downright beautiful, even if I wasn't. That is, I often felt beautiful when I was alone, not when I was the object of a man's gaze.

When I'd finally had enough of my nightgown existence, I walked outdoors for miles, checked out piles of books from the Cleveland Park Public Library, and then came back to the apartment building for a swim. I was in the best health I'd ever experienced. I read for hours, but my reading tastes had changed. Almost no fiction. Nonfiction on esoteric subjects, but primarily science written for the nonscientist. It could be tough going, especially physics, but I soldiered on.

So what was the problem? In our society, you aren't supposed to do nothing. Doing nothing is suggestive of being emotionally troubled or, at the very least, lazy.

How I loved laziness.

As a human being, you are also supposed to enjoy other human beings. Worst case, if you don't happen to be sociable, you have a love for animals or plants. Not me. Solitude was magnificent. I needed no one. And my fake plants were absolutely lovely.

I didn't know what to say to my kids when they implored me to date, to keep up with my old friends, to socialize in some form or another. During a recent phone call with my son, Andrew, I blurted out, "I'm a misanthrope."

Though, of course, that wasn't it either. I didn't hate mankind. In fact, I quite loved mankind. Really.

I couldn't decide if I was bored, sexually deprived, morally suspect, or just disgustingly happy to be doing nothing at all. I went into the living room and booted up my laptop so that a stream of classical music from the Internet filled the room. Late-afternoon sun whispered across the antique Oriental rug. Carefully, I sat down on the couch and debated whether I had the energy to go swimming. If not, my nightgown was just a minute away.

Strange, ethereal music played. I thought about getting up to see what it was. Instead, it mezmerized me. My eyelids closed and I'd started to sag toward the pillows when a voice spoke.

A murder will occur in thirty days. Prevent it.

My eyes flew open and I sat up straight, my breath shallow and rapid. I didn't need to look around the room, because I knew the voice had come from inside my head. The words kept repeating in my memory, and, without conscious thought, I spoke out loud. "In the Kennedy? Washington, D.C.? Where?"

In the Kennedy apartment building. Thirty days. Prevent it.

Okay, so I was mentally ill. That was the obvious answer to my questionable state of joy, even though I found it a little unexpected that I could be so happy and, at the same time, mentally ill. I hadn't thought the two went hand in hand. I dashed to my laptop.

Googling *schizophrenia* brought up so much material that I was reading for a solid two hours before I finally surfaced. Dusk had come and gone. I stood, stretched, and moved slowly around the apartment, turning on lights. Each time a light clicked on, I grew more and more confident that I wasn't mentally ill. I had zero symptoms, except for believing that I'd twice heard a voice in my head.

Relieved, I grabbed my keys and went out to collect my mail on the lobby floor.

One of the more ancient members of our apartment community joined the elevator on the fifth floor. Miss Dora, as we called her, was rumored to be ninety-six years old. She looked it. Crouched over her walker, she shuffled in fake leopard-skin bedroom slippers.

"Hi," she wheezed.

"Hello, Miss Dora!" I yelled.

Her mouth twitched.

I thought about trying to make conversation, but her profound deafness usually made it a hopeless endeavor. On the lobby floor, I held the elevator door open for her.

She glanced up at me, milky green eyes suddenly sharp. "Yes," she said, clear as could be.

"Yes?"

We began to inch along the hallway toward the mail slots.

She stopped walking, her right hand tightened on the walker, and, waving her left hand at me, she indicated that I should go on ahead. I smiled and quickened my pace.

There was no longer any reason to get excited about mail. All I ever received were bills and catalogs, though I did get energized by some of those catalogs. I yanked out my usual pile and wandered to the recycling bins to discard unwanted solicitations. As I unloaded the junk, I made a decision.

I'd imagined the voice. That's all. I'd just imagined it. No problem.

"How're you doing, Anne?" a real voice said.

"Hey, Ivan." Our resident womanizing male god, Ivan Chernislava, was a recent Russian émigré. He was wrapped in a plush terry-cloth robe, his thick black hair soaking wet, slicked back into a ponytail dripping tiny clear drops of water.

"Missed you at the pool," he said.

And you wondered why I showed such discipline in my swimming routine?

"I ate too much at lunch," I said.

"Fab-u-lous," he drawled, grinning.

I wasn't absolutely certain, but it was possible that I could get Ivan into bed. True, he was twenty years my junior, but I was in good shape, and he appeared to have an endless appetite.

Suddenly, with no warning, I thought of what the voice had said. Mind you, I didn't actually *hear* the voice. But I did think about what had been said, even if only in my imagination. *A murder . . . in thirty days . . . prevent it*. Against my will, I watched Ivan as he opened his mail slot and pulled out a single envelope. Not much in the way of mail, especially for a recent Russian émigré. I couldn't keep myself from the next thought: W*as Ivan going to commit a murder in thirty days?* Quickly, I turned and took off without speaking to him again.

When I passed Miss Dora, repeatedly jabbing the key into her mail slot, I hesitated and then stopped. "Can I help you?"

"No, thank you!" she snapped.

I loved moving through the halls and various public rooms of the Kennedy. The apartment building was like a beautiful old woman whose bones exuded wisdom and integrity. With the brand-new wing added to its original structure—the architectural plans for which had been discovered in the bowels of the building—she'd been reinvigorated, reborn, resurrected. She, this building I now called my home, was everything I wanted to be. As my role model, she was obviously sending me conflicting messages. Like, it was okay to simply *be*. On the other hand, I tried to remind myself that the Kennedy was a *building,* while I was a *person*. Presumably, there was a difference.

Back in my apartment, I dumped the mail on the entrance hall table, then picked it all up again and carried it to the mahogany desk in the bay window at the far end of the living room. I stood still, listening to the classical music. Chopin. I felt as if I were sinking into the rug and then the floor below, frozen in place.

The phone rang, a jarring shriek. I jumped, my heart raced, and I grabbed the cordless phone from its cradle.

I took a deep, calming breath before answering.

"Anne, are you all right?" Peter's familiar deep voice blasted.

"Of course," I said. "What did Jonathan say?"

"That you behaved oddly, if you must know."

"He's the one who practically fell into the pea soup when I told him you'd slept with Abigail."

A tick-tock of silence. "You didn't really tell him that, did you?" Peter said.

"Yes, I did. And he *really* almost hit the pea soup."

"Why would you want to hurt him?"

"Peter, he didn't believe me." I sighed so loudly into the phone that the mouthpiece misted over. "No one's ever believed that you would actually bother to sleep with her."

Suddenly he burst out laughing.

"You're impossible," I said, laughing myself.

"What are you up to?" Peter asked.

"Nothing."

"Should you go back to Dr. Armstrong?"

"I'm not depressed."

"Heard from the kids?"

"Just the e-mails I forwarded to you."

"They're great kids, Anne."

"Yes, my claim to fame."

"I gotta run—stay well."

I put the phone down. Probably had an exciting Saturday-night dinner date with a beautiful young woman. I thought about whether I was hungry myself. Nope.

In my bedroom, I closed the cherry venetian blinds and then stripped off my clothes and pulled on a white nightgown. I wafted back into the living room, where I picked up the remote control, pointed it at the gas fireplace, and created flame with the push of a button. I moved into the large dining room, grabbed the remote control for the electric fireplace, and made another fake flame.

This was what kept happening. I was happy. I couldn't seem to help it. I knew I should be lonely, or need to be making a positive difference in the world, or *something*. Instead, I wafted.

Back in the living room, I sank into the sofa and stared at the fire. I remembered my conversation with Peter and wondered how he'd have reacted if I'd told him that I'd heard a voice in my head speak. *A murder will occur in thirty days. Prevent it.* Then I thought about calling my daughter, Laura, and telling her. But I knew she'd be worried by the idea that her mother was hearing voices, and she'd report to her father right away. I'd turned down the volume of the music streaming from the Internet when I was talking on the telephone, so it was barely audible. Though I'd heard the voice while I was listening to music, I now felt obscurely comforted, as if the musical sounds would drown out any attempts the voice might make to speak.

I knew I'd imagined the words in my head, yet I found that I believed them. I guess that was what most of us tended to do with our own thoughts. They had a certain strength, just by virtue of having been our own. Maybe it was a simple case of ESP, a vibe so strong that my intuition gave it voice. Still, it was odd. I'd lived at the Kennedy only a short time, and I didn't know many people. Just the regulars at the fitness center and pool, plus the other stay-at-homes who seemed to meander around the building a lot. So I couldn't quite figure out how I could get to know all the building's occupants, much less prevent the murder of one of them.

Murder didn't even *interest* me. I wasn't a mystery reader, and, frankly, I found it really unpleasant to think about a person killing another person. If a murder was going to be committed at the Kennedy, I definitely wasn't a good choice to serve as detective. Even Miss Dora, who could use her age as a decoy, would be better. She'd get high-powered hearing aids on the sly, then wander the halls. People would say all kinds of things right in front of her because she was practically deaf. I could recruit her.

This was ridiculous. Maybe I *was* crazy—or bored out of my mind, which might be the same thing. I gazed into the fire. Testing.

Suddenly I blurted out, "I dare you—say it again!"

My feet actually went numb as I waited. I wiggled my toes to make the blood flow. When no voice came, I was disappointed. I went into the kitchen and turned on the overhead lights, trying to blast the dark corners with a form of sunshine. The refrigerator was filled with good stuff. Since it was already late for dinner, I grabbed some fresh pasta from Vace's, then quickly assembled the ingredients for an alfredo sauce. I grated fresh Parmesan and melted Danish butter in the saucepan, then slowly added heavy cream when the pasta went into the boiling water. Stirring, I melted the cheese with the butter and cream. I carried the steaming bowl of fettucine alfredo into the dining room and, sitting alone at the round mahogany table, gobbled it down. When I cleaned up the kitchen, I noticed that I'd made enough food for a family of four.

I went to bed at the embarrassingly early hour of nine o'clock.

In the middle of the night, I jolted awake. My eyes shot open and I looked at the small alarm clock, which read twelve minutes past three. I stared around the dark bedroom and listened to the silence. Finally, I made out the dim sound of the wind blowing trees in the park. I was on the ninth floor and I knew it would be impossible for anyone to scale the walls of the building, so I wasn't afraid of an intruder. When nothing happened, my eyes closed and I started to drift back to sleep.

For no reason, just before losing consciousness, I remembered Miss Dora's strangely defiant look as she stood ready to exit from the elevator, how she tilted her head to gaze at me, and her emphatic "Yes."

I timed my arrival at the pool the next day for the exact moment when Ivan threw off his terry-cloth robe and danced on his large hairy toes to the edge of the lap pool. Out of season, the naked skin displayed at an indoor swimming pool was always shocking, but Ivan's thick body, all virile bulges, took the proverbial cake. One particular bulge, given his propensity for sleek European swimsuits, made me decide to act.

I thought this decision had to do with sex.

Like the majority of people, when I looked back at my life it seemed as if sex had always been there, at the beginning, in the middle, and now, near the end. Okay, I knew I was being overly dramatic by implying that the age of fifty is near the end. But it did feel as if the tides and earth's rhythms were a part of our bodies. I mean, all I had to do was look at Ivan's bulge and I was asking him if he'd like to stop by for a martini at five o'clock.

Again, I thought this had to do with sex.

I spent the rest of the afternoon preparing for Ivan. First a quick shower to wash my hair and shave any errant hairs on my body, then a long, soaking bath, and finally, three separate cream applications spaced fifteen minutes apart. It had come to my attention that cream is the secret beauty ingredient for a fifty-year-old woman. My skin seemed to plump out and glow. Unless I was kidding myself, which was possible.

I wore what used to be called a hostess gown, with lacy black underwear underneath. That way, I knew I would find it difficult to change my mind—not that I really wanted to change my mind,

mind you. Or maybe I really did. In fact, as it got closer and closer to five o'clock, and I'd finished setting the stage with a crackling fire, ice bucket filled and martini glasses and shaker displayed, I decided that I was making myself nervous. Too late to back down, promptly at five o'clock Ivan knocked on the door.

His very clean black sweatsuit with black leather slippers made him look almost clerical. As he sauntered into the living room, I knew I'd made a mistake. What had possessed me?

I shook the martini shaker and watched Ivan survey my not insubstantial oil paintings out of the corner of my eye. Suddenly I *knew* that, in fact, this had nothing whatsoever to do with sex.

This cocktail hour, the whole shebang, had to do with murder.

I handed him the martini.

"Is this a Rembrandt?" he asked, gesturing toward a small painting of a woman with a dog cuddled into her voluminous, silky lap.

"Oh, goodness, no." I touched my glass to his. "Cheers."

"*Salut,*" he growled. One black eyebrow rose like a rippling flag. He took a step backward and gestured with both arms extended. "You are the designer?"

Confused by his question, I said, "I'm sorry?" and went to sit down in a corner of the couch.

"Your apartment is very beautiful—I thought you were, perhaps, a home designer?"

I laughed. "No, no!"

Ivan crossed the room and sat down opposite me, in a wing chair that looked too small for him.

"What brought you to the States?" I asked him.

"Oh, I'm attached to the embassy."

"In what capacity?"

He shrugged. "Administrative—nothing that interesting as yet. But I have aspirations."

"Somehow I don't doubt that, Ivan." I laughed.

We both sipped at the martinis.

"Excellent vodka," he said.

"I forgot that you'd be a vodka expert!"

Maybe it was the drink already meandering through my body, but I wondered whether, perhaps, I *did* want to have a quick sexual interlude with this Russian stud. I tried not to consider the moral-parameters.

"You have two children, yes?" he asked.

I nodded. "Laura is at Juilliard, a freshman. And Andrew is a senior at Swarthmore."

"I know about Juilliard," Ivan said. "She plays?"

"French horn."

He laughed.

"Why are you laughing?" I asked.

Ivan waved both hands apologetically. "Really, you must be very proud." He still giggled.

I demanded, "*Why* are you laughing?"

"The French horn is so, well, *large*."

"It's a beautiful instrument!"

He made a valiant effort to stop the amusement leaking from his voice. "I think I saw her at the pool one day. She's lovely." Then he repeated, "You must be very proud of your children."

"I am, but mostly because they're both good people."

"And what, for you, does it mean to be a *good person*?"

I watched his thick red lips take a gentle slurp from the martini, then the way they pursed together with pleasure. The gas fire floated heat against my lower legs, and I shifted them away.

I liked that he wanted to know, though it was always difficult to succinctly summarize a philosophy like that. Still, I accepted the challenge. "I guess I'd say that there's one word to explain it."

"One word?"

"There's a single word that describes a good person."

He smiled. "Are you going to tell me the word?"

"Are you going to try to guess?" I sipped my martini and smiled back.

Ivan screwed up his face dramatically so that I'd be sure to understand how hard he was thinking. "A good person," he muttered. Then, in Russian, "*Khoroshi chelovek.*" To my surprise, he was quiet for a long time. I'd expected that he'd jump right in, spurting out one possibility after another.

Finally, he held up one fat index finger. "Love," he said.

I shook my head no.

"Love is no?" he asked.

"For me, love is not the word," I said quickly. I felt a bit defensive. "I was thinking of the word *kind.*"

"*Dobry,*" he said.

"To be kind."

He smiled gently. "I think it is the same thing as love."

"In English, the root of the word *kind* comes from *kin,* meaning family. So my children are good people because they treat others with kindness, as if even strangers are family."

"The same as love."

"I'm not saying that they *love* everyone," I said. "Your way means a good person *feels* love for all other human beings."

Ivan nodded eagerly. "Exactly."

"I mean that they treat others with kindness, even those they *do not* love."

"Okay, yes, I understand your point," he said. He looked absolutely furious.

I said, "No one can love everyone in the world."

"I do," Ivan said. "I love all."

He tipped the martini glass, draining the last vestiges of vodka and using his brown tongue to fish out the olives resting in the bottom of the glass.

I smiled, trying to lighten the mood. "You love all?" I teased.

He held up his glass. "May I?"

I nodded.

Ivan rose in a fluid rush and moved to the marble-topped bar. He fairly shouted over his shoulder, as he packed ice into the martini shaker, "I love you, for example."

I felt the red flush instantly pulsing in my cheeks. *Here we go.*

"Do you want another martini?" he asked.

I held up my empty glass, momentarily too weak to speak.

With the shaker creating a cacaphony of noise, he grabbed my glass.

Ivan gave me my martini and then leaned against the fireplace mantel, gazing at me. "So, I love you—what do you say about that?"

"You're a lover; that's what you do."

He gulped at the martini. "I am a lover, of course, but I do love *you.*"

I smiled, feeling my way. "Okay, okay."

"You." He pointed at me with the martini glass.

Desperate, I burst out, "Perhaps we're having a cultural misunderstanding."

"A cultural misunderstanding?" Both black eyebrows shot up.

Physically, he really was a god. I felt sick to my stomach and wondered whether he'd still love me if I puked at his feet. "I think you're talking about love in a generic, widespread way," I explained.

Ivan's large head shook back and forth, reminding me of a nearsighted hippopotamus.

"No?" I asked. Sweat poured from my armpits and rolled down my sides to collect at my waist.

"I fell in love the first time I saw you."

I tried to remember when I'd first seen Ivan. I had no recollection. But maybe, I thought, this was what he believed had to be said for an effective seduction. "Ivan, you don't have to—-"

He interrupted, "I am not saying this to get you in bed. Of course, I do hope to get you in bed one day, since that is such a beautiful expression of love, but that is not why I love you."

The second martini was beginning to make me feel like I was in two places at once. So, I had to admit that in my head I began a phone conversation to Laura. *You will not believe what happened, Laursie. Your mother has a Russian god in love with her. Truly.* I was awfully pleased with myself, even though I figured he must have lost his beautiful mind.

"You don't believe me." Ivan sat down in the wing chair and looked at me carefully.

"I'm afraid that's right." I grinned. "But thanks for trying."

He didn't smile.

I extended my bare foot and touched his black slipper gently. "Give me a break. I'm fifty years old and doing my damnedest to remember that fact."

To my astonishment, he slid off the chair so that he was kneeling in front of me. His arms wrapped around my lower legs and he stared at me. (And, yes, in my mind I continued to describe everything to Laura. *And then he actually grabbed my—*)

"You are not fifty years old," he declared melodramatically.

I might be able to kid myself from time to time about how I didn't really *look* fifty. I bet there isn't a fifty-year-old woman in this country who actually thinks she looks fifty. You simply can't *be* fifty and accept *being* fifty. It's one of those impossible paradoxes. But, all joking aside, it's a rather painful paradox, too. I had to restrain myself from kicking both legs forward in an effort to dislodge him.

"You are a beautiful girl, timeless and eternal."

(*And then he said, "You are a beautiful girl, timeless and eternal"*. I could hear Laura's peals of helpless laughter at the very idea that her mother was a girl, just like she was.)

"Ivan, I am not a girl. I'm a fifty-year-old woman, divorced and with grown children. I confess that I did imagine having a fling with you. But I know that probably wouldn't be a good idea, anyway." His deep, endless brown eyes gazed into mine. "I've been a little lonely, and I thought—"

He let go of my legs and sat back in his chair. Calm, he sipped his martini. "I cannot have a fling with you." He pronounced the word *fling* as if it were disgusting. "I could have a fling with your daughter, but not with you."

"Now *that's* disgusting!"

"I am always honest."

Since I never drank two martinis in a row, I was beginning to experience a profound physical reaction. My lips were like cartoon lips, moving without any conscious knowledge on my part. I also noticed that Ivan's declaration of love had begun to make me swell. My breasts puffed out like two loaves of yeasty bread rising near a warm oven, and my buttocks, on which I firmly sat, inflated so conspicuously that I was elevated several inches.

I've never been socially adept. I could now see that in any effort to either (1) get laid, or (2) investigate some putative murder, I was going to ram into my poor social skills as if they were a massive stone wall erected between me and others. I resolved to address this little difficulty *sometime,* but meanwhile Ivan Chernislava had completely flummoxed me. I could no longer make my lips smile or speak.

Ivan stood up, drained his martini with a flourish, and picked up my limp left hand where it had settled in my lap. "You will give this some thought." He bent over and kissed my hand with his wonderful red lips.

Of course, given my overall numbness, I didn't really *feel* the kiss, which was a shame, since no one had ever before made such a romantic gesture toward me. I knew I'd want to remember the glorious moment when I was fifty and a young Russian god kissed my hand, but even while it was happening, I wasn't really there. I was drunk as a skunk.

Before I could even struggle to my feet, he was moving through the living room. Distantly, I heard the door to my apartment opening. Given Ivan's physical presence and character, I expected the door to dramatically crash shut. But he must have turned and carefully latched it, soft and, yes, kind.

Though my beautiful Kennedy apartment building was, as I described, a venerable complex in Washington, most of the apartments in the old part of the building had no laundry facilities. Rolling my hamper of dirty clothes down to the basement was a throwback to my early married days in Chicago, when Peter had been clerking for a state supreme court justice. Every Friday night, we'd lug two bulging bags of laundry five blocks away to the local Laundromat. While Peter scribbled briefs on a yellow legal pad, I read novels. We folded together.

Sometimes I made the mistake of taking a memory like that, still in its pristine bubble, and trying to pop it. I would jab and jab, eager to explode the bubble with my pointed hurt feelings, not to mention my even more pointed guilty feelings. I'd finally begun to learn that popping the bubble hurt more than the original memory.

The Monday morning after my debacle with Ivan, I loaded my meager pile of colored clothes in one machine and the mountainous whites into another.

Oddly, because of the way the ground sloped away from the building, the basement was above ground, with huge windows looking out onto a view of the park's massive trees. That was the laundry room's only saving grace. Ductwork, ratty linoleum, and uneven walls painted a dull yellow, plus the constant thrub and throm of the washers and dryers and an indescipherable ancient odor, created a singularly unattractive place. Plus, there always seemed to be one or several machines out of order.

Next door, the management had organized a small library with nice carpeting and funny old wing chairs. I wandered in and gazed at the books, but when nothing appealed to me, I sat in a chair close to a window. A few minutes later, I heard the elevator doors open and, glancing behind me, caught sight of one of the several cleaning ladies who worked in the building. She was an African-American woman of what can only be described as grand porportions. I usually ran into her every week, and I'd introduced myself early on, but she always waited for me to greet her.

I waved from my chair, so that she'd be sure to spot me. "Hey, Mary!"

"Hullo, Anne," she sang out before disappearing into the laundry room.

On her way back upstairs, she stopped in the library. "You're still not interested in someone to help you clean that big apartment of yours?"

"You know what?" I said. "I like to clean." I wasn't kidding, either.

She shook her head, laughing softly. I enjoyed watching Mary move, because every gesture undulated like a barely contained flood of water.

"What about you?" I asked.

"Huh?" She chortled hard enough to make her chest and stomach ripple.

"Do *you* like to clean?"

"I sure hope so!"

"But *do* you?"

"Yeah," she said, the laughter winding down, "I do."

"That's good." I stood up and started for the laundry room to check on my loads.

When Mary and I both had clothes in the dryer, we set ironing boards close together and plugged in the irons. Then we started snatching various items from the dryers, before the wrinkles set in, and ironing them one at a time. I felt Mary assessing my ironing skills, so I worked at developing good form, which, in ironing, means gracefully wielding the unwieldy.

"Not bad." She chuckled.

I bowed. "Thanks."

Mary shook her head back and forth. "You're unusual; I'll say that."

"Little do you know." I waited for a few minutes, then spoke again. "Are you married?"

"Ummm, yes," she murmured.

"I used to be, but no more."

She nodded at my laundry. "I could tell."

Swish, swish, went our irons. Maybe I was nuts, but it seemed like we were in unison.

"I got one of those marriages where he comes and goes." There was no judgment in her voice.

"You mean he travels for his work?"

She laughed. "Right, that's it; he travels for his work."

"My husband traveled for his work, too." I caught her eye and we giggled like silly kids.

"These men, they gotta work so hard with their traveling," Mary said.

I grabbed a hanger and hung the blouse I'd been ironing from a handy iron pipe. Thrusting one hand into the dryer's whirling damp clothes, I pulled out two king-size pillowcases.

"Oh, Lord, you iron the bedding," Mary said.

"I bet you do, too."

"I iron Mrs. Janus's bedding; that's for sure."

"And your own."

"Maybe."

We were quiet for a few minutes, and it suddenly occurred to me that Mary could be very knowledgeable about the building's news. I almost asked whether she had any good gossip, but even my underdeveloped detective skills were good enough to make me realize that blurting out a question probably wasn't the best way to find out anything. I glanced at her, debating what to say.

Unexpectedly, Mary said, "Something bothering you?"

I stalled by going over to the dryer for the top bedsheet. Mary let go of her iron and reached for one end of the sheet. Together, we folded it in half, and then I started to iron.

"I hope you don't think I'm crazy if I tell you," I said.

Mary sprayed starch on a man's gigantic shirt. "You're not crazy," she said, "no matter what you say. I have a working knowledge of *crazy* and you don't fit the description."

"I never thought so either," I said, still hesitating.

She started to hum under her breath, which relaxed me.

"I heard a voice in my head," I blurted out.

"Was it the Lord?" she asked.

"Was it . . . who?"

She giggled. "The *Lord*—that's usually who starts speaking."

"I never even considered the possibility."

"Then it wasn't. The Lord tends to say so."

"I thought it might just be myself."

"That's what we got thoughts for."

Confused, I glanced at her.

"Thoughts are instead of talking, right?" she said. "Why would you *say* your thoughts when you can just *think* 'em?"

"I guess that makes sense."

"What did the voice say?"

I turned over the bedsheet and positioned it across the ironing board. "Okay, here are the exact words." I looked at Mary and was pleased to see that I had her complete attention. " 'A murder will be committed in thirty days. Prevent it.' "

Mary's iron stopped moving. She stared at me.

"So I asked, *'Here at the Kennedy, in Washington, D.C., or where?'* "

"What did the voice say then?" Mary held the iron high in the air, midstroke.

"It said, *'At the Kennedy. Thirty days. Prevent it.'* "

Mary's deep brown eyes swam. Or mine did. I wasn't sure which.

"Do you think I'm crazy?" I said.

Briskly, she picked up the starch and made a sweeping gesture so that beads of starch floated through the air like a thin rain. She heaved the iron down hard.

"I guess you *do* think I'm nuts." I pressed my own iron on the sheet and held it without moving while the steam hissed.

Mary sighed. "I said you weren't crazy, and you aren't. I have to assess this. It's a si-tu-a-tion."

She pulled out the word *situation* in a way that I found reassuring.

"You're right—it's a situation." Again, I felt comforted, not so much because I'd finally confided in someone about the voice, but because Mary seemed like the right person to have told.

"I'm not convinced there's going to be a murder," I said.

"Why the hell would the voice tell you there was going to be one, then?" she exploded.

"I don't know!"

The irons traced rapid arcs through the air.

"Will you help me?" I whispered.

"What am I gonna do?" she asked. "Pretend you didn't tell me and wait around for someone to get killed?"

I shrugged. "I was considering exactly that."

"No, you weren't—that's why you dragged me into it."

Mary went over to the dryer and pulled out a woman's blouse, which she flapped hard in the air and then tugged straight over the end of the ironing board.

"I haven't told anyone else."

Mary started to laugh so hard that she stopped ironing, leaned over the board, and gasped for air. "Thanks for sharing," she finally managed to say.

I clomped the iron on its end and felt the waves of helpless laughter roll up from my stomach. I looked at Mary and, possessed by her laughter, collapsed to the floor, howling with my own. Tears streamed down my face. We just kept laughing and laughing. I could hear her gasping for breath, and I finally got worried that she might have a heart attack, so I started to wind down.

Standing up, I said, "I'm going to get some toilet paper."

"Bring me some," she said in a strangled voice. Then she swiped at her running nose.

I rushed to the bathroom, yanked off reams of toilet paper, and tore back to the laundry room. We both honked and wiped.

"We need a plan," I said.

"I'm done with Mrs. Janus at three o'clock," she said. "Can I come by then?"

Mary had unplugged the iron while we were laughing, and now that it was cool she placed it in the bottom of a plastic basket. Carefully, she draped the ironed items across the top.

"I'm number nine-oh-two," I said.

"That's a big apartment," she said.

"I don't need any help!" I yelled.

She nodded. "Uh-huh."

I finished my ironing in a flash, folded up the ironing board, and lugged it to a distant corner of the room, where it leaned against a large wooden cupboard. I kept meaning to explore the innards of that cupboard, since it had a strange, mysterious aura, and I could imagine it leading to the land of Oz. But today I was in a hurry.

I tore back to my apartment to do a quick dusting and vacuuming as proof to Mary that I was a good cleaner. Then I whipped up some banana-nut muffins, grateful that I had fresh buttermilk, and popped them into the oven. It felt good to think of having a visitor, which surprised me. I was so busy that, briefly, I forgot about the si-tu-a-tion with Ivan Chernislava.

When the muffins were out and cooling, I ground the coffee beans and made a pot of coffee.

Okay, I know it's uncommon for a woman like me not to have a good girlfriend, someone to whom I would tell absolutely everything, especially something as deliciously weird as the scene with Ivan. So . . . I used to have that girlfriend. I'd lost my best friend because she took my ex-husband's side. Indeed, she read me the proverbial riot act about how I'd never deserved him, blah, blah, blah. Not worth rehashing here. Though I forgave Peter for his transgressions, I couldn't seem to forgive my best friend. Dr. Armstrong, my shrink, challenged me about this, and he eventually got me to see that I was actually not forgiving myself for my own goof-ups in the game of marriage.

Since Mary didn't fit into any previously known category—she wasn't really a friend yet; nor was she my boss or my employee—I assumed she couldn't hurt me the way a best friend who tells you all your faults can hurt you. I knew that my logic was deeply flawed and that Andrew, immersed in troubling work on string theory at Swarthmore (if you know anything about string theory, you'd have to call it troubling), could easily zero in on the illogic. It didn't matter. The coffee and muffins smelled wonderful, and I was relieved to have shared the secret of the voice with a woman who didn't think I was a lunatic.

Nevertheless, when I opened the door to let Mary in, I said, "Have you decided I'm crazy after all?"

"Stop with the crazy talk." She breezed in and started walking through the living room as if she had a specific destination in mind.

I was so nonplussed, I didn't say anything right away. At the far end of the living room, she turned left into the library, disappearing from view.

"Hey, what are you doing?" I said, running after her.

"Looking around," she said.

I caught up with her as she catapulted through the French doors into the dining room, where she stopped dead in front of the marble fireplace between two windows. No other apartments at the Kennedy had *two* fireplaces.

"What's that?" she asked.

"It's a fireplace."

"I *know* it's a fireplace, but how'd it get there?"

I picked up the remote control. "Watch this!" I made the fake flame turn on with a push of the button.

Mary leaned over and peered at it. "Is that real?"

"Nope, it's an electric fireplace I installed."

"Holy mackerel," she swore under her breath.

Oddly pleased with myself, I made the flame explode to its highest ability.

Mary ignored it and kept marching from the dining room into the kitchen.

I said, "I made a snack. Would you care for something?"

She glared at the muffins displayed on a platter. "You make those from a box?"

"That is such a rude question," I said, "but since you ask, I made them from scratch, and they're delicious."

Her brown eyes slid in my direction, and I saw a wave of amusement. "Unusual, that's for damn sure."

"I'm not alone." I picked up the coffee and poured two mugs full, one of which I handed to her. Then I gestured to the silver creamer and sugar.

After we'd both fixed our coffee and taken a muffin, I led the way back into the living room. Mary dropped easily onto one end of the couch, and I sat opposite her.

A bit defensive, I stared at her as she took a gentle bite of the muffin. She swallowed and picked up her coffee. Then she looked at me, nodded, and said, "Pretty good."

I grabbed my own muffin and took a big bite. I'd skipped lunch because I'd been so busy bustling to impress her. Mary looked around the living room, her eye stopping at each painting and object.

Finally, she said, "You'll have a big party."

"I'll . . . what?"

"You'll have a party and invite the whole building. I'll be here, working for you, and we'll put out some feelers, start nosing around."

"I don't want to have a party," I said. "I'm really not a party kind of person."

Mary licked her lips, which I felt was a sign that she'd enjoyed the muffin.

"Would you like another one?"

She put a hand on her stomach. "Best not."

"I was thinking we could start brainstorming about everyone in the building," I said. "Make a list and share our information."

"You're going to have a party," she said.

"What a bossy-boots," I said.

She grinned. "I've been bossy since I was a little girl. I *enjoy* being bossy."

"I don't particularly enjoy being *bossed,*" I said.

"Yeah, you do."

"I do not!" I swallowed some coffee and felt the heat rising into my cheeks.

"Everyone I know likes being bossed by me," Mary said.

"They give you that impression because you scare them, but they don't really like it at all."

Her eyes opened wide. "I don't scare people."

"Actually, you do." I stood up. "I'm having another muffin—sure you don't want one?"

"Please," she said politely.

As we ate our second muffins, I felt an unusual sense of peace in the room. "It was about this time of day when the voice came," I said.

Quiet, Mary nodded her head up and down. "Umm," she murmured.

"You think this is for real, that if we don't do anything a person will be murdered within thirty days?"

"Indeed, I do," she said.

"What makes you so sure?"

Mary shrugged. "Look at it this way—it's always fun to have a party."

I started to argue, but when I glanced at her, she was grinning. And this much I'd learned real fast: When Mary smiles at you, you smile back, big-time.

That night, at a Kennedy Center performance of the National Symphony playing an all-French program, I saw one of the more illustrious of my apartment's tenants. Paul Hammer, a former democratic senator from Florida, looked a million years old. He'd been widowed the year before, and I thought he might decide I'd be a good candidate for the next Mrs. Hammer. His politics were acceptable to me, and the extraordinary rumor was that he'd been faithfully faithful to his wife for fifty-three years. This was especially remarkable, because, though I shouldn't be catty, she'd been a deeply unattractive woman.

During the intermission, I threaded my way through the crowds, barely registering the explosions of political gossip all around me, to grab a white wine and then station myself right next to him.

"Senator Hammer?" I said with a big smile.

His head, which had been tucked turtlelike into his chest, swiveled. "Not anymore," he wheezed.

I held out my hand. "I'm Anne Johnson, one of your newer neighbors at the Kennedy."

"Charmed." His pale blue eyes looked at me directly, and his hand squeezed mine. His skin, loose on the bones of his hand, felt warm.

"What apartment have you got?" he asked.

"I'm in nine-oh-two."

He nodded judiciously. "Washer and dryer?"

"Nope, but the view and floor plan are worth it."

"Absolutely." He smiled broadly. "Are you enjoying the music?"

"I've come late to discovering French composers," I said. "But I'm learning."

He nodded. "Good, good."

I went on, "I wanted to mention that since I'm new in the building, I'm planning a cocktail party this Friday. An open house, actually, with everyone invited."

His sleepy narrow eyes popped open. "What a wonderful thing to do! We need to get to know one another."

"You've lived there for a long time—you must know a lot of people."

He winked. "I know a lot of people, and I know a lot *about* them."

I grinned. "I bet!"

"There's plenty of hanky-panky going on in that building." He smiled and lost twenty years in doing so, but that still put his appearance at 999,980 years old.

I touched his arm. "If you don't tell me, I'm going to *uninvite* you."

"Hang out in the laundry room." He winked.

Just then the houselights blinked, warning us to start finding our places.

He continued, "Good location for meeting in the wee hours of the night."

I escorted him to his seat and repeated the date of my party over and over again. He promised he'd be there.

In my seat, which was significantly farther back, probably because I wasn't a former U.S. senator, I imagined the laundry room at three o'clock in the morning. It had never occurred to me that I could do my laundry at that hour, but I decided that I might have insomnia that night and need to wash all my towels.

During the second half of the program, featuring Ravel, I debated whether I should actually descend to the bowels of the building to wash my towels simply because an illicit coupling might be going on. For one thing, if I were doing my laundry, I don't think the couple would couple. Something about the music, which involved a characterization of Pan and his wicked pipe playing, made me worry that I was wasting my time. Maybe I was being led astray, not by a devil or anything supernatural like that, but by my own overactive imagination.

Yet . . .

I saw a woman turning over in bed and discovering that her husband wasn't next to her. Worried, she meandered through the apartment, searching for him. When she didn't find him anywhere, she threw on a robe and slipped bare feet into slippers.

Hesitant and scared—about what, she wasn't really able to articulate—she grabbed a kitchen knife and left the apartment. Gliding through the silent halls, she took the stairs and searched through all the public rooms of the Kennedy, those glorious spaces that were recently renovated back to their original beauty. She could almost hear the echoey music of the old innaugural balls. She was so quiet that the doorman at the front didn't hear her. Finally, beginning to feel silly, she tiptoed into the laundry room. Oddly, the dryer thrummed, and she heard the load of wet clothes *thwap*ping back and forth.

Her gaze traveled to the dryer, and she saw the woman's naked back held by her husband's hands, then his face pressed against her blond hair, with his eyes closed in ecstasy. She glided forward, ever silent, and plunged the knife into the woman's back.

I swallowed and felt the pinpricks of sweat dotting my forehead. If I caught the guilty twosome first, they'd be warned, and the woman's murder wouldn't happen. The music ended and the audience burst into applause. I jumped with surprise. I felt disgusted with myself, though not because I'd been capable of imagining such perfidy. The problem was that I was excited by it. I was turned on by the idea of being screwed against a thumping dryer. No question about it. In fact, I was so sexually charged that I was afraid to move. I could have an orgasm instanteously.

You probably think I'm exaggerating. But the truth is that I've always been wildly orgasmic. To an absurd degree, quite frankly. All I had to do was wait for the right situation or fantasy and then let 'er rip. It was embarrassing, and this was not information that I shared with many people. Peter had known, of course, and my former best friend, Betsy (the one who somehow felt it necessary to tell me that I was totally at fault in my relationship with Peter) had quizzed me mercilessly. We'd concluded that it was something anatomical. Betsy had actually suggested that I should volunteer myself for a medical study, to further research on why certain women were so lucky.

I stayed glued to my seat. I was small enough that I could curl my legs sideways and let people push past me. When I finally moved up the center aisle, I felt wonderfully satisfied, as if I'd actually experienced the orgasm. For the first time in months, I didn't wonder who I was and what I was doing with my life. I simply had a murder to prevent. I was finally *called* to something higher than, or at least different from, my former calling to motherhood. The fantasy of that poor woman discovering her husband in the laundry room had thrown open my mind. I knew it could happen. The possibility of its happening might be low, admittedly, but it *could*.

I got home by eleven o'clock. Though it was past my bedtime, I was so energized that I started the gas fireplace in the living room, made myself a cup of tea, and settled into the couch with a notepad on my lap. I listed all the liquor I'd need for the cocktail party, and then brainstormed food possibilities. Finally, I drafted the text of a small poster I'd design on my computer, announcing my housewarming party on Friday from seven o'clock to nine. I toyed with the language, trying to hit on something that was amusing and clever, as well as enticing. I finally figured out that I was trying too hard and ended up with a straightforward invitation.

At midnight, with a list of food and the ingredients I would need, I turned off all the lights and the gas fireplace. My body headed for the bedroom, then abruptly veered in quite the opposite direction. Before I knew what was happening, I had snatched up my keys and opened my door. The elevator was directly outside my door. I pushed the down button and cringed at the loud noise as it lurched into service. It seemed like the doorman would have to hear it. Big mistake, I suddenly realized. I dashed down the hallway, toward the stairs. Nine flights turned out to be somewhat exhausting, but I decided that a detective who meant business couldn't use an elevator. Since I was still wearing my dress shoes from attending the concert earlier that evening, I took them off and held them in my hand.

At the door into the laundry room, I put them back on and took a deep breath. I didn't expect to actually find anything, in all honesty, especially since it wasn't very late, but I had a sense that I was just practicing, honing my skills at investigating. And, frankly, I was enjoying myself. I pushed open the door and crept forward. A single light shone, so it wasn't completely dark. No washers and dryers were in use. I heard the quiet as if it were a loud noise, or perhaps it was my heart beating faster and faster.

Laundry areas of large old apartment buildings, at midnight, are very scary places. Machines loomed and their edges dissolved into the dusky darkness so that they might easily be imagined as animals or very big, dangerous men. The huge windows gleamed deeply black, and funny little gleaming lights shot here and there. I stood still for a long time, too nervous to walk forward until I'd successfully defined what everything was. Eventually, as my eyes adjusted, I felt comfortable enough to venture all the way into the center of the room.

I placed one hand on a washing machine and didn't move. Slowly, I turned around in a circle, looking and looking. No, I didn't have any idea *what* I was expecting to see, since the large room was dark and deserted. Why didn't I leave, or at least walk directly into the little makeshift library? It occurred to me that I was hoping to hear the voice. *Lead me,* I said in my head. *Show me what I need.*

That was when I noticed something that I couldn't decipher. Hulking and dark, it seemed to rock in place. I checked my nerves and thought, *Okay, it's a furnace or air-conditioning unit that subtly moves when the power is on.* I leaned forward and squinted slightly. It wasn't making any noise, however, which tended to discount my idea. Seconds before it moved in a *big* way, fear surged through me like I'd been plugged into an electric current.

"Who's there?" came a deep male voice. He shifted forward, quickly transforming into the shape of an enormous man.

Everything went dry. My mouth, eyes, nose, and even my ridiculous vagina. Sucked dry with fear.

He said, "You come to do laundry at this hour?"

"No," I squeaked.

"What then?"

Mercifully, he didn't move any closer. I could tell from his accent that he was German.

"I needed a book to read," I said, pointing in the general direction of the library.

"Huh."

"What are you doing down here?" I said.

"Night watchman."

"I didn't know the Kennedy employed a night watchman."

It occurred to me that in America we use the term *security guard*.

"Management keeps it quiet."

"Oh." I started walking toward the library, where I switched on the overhead fixtures. They buzzed and flickered for a minute before exploding into bright light that momentarily blinded me. When I could, I checked behind me. He still stood in the shade of the laundry room, unmoving except for that slight rocking motion.

I pretended to peruse the titles of the books, my head tilted to the side, but I didn't register any of the words. I was thinking that it was highly unusual for an establishment like the Kennedy to have a night watchman skulking around the building and not to warn the building's inhabitants. Plus, usually you announced the presence of security so as to deter crime. Why wouldn't they have told us?

I grabbed a book and headed in the direction of the elevator.

"Good night," I said in a neutral voice. He didn't reply.

Tuesday morning, I was in the management office right at nine o'clock.

Angela, the assistant manager, sat behind a massive desk nursing a mug of coffee. She always looked out of kilter in the office, because she was one of the tiniest women I'd ever known, and her desk was one of the largest. I guessed she was about four-ten, and her head, arms, legs, and feet were in perfect, minuscule proportion. Her brown hair was cut short and curly, carefully wild. Her small smile curved around the edge of her mug.

"How's it going, Angela?" I asked.

"I am in recovery, deep recovery."

"From what?"

"A date last night."

I plopped into the chair on the other side of the desk. "Tell me, please. I love date stories."

"Okay, so I met him through one of those online dating services, eHarmony-dot-com."

I nodded enthusiastically.

"Have you tried it?" she asked.

"Not yet."

One little hand, tipped with perfectly manicured nails, rose into a stop sign. "Don't!"

"You've already convinced me."

Angela sipped more coffee and ignored a buzzing telephone. "We did about three e-mails back and forth. Usually, I wait longer, but this guy sounded so perfect that I couldn't." She pointed an accusing finger at my nose. "I'm gonna tell you something. I thought I'd fallen in love!"

"What was so great about him?"

"He was funny!" she screamed. "Do you know how hard it is to find a guy who can make you laugh?"

Angela had never struck me as a young lady with a strong need for comedy. She dressed conservatively in thick fabrics, and her makeup gleamed so that it looked baked on. Only her curly hair, hinting at disorder, suggested otherwise.

She leaned forward, and I found myself drawn toward her. Our heads were about a foot apart, in the center of the desk, as she whispered, "When I was a kid, my shrink told me I had to have at least three rip-roaring laughs a day." Angela paused. "For my health."

"You mean like the daily requirement for eating five servings of vegetables and making one bowel movement?"

Her eyes widened. She sucked in a deep breath and then she cawed a giant laugh. I'd never heard anything so fake in all my life.

I tried to join in, just to ease what I considered an awkward moment, but Angela deemed me irrelevant. Her laugh lasted long enough that I got impatient. From another office, tucked around a corner and down a short hall, the manager, Michael, yelled, "Cut!"

She switched off the laugh while it was still full throttle. "I'm going to have to find another job if I don't stop right when Michael tells me to," Angela explained.

By this time, I felt we had drifted so far from the real purpose of my visit that I decided I wasn't all that interested in her terrible date. I stood up. "I have an appointment, so if you'll excuse me." At the door into their offices, I turned. "Why do you have a security guard in the laundry room at night?"

Angela put down the coffee and tapped its porcelain shell with one fingernail. "Who said we had a security guard in the laundry room?"

That was the moment I learned to be a private eye.

I said, "No one."

In my apartment, I called Mary's cell phone. When she answered, I could hear the roar of the vacuum cleaner. "We need to talk," I yelled.

"I can take a half-hour break at twelve," she said.

"Want a tuna-fish sandwich?"

"I got my lunch."

"Okay, see you at noon."

I went to make my bed, and on the way decided the bathroom needed a good cleaning. While crouching over the ancient bathtub, sprinkling bleach cleanser vigorously, I heard the phone ring.

Laura sobbed into the phone, "Mom?"

"Sweetie, what's the matter?"

"I had the worst weekend. I hooked up with this senior, and I honestly, truly, fell in love, and we spent every minute together since Friday night, but he just sent me a terrible e-mail saying he wasn't ready to have a relationship with someone, particularly a freshman, and—"

I interrupted, "I'm so sorry."

"Plus, I know I drank way too much."

"Did you get sick?"

"I vomited Sunday morning, but I'm okay now."

I heard gulping swallows and loud sniffs.

"I want to come home this weekend."

I'd never imagined that Laura would choose to leave college to visit her mother, and I wasn't sure what I thought of the plan. Or maybe, to my own surprise, I wasn't sure that I liked the idea. It seemed like I'd just gotten over the shock of her absence.

"Of course, I'd love for you to come," I said, "but I've planned a big cocktail party for Friday night and invited the whole building. You might not enjoy—"

"Mom, that's great!" she said, cutting me off. "I could help!"

"Sure, if you don't mind."

"You know I love parties."

"So you'd take the train down?"

"I can skip my Friday-morning classes and be home by four o'clock."

"I don't think it's a good idea to skip—"

She started to cry again. And, yes, I knew that growing up meant that she had to make her own decisions.

"Okay, it's your choice," I said.

"Since you'll be getting ready, I'll take the Metro from Union Station."

Always the mother, I said, "Have you had breakfast this morning?"

"I just woke up and got his e-mail!"

"Go to a coffee shop and have a big pile of eggs and sausage." Laura had a tendency to waste away, especially when she was upset.

I went back to scrubbing the bathtub and tried not to think about my darling little girl having sex with a college senior. Motherhood could be a bitch.

Mary and I sat at the dining room table, eating our sandwiches. I showed her the invitation I planned to post on the bulletin board later in the afternoon, and she approved it. Then, after we'd both finished half a sandwich, I told her about Senator Hammer's laundry room insinuations, and how I'd made a midnight visit down there. When I described the hulking man suddenly speaking with a German accent from a dark corner of the room, Mary jumped and gasped.

"Holy Mother," she said.

"You're telling me," I said. "But here's the real puzzle. Angela, in the management office—"

She nodded. "I know Angela."

Mary didn't sound like she approved of Angela, which I found intriguing.

"What's the matter with Angela?"

"Keep on the subject."

I glared and deliberately took a big bite of sandwich. Finally, after laboriously chewing and swallowing, I said, "According to Angela, they *don't have* a security guard in the laundry room."

Mary's eyes widened in an extremely satisfying way.

"Do you know anyone who lives here who fits his description?" I said.

Her eyes searched the room. Finally she shook her head slowly. "Can't think of anyone, but that's why you're having the party. We're going to flush 'em out."

I gazed at her admiringly.

"What are you planning to serve?" she said.

I described the menu.

"You need one item to be passed. I'll be able to eavesdrop. No one ever thinks the help listens."

"We can heat up some of those weenie dogs."

Mary grinned and held up two fingers, leaving about an inch of space. "Weenie dogs, huh?"

"I happen to like weenie dogs!"

"That's because you're such a little woman."

"I'm not that little, just compared to you."

"Are you saying I'm *big*?"

"Let's put it this way," I said, laughing. "I imagine you're not too fond of weenie dogs."

"You got that right!" She drank from her can of diet soda. "Speaking of hot dogs, I was thinking we should have my husband bartend."

"He's not traveling?"

"Not at the moment."

"Okay, if he's willing." I took another bite of sandwich and tried to remind myself of anything else we needed to discuss.

"My daughter's coming home from college for the weekend, so she can pass something, too," I said finally.

"No, that won't work," Mary said. "She should focus on talking to a couple of people we think seem suspicious. We can send her in their direction."

"One problem."

She opened her eyes too wide, like she was a gigantic insect. A dare?

"It *is* a problem," I said.

"What?"

"If Laura, my daughter, is part of our investigation, she'll have to know why we think there's going to be a murder."

"Right," she said, eyes still huge, and the long lashes curling outrageously toward dramatic black arches.

"You may not think I'm crazy, but Laura will."

"She'll take issue with the Lord speaking to you?"

"It *wasn't* the Lord, remember?"

She muttered, "I don't know who else it was."

"You told me that the Lord identifies himself, so it couldn't be him."

"Maybe male lords always identify themselves—you know, it's an ego thing. But a female lord prefers to be anonymous."

"I don't believe in God," I said.

"You heard Her voice and you don't believe?" she asked.

The strangest thing happened then. I started to feel like I was going to cry, not an activity I get into often. First of all, in general, I don't approve of crying. I have that WASPy, stiff-upper-lip attitude. Which is not to say that I *never* cry. I completely lost my mind when I found out Peter had slept with someone other than me. I cried forever. Those endless tears catapaulted me into divorce, and I am strangely grateful. So, yes, I can see the value of crying, though on general principle I think people cry too much.

I stared at Mary. The feeling gripped my chest like a big hand clutching and then squishing my lungs together. I couldn't quite breathe. I gulped for air.

"Honey, I'm sorry," Mary said. "You don't have to believe. That's okay. I got enough for the both of us."

"Enough what?" I managed to say.

"Faith." Her hand reached across the table and patted mine.

"Is it faith that keeps you with a husband who 'travels'?" I'm afraid I sneered the word *faith*.

She shrugged and gave a mighty grin. "I moved beyond. That's just his body, doing the thing men's bodies are made to do."

"Okay."

"So you don't want to tell your daughter about the voice?"

"I might be able to," I said after a moment. "Maybe if I make a funny story out of it."

Mary rolled those eyes of hers before standing and picking up her lunch things to carry into the kitchen. "You want my opinion?"

I trailed after her. "Yes," I said doubtfully.

"You gotta tell her."

"Umm," I said.

"She must be a smart child," Mary said.

"Very."

"I got a son in high school. He's very smart."

She turned from the sink, where she'd rinsed out her glass.

"I'd like to meet him."

She nodded her head slightly.

After Mary left, I posted the invitation on the bulletin board next to the mailboxes. As I was about to go back upstairs, the postal delivery person, a slim woman plugged into little iPod earbuds, arrived. I loitered as inconspicuously as possible by reading other notices, but I watched as she inserted a key and swung the entire steel front of the boxes open. She bounced slightly on her knees, obviously moving to the rhythm of the music filling her head. I edged closer and tried to see into my own box. Instead, I noticed a single red dot on the lip of one box. I searched all the other boxes and couldn't see another dot.

I moved even closer and reached for the catalog she'd flipped into my box moments before. To my surprise, the mailwoman reacted by snapping me a disapproving look.

"You're not allowed to take mail until I'm finished," she said.

"Oh, I'm sorry!" I shoved the catalog back into my box. Then, since I had her attention, I pointed and continued, "What's that red dot mean?"

She yanked out one earbud and said, "What?"

I repeated the question, but this time I touched the red dot with my forefinger.

"Not my business." She shrugged and turned so that she was more effectively blocking my view. "You'll have to step back," she ordered.

I had a sense that she was probably within her legal rights to require my distance from the undelivered mail, so I stepped back and away. I decided it wasn't too far-fetched to imagine that a red stick-'em dot might be a communication of some sort. I wandered down the hallway and tried to develop more ideas about why someone would need a system of red dots. I took the elevator up to my apartment, feeling swamped by the messaging possibilities in a single red dot, though I also recognized that only a person with a key to the mailboxes could use it. So, a mailman, unless management had a key, which they probably did.

In my apartment, I lay down on the green velvet couch under the windows in the library and stared out at the trees. It had been a cloudy morning, and now, as if on command, rain splattered against the panes. Mesmerized, I watched the droplets of water roll down the glass. I halfway expected the voice. Okay, maybe I halfway wanted the voice. I tried to imagine it, but it was fairly unimaginable.

It was possible that I was lonely, even though I didn't really want to admit to such a possibility. I could still be married to Peter. I could be back in our old house, with my life rotating around Peter's schedule. I'd be planning what we'd have for dinner and maybe be on the phone with our travel agent, arranging our Christmas trip to the Caribbean. In some ways, I think I missed him, and I wasn't sure why, since I didn't miss our life together. Well, it was *his* life. I'd merely been attached to it. I liked being on my own.

And, things were perking up. The Russian god had declared himself in love with me, and I'd been tapped to prevent a murder.

I blinked, ready to get down to business. First, I had to find out who the man with a German accent was. Second, why was he lurking in the laundry room at midnight, and why did he lie about what he was doing there? Third, was I actually interested in a relationship with Ivan? For a moment, I started to lament that I didn't have a friend with whom to discuss Ivan. Then I felt a surge of liberation. I could decide for myself! I didn't have to listen to anyone else's opinion! And, if I happened to make the wrong decision, I wouldn't have to confess to anyone afterward.

Thrilled, I watched the rain.

Moments later, I hopped up and headed back downstairs, clutching a homemade chocolate-chip cookie. The day doorman, Max, had been at the Kennedy forever, and though he ought to be the soul of discretion, I had the sense that he might be quite the opposite.

"Hey, Max, I brought you a little sunshine on this rainy afternoon." I held out the cookie, centered on a white paper napkin.

"Why, thank you!"

His wrinkled face creased into an even deeper grin, which was difficult, since he normally wore a constant smile.

I leaned against the wall, making myself comfortable. "Everything okay at the Kennedy?" I asked.

He nodded, chewing the cookie.

"I had a funny thing happen at midnight the other night."

Max said sharply, "What?"

"I couldn't sleep, so I went down to the library to find something to read." I opened my mouth in a big yawn, as if to convince him. His expression was suitably nervous. "And there was someone in the laundry room."

"People can be self-conscious about their dirty stuff, you know? Don't want the whole world to see their underwear." He guffawed. "I don't have that problem myself."

"He wasn't doing his laundry—in fact, the lights were turned off."

"That's a little strange."

"You're telling me."

"Did you talk to Michael?"

I shook my head. "I don't want to get anyone in trouble. I thought I'd ask you."

Max clearly liked the idea that I respected his opinion. He thrust his hands into both pockets and rocked back on his heels. "Did he speak to you?"

I nodded. "He had a German accent."

With a squirrelly look, he sighed. "Probably Lukas Bauer—was he a big guy?"

"Very." I wrapped my arms around myself. "Frankly, he really scared me."

"That'll be Lukas."

Silence.

Finally, I said, "So why would he have been standing around in a dark laundry room at midnight?"

Max had gone dead on me. His face was blank and bored. He spotted someone approaching the front door, a long way off, and he hopped to attention. Holding the door wide open, he stepped outside while simultaneously unfurling a huge umbrella.

"I guess I *should* speak to Michael," I yelled.

My gambit failed.

"Good afternoon, Mrs. Schwartz!" he shouted to the approaching woman.

I ambled through the reception hall, down wide steps into one of the grand living rooms where no one ever seemed to be. Large windows to the right showed the dark, rainy afternoon. I found a wing chair tucked discreetly into a corner and plopped down.

So far, my detective skills weren't exactly overwhelming me with successful results. Okay, I thought, I'd have to go where the people were. That meant the swimming pool, fitness room, and the laundry facilities. I could do my swim early and not run into Ivan, but I sort of wanted to run into Ivan.

It wasn't impossible that he'd truly fallen in love with me at first sight. Why not? Just because I was fifty, postmenopausal, and not the type men usually fell for didn't mean I couldn't entertain this rather delightful fantasy. And it wasn't even my fantasy. Ivan had declared himself. I didn't make that part up.

Yet . . . it was admittedly suspect.

Fifty years without a truly romantic experience. I'm not romantic, basically. I am basic. In college and my early twenties, I was the woman with a crew of male friends, but no boyfriend. I hasten to add that this had nothing to do with my appearance. Though, perhaps, it had everything to do with my style. No-nonsense. No makeup. No hair. I wasn't *without* hair, but I wore it in a long, messy ponytail. Brown hair, pale skin that never tanned, and a size-too-large pair of jeans and T-shirt/sweatshirt combo. In retrospect, I guess I looked like a female boy, and I suppose I didn't think too highly of myself. I've never understood, until the last several months, how some people could be so enthusiastic about themselves. My whole life, I'd been a black-and-white photo. Launched as a divorcée, I suddenly saw myself in color.

I'm capable of wearing more feminine clothes now, and I put on makeup to cultivate the "handsome older woman" look. I stared down at my lap, away from the depressing view, thinking. Finally, I stood up and headed back to my apartment. I was being forced to go shopping.

Most people remake themselves at significant moments of their lives. I was at a significant moment. I was divorced. I was fifty years old. I'd heard a voice warning me that someone would be murdered. It was up to me. Sometimes you work from the inside out, and other times you have to go the other direction, from the outside in. I threw on drawstring black silk pants and a matching blouse that hung to my knees. Brushing my hair, I searched for white strands and found nary a one. Very weird. I didn't color my hair, so why wasn't I going gray? It was disconcerting. I braided my long hair and stared into the mirror.

And now I was being forced to get my hair cut. It was too long. It dragged my face to the floor. Promptly, before I could think about it any more, I called Elizabeth Arden.

The receptionist said, "Oh, my God, you're so lucky; we just this second had a cancellation from a very important client, and Lagos himself has an opening."

I thought, *Lagos?*

"I'll take it," I said.

"I should tell you, a cut with Lagos is two hundred and fifty dollars, with the blow-dry extra."

"No problem."

"See you at three o'clock."

Since I had some time to kill, I checked my e-mail and was surprised to see something from Peter.

> Dear Anne,
>
> Heard you're having a big party Friday night. Can I come?
>
> Sincerely, Peter the ex

I started to laugh. Laura must have told him.

> Dear Peter the ex,
>
> Sure, but only if you bring a date.
>
> Sincerely, Anne

I didn't want any possible romantic or sexual partners to think Peter and I were getting back together. Within seconds, my computer make that *boing* noise, telling me I had a new e-mail message.

> Dear Anne,
>
> If you insist. Her name is Ann.
>
> Sincerely, Peter the ex

I said he was impossible and I was right. Still, I had to laugh again. He'd always been great at making me laugh. I imagined his new Ann as a Yale-educated lawyer, about thirty-five years old, beautiful blond hair twisted into a nonchalant sexy bun. She wouldn't be thrilled at having to attend his ex-wife's cocktail party, but she'd learn that Peter was nothing if not complicated.

I shot off an e-mail to Laura.

> Hi, baby,
>
> Hope things are a little better. Don't forget to eat. I'm going to Elizabeth Arden to have all my hair cut off.
>
> Love you , Mom

When I was ready to go, I noticed that the skies had lightened and the rain had stopped. So, though I owned a dashing little convertible, I took the Metro from Cleveland Park to Friendship Heights. I'm a bit weird about driving. I can do it well, but I find it constantly unnerving, as if I'm possessed by someone else's skin and bones when I'm behind the wheel. Plus, I love to eavesdrop and watch strangers, and the Metro is great for people watching.

As I descended on the long escalator into the bowels of Washington, I spotted the broad back of Mary much farther down. Quickly, I moved to the left and rushed down the moving stairs.

"Hey," I said, stopping on the step behind her.

I saw the way her skin shivered with surprise. There was

something about that escalator ride that put you into another world. Maybe we all secretly imagined we were on our way to hell. I rested a hand on her left shoulder and whispered into her ear, "It's the Lord, otherwise known as Anne!"

She swatted at me, but she was laughing. Twisting around, she said, "Where are you going?"

"To get my hair cut for the party."

She nodded. "I've got to pay a visit to the beauty parlor myself."

We stepped off the escalator and moved toward the turnstiles. I was quiet, waiting to see if she'd begin the conversation. I'd begun to feel like a pesky yellow jacket, buzzing around her.

"Have you got a boyfriend?" she asked suddenly.

"No, do you?"

Mary chortled. We fed through the turnstiles, with Mary barely fitting.

"I got a boyfriend," she said.

"You really do?" Needless to say, I was astounded.

"Yup."

We boarded the next set of escalators. This time, I stood next to her.

She gave me a severe look. "Can you keep a secret?"

"I'm excellent about secrets."

"How come?"

"I just am—I'm not going to try to prove it."

We left the escalator and headed for the same platform. "Where do you live?" I asked.

"Off Shady Grove Road in Gaithersburg."

"That's a long ride."

"I enjoy it."

We found two seats together on a bench.

"So," I prompted her. "I keep secrets."

I was busy trying to imagine Mary in bed with a boyfriend.

The whole concept somewhat boggled my mind. Then I broke through. I saw her large brown body undulate, the breasts spilling and flowing, the stomach like the hilly sands beneath the sea.

"His name's Jerome," she interrupted my vision. "I figured, Well, my husband *travels,* then so can I. But I'm monogamous with Jerome."

"What's he do for a living?"

"That's the really secret part."

"Okay."

"He's an English teacher at my son's high school."

I slapped her arm. "That's playing with fire, all right."

She sighed. "I know, I know—Lord knows we tried to keep it from happening, but sometimes these things can't be controlled."

"I hope your son doesn't suspect."

She shook her head vigorously. "Not a clue."

I fell silent, trying to take it all in.

"You disapprove," she said.

"I disapproved when it was my husband, but it's harder when it's you."

She nodded. "I know what you mean." A massive sigh escaped her. "But you don't have any reason to be lonely—you're not even married anymore."

"I'm not lonely."

The lights embedded in the cement alongside the subway tracks started their quiet, rhythmic flashing, the signal that a train was approaching. We both stood up.

Mary sent me a glance full of mystery and amusement.

"What?" I practically yelled.

"Nothin'."

The rush and clamor of the approaching train filled the tunnel. After the train expelled several people, we marched on and found two seats together. The doors shut and the train left.

Mary nudged me with her elbow. "You *do* take the cake," she said.

"I don't take the cake, and, furthermore, I'm not lonely."

"All right, all right."

"Are you in love with this Jerome?" I asked.

Her eyes closed briefly. "Possibly," she said finally.

Long pause before she added, "Probably."

We didn't try to talk over the noise at the Tenley stop. But since I was getting off at the next one, I rushed to fill her in about my interrogation of Max the doorman. That's what I called it. An interrogation.

"Whiffy-sounding, huh?" Mary said.

"I sure think so."

"I'll ask Mrs. Smith tomorrow if she knows this Lukas Bauer."

Then I told her about the red dot on the mailbox.

"I doubt it means anything," Mary said.

"I guess you're right." Suddenly the red dot shifted in my imagination from its location on the mailbox to the red dot Hindu women wear over their third eye. I blinked and it shifted yet again, becoming a small diamond that twinkled just like an eye stuck in the same place on the forehead.

The subway screeched to its next stop.

Mary said, "I'm glad you're getting that haircut—increase the odds of you finding a boyfriend."

I swatted her arm, hopped up, and ran for the door.

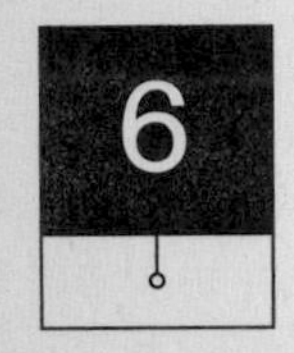

"Lagos is running a little behind." The receptionist eyed me as if trying to read my bank account from my clothing.

I remembered why I grew my hair long in the first place. Beauty parlors gave me the creeps, big-time.

"I left my Rolls with the parking attendant and *promised* I wouldn't be late."

Her eyes widened. "Why don't I try to find out exactly how long it'll be?" she offered.

"That would be utterly great." I tapped a finger on the marble console, wishing I'd worn my major diamond ring, the one I kept in a safety-deposit box because it seemed to demand something of me that I was inherently unable to provide. I'd have to remember next time.

Surprise, surprise, the receptionist rushed back and said Lagos would be with me in five minutes. Meanwhile, I could go right in to the shampoo girl. Personally, I wouldn't want to be called a shampoo girl, if that was the job I performed at Elizabeth Arden. As I changed into a smock, I tried to come up with a better designation and failed. I'd have to tip her extravagantly.

Despite my long, thick hair, which must have been terrible to wash two times, then condition, the shampoo girl was lovely. She gave a great scalp massage, so I felt she definitely earned the twenty-dollar bill I slipped into her pocket. She turned pale and murmured, "Thank you, madam."

I was escorted to Lagos's chair, like a queen being led to her throne. Only, whoops, this throne belonged to his royal highness, Lagos. I hated the man immediately.

"Dear one, dear one," he intoned, lifting my heavy, wet hair in both hands. "What on earth has happened here?"

I knew I should continue the haughty act, but I was tuckered out by the effort. Acting exhausted me.

I shrugged. "Lethargy."

He knew he'd been had by the receptionist, but he was stuck with me now. Still holding my hair in the air, making me look like I'd been electrocuted, he said, "What do you wish to do?" He sounded bored silly.

For a moment, I examined my face in the mirror. It was a damn good face, damn it. Excellent bones. Nice nose.

"What do you recommend?" I said.

He must have felt my own positive assessment and taken a real look himself. His small bald head tilted to the side.

Suddenly feeling magnanimous, I said, "You've got good bones, too."

Lagos smiled. "How old are you?"

"Fifty."

"No gray at all." His fingers combed through my hair.

"I know, it's really weird."

"I'd cut it all off, truly short, very *mignon*."

"Are you French?"

"Yes, of course, what did you think?" He kept scraping his fingers all over my head, which felt fantastic. I was starting to like him.

His fingers began a little dance across my forehead, in front of my ears, across the nape of my neck. "Wee little tendrils here and here and here," he said. "I'm telling you, it would be marvelous." Then he shrugged. "I understand this is very daring, and you may not wish for it. *Bien, pas de problème*. I am simply giving you my opinion, as you requested."

"Do it."

He dropped my hair. "Really?"

"Oui!"

And so he began to cut off all my hair. We chatted, and Lagos discovered I lived at the Kennedy.

"Ah, then you must know Mrs. Cadwallader?"

I'd naturally heard of Mrs. Cadwallader, because she was one of the major women of Washington society, but I certainly didn't know her. "I'm having a large open house this Friday," I said, not answering.

"She comes in first thing Friday morning—I will tell her how charming you are." He smiled at my reflection in the mirror.

"That would be great." I debated. "I've been getting some strange vibes in that building," I said finally.

"I believe in all that stuff, ESP, reincarnation, psychic phenomena," he said. "What kind of vibes exactly?"

I watched my hair tumbling to the floor. The shampoo girl appeared, picked up the long swatches of hair, and put them into a clear plastic bag.

"I hope you don't mind—I make a donation to Locks of Love when I cut such long, healthy hair."

"That's wonderful, Lagos."

"The vibes?" he prodded.

"Negative, as if something bad might happen there."

"Maybe you're picking up on something from the past, like the murder ten years ago."

"There was a murder at the Kennedy?" I practically shouted.

He dropped his voice. "Yes, nasty business."

"Can you tell me about it?"

"No," he whispered. "I'm sorry; I can't talk about it."

To my amazement, his eyes were full of tears.

"That's okay," I said hurriedly. I wanted to know the story, but I also didn't want Lagos to ruin my haircut.

I waited a few minutes. "I never thought I was psychic before. I don't think I believe in anything like that."

Funny how easy it was to tuck the memory of the voice away.

"I am a little psychic myself," Lagos said.

"Really?"

"For example, I know you don't have a Rolls Royce." He grinned.

I grinned back. "Bingo."

"And I feel you *are* a bit psychic, whether you believe in it or not."

"I don't see how I can be something I don't accept exists."

He shrugged in that exaggerated Gallic way.

"And you aren't French!" I said.

"Bingo."

He patted my shoulder. "We were meant to find each other. I am going to make you look so smashing it will be quite disgusting."

I laughed, jerking my head.

His hands rushed to surround my head, holding it in place. "Stay very still," he lectured.

I drifted into trying to dredge up some memory of a murder at the Kennedy, while also leaving Lagos alone as he cut. My eyes closed. I didn't want to assess the work in progress for fear it would cause heart palpitations.

Sharp odors crawled up my nose, probably the chemicals associated with dyeing hair, straightening hair, and generally controlling hair. I thought of Mary and her careful hairdo, glistening black swept high and dramatic, giving her even more stature. I wondered what Jerome was like. I'd been imagining him as an African-American, but suddenly it occurred to me that he might be white. Could I just ask her, "Hey, is he white or black?" I had no idea if that was an acceptable question.

Lagos's fingers zipped over my scalp, lifting and parting and easing the hair every which way. It felt good.

He said, "Are you getting nervous?"

"Yes."

"Can't say I blame you." His chuckle vibrated around my head.

"That's not reassuring," I said.

"Just think happy thoughts!"

"Now you're Peter Pan."

"You're going to look a little like Peter Pan," he murmured. His fingers still danced all over the place.

Try as I might, I couldn't work up too much worry about this.

"Your wardrobe will need revising," Lagos said.

"I don't really have a wardrobe."

"All the better."

There was silence. *Snip, snip, snip* went the scissors.

"You might want to peek," he said.

"No."

I heard the scissors clunk down on the shelf under the mirror. Now his hands jumped over my head, like I was a rock in the middle of a fast-moving brook. Finally, gentle pats. A sharp twitch here and there.

"Okay, I'm done."

I opened one eye. The view wasn't all that good with one eye, so I opened the other. Then, immediately, I burst into tears.

"I know, I know," he said, patting my shoulder.

People began to collect around Lagos and me. Murmurs moved like a breeze blowing through an open window.

I swiped under my eyes, clearing the tears.

"I look b-e-a-u-t-i-f-u-l," I choked out.

Humbly, Lagos murmured, "I know, baby, I know."

The voices around us grew louder and stronger: "Absolutely extraordinary. Did you take a before picture?" "She's a knockout. How did you handle the layering at the crown?" "She looks like a different woman."

I blinked and turned my head left, then right. The shampoo girl handed me a mirror, and I held it up to see the back, then each side. Returning to the front view, I saw that my face leaped forward. It's a strange thing, and maybe this is not something that's politically correct to say, but I knew I'd fallen in love with myself. Simply and utterly *in love with myself.* That had always been the problem with my marriage, of course. Its failure hadn't been a failure to love Peter. I'd just failed to love myself. I dropped the hand mirror into my lap and both hands rose to open in a questioning pose.

"Is this really me?" I said.

Laughing, all those strangers nodded yes.

After divesting myself of hundreds of dollars—*hundreds*—I bounced across the street to Neiman Marcus. I floated up the store's escalator, absolutely convinced that every eye was on me. When I glanced around, I noticed that no one was noticing me at all.

On the second floor, I moved from designer to designer, trying on various outfits. I didn't want something too formal for my party, but I certainly thought *festive* was the operative word. I've always felt politically opposed to clothes. Okay, I know we can't go naked all the time, if for no other reason than because we'd freeze and develop painful chapped spots on our butts (or so I'd imagine). But I still didn't understand people's need to so violently express themselves. I started to space out as I flipped the clothes along their racks. Then I caught sight of myself in a strategically placed mirror and I blinked with astonishment. I looked like a person. Sounds ridiculous. After all, I've always been a person, particularly a wife-and-mother kind of person, but this was different. I looked like a person, with a capital P.

Person.

So, though shopping usually exhausted me, the new haircut empowered me to perform like an outboard motor. I plowed into a section of clothes designed by someone called Eskandar. I'd never heard of him, if he was a he and not a she, but I obviously wasn't an expert. I found exactly what I was looking for: wide burnt-orange raw-silk trousers and a matching blouse that flowed off my shoulders like a waterfall and buttoned high up my neck.

Clutching my bag, I left the rarefied, slightly sickening environment of Neiman's. I stood still on Wisconsin Avenue, assessing what to do about getting some dinner. Somehow I was too excited to go back to my apartment and my leftover fettucine alfredo. I could stop for Indian takeout, but that, too, didn't fit my celebratory mood. I wanted to have an elegant meal. It was always tricky for a woman to contemplate eating in a good restaurant alone. I tended to need to dredge up a spurt of courage, and I always fell back on takeout instead, or making a fancy dinner for myself. I gripped the Neiman Marcus bag. A breeze blew around my head. I felt so *light*.

Decided, and yes, determined, I hopped the metro to the Woodley Park/Zoo stop, crossed Connecticut Avenue, and marched into Petits Plats, a small French restaurant. Every day they posted a prix fixe menu on a charming little display next to the sidewalk. Often, the dessert was *îles de flotante,* or floating islands, my all-time favorite. They seated me with gratifying fanfare at a tiny table next to the front window. I ordered a glass of white wine, the Montravel 1996. Then I tried to stop grinning. One hand rose to touch my hair; I wondered how it looked. The waitress arrived with my wine.

"Cheers," I said, immediately taking a sip.

Slowly the restaurant filled with people, almost entirely couples. By the time I'd finished my salad course, I'd begun to feel just the slightest bit beleaguered, even though the arrival of an elegant Dover sole, delicious and perfectly cooked (that is, not overdone) was everything that it promised. I drained the last of the wine, sat tall in my chair, and tilted my chin toward the ceiling. I gazed boldly at the other diners and concluded that when you were alone at a fine restaurant, it didn't matter if the couples around you were gay or straight, because you still felt out of place. I tried, but even the *îles de flotant* didn't really float for me. I was lonely. I settled the bill quickly, happy to hit the street again.

The Kennedy was about four blocks north, past the zoo's entrance. I trudged along, defeated. The evening doorman held the door open and said, "May I help you?"

"Carlos, it's me—Anne Johnson!"

He was a skinny little guy with a face scarred by acne and a smile so huge that the lips curved to touch the corners of his grinning eyes. "Ms. Johnson?" he said.

"I got my hair cut," I said weakly.

"You look fantastic!"

"Really?"

"Holy smokes, I can't believe it!"

Since Carlos was being so friendly, I blurted out, "Do you know why there's a security guard posted in the laundry room at night?"

His eyes opened with mock surprise. "I don't know about that, but I'm always the last to know anything. My wife was five months along before I got wind of a baby coming—turns out everyone else knew about it for ages."

"I was told by—"

Carlos interrupted, "See, I didn't know you were Ms. Johnson, just for example. Thought you were a visitor or something. That's what I mean; I don't seem to have the eyes God gave me."

I looked into those eyes of his and figured he was probably right.

When I got into my apartment, I turned on the small lights framing the gold mirror in the entrance hall and stared eagerly at my image. I hadn't seen it for a good hour and a half. *Wow*.

I checked for phone messages and got one from Laura. "Mom, don't get your hair cut! This is just a midlife, postdivorce blip you're going through. Don't do it—you'll regret it!"

When I looked at my e-mail, she'd also fired off a warning in answer to the e-mail I'd sent before leaving. I started to laugh, but it sounded so hollow in the empty apartment that I stopped. Restless, I hung up the new outfit and decided that I'd go for a swim. Swimming with short hair—what a luxury. On the other hand, what if it looked terrible without Lagos's special touch? He'd assured me that it required nothing. "Its beauty is in the cut—I am a master!"

I stripped off my clothes and looked at myself naked. For a minute, I was worried that I'd taken on the appearance of an ant, with a tiny head on a more substantial body. I yanked on the blue tank suit I used for swimming laps and felt better.

The fitness center was busy, but everyone's eyes were glued to the multiple television sets. The pool was quiet, since it was late for most swimmers, including, I hoped, Ivan Chernislava. I dove in and the water flowed over my head. I surfaced, gasping. It was the best feeling.

In all the excitement of the haircut, then shopping, and dining at Petits Plats, I'd forgotten about Lagos's reference to a murder at the Kennedy ten years ago. The swimming pool and fitness center were located in the new addition, completed only a year ago, so I didn't expect to get any ghostly vibes underwater. But I wondered whether the voice warning me of a murder in one month was really, somehow, from the past. I knew enough about physics in my reading of recent books like *The Fabric of the Cosmos* by Brian Greene to know that, basically, we don't know squat about how time and space really work.

Maybe it was like I picked up on a radio transmission from more than ten years ago, a message delivered to someone else entirely, and it had been referring to the murder about to happen *then*. In which case, I was off the hook. The murder had already occurred. Hadn't it? I stopped swimming at one end of the pool and lolled against the wall. This was too complicated to think about while simultaneously moving my body. So, perhaps, in that strange moment when I'd heard the voice, a wormhole had opened up and I'd been privy to information from the past. I sat with the possibility for a while. I finally concluded that it was possible. And that left me wondering what to do. Except I was committed to having the party, and I was even enthusiastic about it. I swam for another twenty minutes, putting all thoughts to the back of my mind.

I climbed out of the pool and was just emerging from a total-body towel experience, blinking like a mole, when Ivan's voice exploded nearby.

"Impossible!"

I'd probably cut off all my hair simply to discourage Ivan. Whirling around, I saw him standing about six feet away wearing only those skimpy black briefs that made him look like he was preparing for Olympic swim trials.

With the towel draped around my shoulders, and keenly aware of my bare thighs, I lifted my hands and riffled through the short hair. My intent was to make the hair and myself appear absurd. "Still love me?" I asked.

What a dumb thing to say. Why did I always do that? At the most important moments, when I was determined to play things perfectly, why did I make stupid mistakes?

"Fantastic!" Ivan exclaimed.

"Oh, come on, admit that you like women with long, flowing hair." I wrapped the towel around my upper body, under the arms, and tucked it in firmly.

He advanced on his tippy-toes. "May I touch it?"

"No!"

I couldn't take my eyes off his nipples. They were absolutely huge. I'd never seen such robust nipples. Mine, despite being attached to full-blown breasts, were like baby nipples compared to his.

But, naturally, he did touch my hair. Those sausagelike fingers of his twitched twice over the front of my head. "You look two years old," he said.

"Is that good?" I seemed to be obsessed with the devilish desire to flirt with him.

He grinned. "So, let's see, you cut off your hair and you give a big party. Interesting."

"Not really." I pulled on my terry-cloth robe, over the towel, and belted it tightly.

It looked like Ivan was about to reach out to ruffle my hair again. To deflect him, I burst out, "Do you know Lucas Bower?"

In retrospect, I don't know why I asked him. I probably had a vague sense that two foreigners in the same building might have been connected, which was a silly thought, given the high numbers of foreigners living in D.C. But beneath that initial idea, my instinct was continuing to make me suspicious of Ivan. Much as I *wanted* to believe that he found me utterly desirable, I knew it was bull.

His face went still, not as severely as the expression on Max, the doorman, but more as if his thick, handsome features melted into a mask of indifference. For such a lively face, the difference was every bit as startling. Both shoulders, muscled and firm, rose and fell. His famous nipples puckered tight, like they wanted to cede from union with Ivan's body. Then he strode to the end of the pool, ready to dive in.

"What kind of answer is that?" I said.

"The name doesn't ring," he yelled too loudly. The echo created from the pool's water sent his shout leaping around the room.

Ring, ring, ring!

He crashed into the water with a flat dive, causing waves to smack the sides of the pool and splash over the edge.

For a moment, I stood there, unmoving and stunned. What had that been about?

* * *

In my apartment, I took a quick shower, stared at my short hair for about a minute, still amazed by it, then pulled on a warm flannel nightgown. I put on the gas fire in the living room and checked my e-mail without much interest. Finally, I settled on the couch, pulling a fur afghan over my lap. The loss of hair on top was making me chilly.

Something was definitely going on with this Lukas Bauer guy. Disgusted by my poor detective skills, I jumped up and ran to my laptop, where I Googled "Lukas Bauer."

There were an amazing number of Lukas Bauers in the United States, and one in Washington, D.C., who turned out to be dead. I was surprised, until I remembered that I didn't really know how to spell either his first or last name. I began with different spellings of his first, adding new spellings of his last name. It got pretty complicated, but I kept at it, and finally found him. Lukas Bower was a German citizen, attached to the World Bank. He'd moved here six months ago, and he was high enough at the bank to have warranted a quick mention in the *Washington Post* when he arrived.

Why would a high official in the World Bank be lurking in the laundry room, and then lie about it? And why were both Max and Ivan so weird when I mentioned him?

Though I was feeling incredibly cozy in my nightie, I knew I had to continue to figure out what was going on. I might discount the voice I'd heard, or even write it off to a wormhole that opened up and allowed me to access information from the past, but I couldn't ignore what had happened since then. I changed into a red sweat suit and checked my hair, prepared for it to have suddenly gone flat and ugly. Instead, it looked pixieish. If I'd still had my long hair, it would have been dripping wet and cold all over the back of my sweatshirt. I slipped on black Chinese slippers, thought for a minute, and then headed for the kitchen.

I felt ridiculous as I stood in front of the knife drawer. Even if I were attacked, I doubted that I'd be able to stab someone with a kitchen knife. Either they'd overpower me before I got a chance, or I wouldn't have the strength to do any significant damage. I closed the knife drawer and, before I could get the heebie-jeebies, rushed into the hall and down the back stairs to the laundry room.

Lights blazed and machines humped and bumped with loads of laundry. Two twenty-something women sat up on washing machines, mouths moving fast. Apparently, one of them had been dumped by her boyfriend that morning. She glowed with so much anger that I had to admire the friend trying to help her.

I marched over to a distant washing machine, opened its door, and peered inside as if searching for a lost item of clothing. Oddly, I found a black sock, which I waved triumphantly while glancing into the far corners of the room.

"He told me *last week* that he loved me," wailed the woman who'd been dumped. "Why would he *do* that?"

I waited impatiently to hear what her best friend had to say. Why did the schmuck say he loved her just a week before?

"Something must have happened," the friend said. "Like, maybe an old girlfriend called him up, a chick who'd dumped him and now wants to get back together with him."

"He told me he'd always been the dumper and never the dumped."

I leaped into the conversation, unable to contain my wisdom for another second. "That should have clued you in."

Both women swiveled their heads in my direction, and I felt like I was a deer caught in two sets of headlights.

"You know?" I added lamely.

The best friend glared at me. "I know this is a public space, but—"

"It's okay," the other woman said. "She's right."

"Some people are naturally cruel," I said. "Don't take it personally."

The woman's eyes filled with fresh tears. "How do I *not* take it personally?"

I stuck my hand into the black sock and held it up in the air, manipulating the fingers so it seemed to be a mouth. In a deep voice, I said, "Don't be such a baby."

"Leave her alone!" the best friend said.

I continued, "You're just a crybaby. No wonder I dumped you."

The tears in the woman's eyes seemed to freeze. Then she yelled, "You son of a bitch! I am *not* a crybaby. I'm a gentle, kind soul who's been jerked around by a gigantic asshole!"

I made the sock's mouth open and close without any words. Both women burst out laughing.

"As an older woman, with some experience, I have two words of advice," I said.

"What?" said the friend.

I said, "Forget pain."

They blinked in unison.

"How do you forget pain?" said the dumped one.

"You just do."

I walked up the aisle formed by the oversize machines. "Every time you begin to feel the pain, catch it in your hand and throw it away." I used the black sock on my own hand to pretend I was snatching at something and then tossing it toward the ceiling.

"I've tried to do that, and it doesn't work," said the best friend.

"You don't want it to work." I yanked off the sock and dropped it in the lost-and-found basket by the door. "Most people love their pain. Take it away and they feel empty."

As I waited for the elevator, I heard the best friend hiss, "Who asked her, anyway?"

I smiled, pleased with myself. I was the expert on how to live one's life. *Forget pain.*

Right.

In my apartment, I put my nightgown back on and prepared my bed by plumping two goose-down pillows and laying them in the center. Then two more pillows on either side of them, so that I felt like I wasn't really alone, though, of course, I knew perfectly well that I *was* alone. I turned off the light and climbed in. Soft flannel sheets caressed my bare feet. I was exhausted, but I lay on my back with my eyes open, staring at the dark ceiling.

The phone rang, and I felt my body jerk with surprise.

I groped around for the cordless phone and finally found it by knocking it to the floor. When I'd reclaimed it and managed to push the talk button, the person calling had hung up. I waited a few minutes, until a message might have had time to be registered, but there was no message. I punched in *69 and got the recording saying that they couldn't reveal what number had been calling me.

I got out of bed, put on slippers, and went into the living room to check my e-mail.

Nothing, so I wandered into the library and knelt on the green velvet couch, pressing my face close to the dark window and cupping my hands around my eyes to peer into the dark night. I saw only the shadowy outlines of trees.

The phone rang again. This time, I leaped for it and said, "Hello!"

The sound of heavy breathing came through the receiver. Harsh and labored. In and out.

"Who is this?" I yelled.

The breathing quickened and became louder.

"You don't scare me one bit," I said.

The breathing stopped.

I waited a moment, curious until I realized that curiosity would encourage him. (I admit that I thought it was a man.) Abruptly, I hung up and headed back to bed. As I lay there in the dark, I told myself the phone call had nothing to do with my sleuthing and the possibility of a murder at the Kennedy. I closed my eyes and nestled my head into the pillow.

The phone rang and I grabbed for it. Heavy breathing again.

I slammed down the receiver, hopped out of bed, and groped my way into the living room, where I turned on a table lamp and took the receiver off the hook of the telephone in there. I buried it behind a sofa pillow so I wouldn't be able to hear the loud beeping noises, warning me a phone was disconnected. Finally, I settled back into bed.

Even though I knew it was impossible for the telephone to ring again, I couldn't help waiting for it. In fact, just before I drifted to sleep, I *did* hear it ring. I jumped and grabbed for the receiver and barked, "What?" Of course, there was no dial tone, but I felt the vibrations of the ringing still radiating through the room. I closed my eyes, listening as they grew fainter and more distant.

The next morning, I had a quick cup of coffee, then dressed in jeans and a black cashmere turtleneck sweater. When I greeted Angela in the office downstairs, she gasped.

"Anne?"

I ruffled my hair with both hands. "Yup."

"It looks fantastic," she said.

"Thanks," I said. "I need to speak to Michael."

She raised one eyebrow, obviously hoping that I'd tell her why I needed to speak to Michael, but I stared at her without adding another word. She glanced at a calendar and said, "He's free right now—go on in."

The manager of the Kennedy, Michael Callahan, was handsome in that Irish-rogue way. Black curly hair and bright blue eyes. He seemed too young for his job, but I was at the point where I thought most people were too young for their jobs.

I said, "Do you have a minute?"

"Sure, sit down. Everything okay?"

"I had a strange encounter in the laundry room the other night—" I began.

He interrupted, blue eyes dancing with amusement. "Mr. Bower came to see me. Said he was afraid he might have scared you."

I waved my hands, as if to make light of it . "Oh, not really scared. It was just peculiar. Why did he tell me he was a night watchman for the building?"

Michael smiled. "Because he is."

"He is?"

Big nod. "We don't advertise it, because we don't want the residents to start imagining there's some specific reason."

My thoughts scattered all over the place. "But I thought he worked for the World Bank."

"Must be a different person." He smiled at me as if I showed symptoms of early dementia.

I stood up and turned to go. Then I remembered what I'd been scrambling for. "Michael, do you know anything about a murder in the Kennedy that happened ten years ago?"

He grinned and opened his hands wide. "Before my time."

"But have you heard of it?"

"I think it's one of those rumors."

"I guess so."

He came around his desk and walked me across the office. "I'm looking forward to your open house on Friday," he said.

"Glad you'll be there—I like to have the support of management in case we get rowdy."

For the rest of the morning, I threw myself into shopping for the party. I didn't remember to reconnect the phone until mid-afternoon, when I discovered that I had twenty-three messages on my voice mail, all of them heavy breathing.

I was breathing heavily myself as I dialed Mary's cell phone number.

I figured it was my own panic that made it sound like *Mary* was breathing heavily as she answered her phone.

"Are you all right?" I said.

"I'll be fine," she said. Pant, pant.

I carried on: "Something has totally freaked me out."

"Can't compare to what I've got happening."

"What?" I said.

"I found my Wednesday dead."

"Today is Wednesday."

"Yup—*dead*."

"How can Wednesday be dead?"

I walked with the phone into the kitchen and started to lay out the ingredients for my famous cheese puffs, though, in truth, the recipe came from my grandmother. Despite all those phone messages of heavy breathing, Mary was already making me calm.

"My Wednesday job," Mary said, exasperated.

"The job is dead—they're letting you go?"

"You could say that." Pant, pant.

"You mean the *person* you clean for on Wednesdays is dead?"

"You did graduate from college, right?" she said.

"Who is it?"

"Senator Paul Hammer." She paused, then lowered her voice. "The police are on their way."

"What happened?" I whispered, remembering the courtly gentleman I'd talked to at the Kennedy Center just two days earlier.

"I came back upstairs from the laundry room and found him in the bathroom, dead."

"Was he—"

Mary interrupted, "Yes, on the john."

I couldn't help it. I started to laugh.

"Don't get me started," she said. "What are the police going to think if I'm laughing my fool head off?"

"I'm sorry." I gasped. "Give me a second."

The phone went dead. I held it away from my ear and stared at it, then gently poked a few buttons. Finally, when nothing happened, I pushed redial. Mary's cell went straight to voice mail. I considered leaving her a message of heavy breathing and then seriously questioned whether my insensitivity had hit an all-time low. It couldn't be pleasant to find someone dead on the toilet, especially someone famous like Paul Hammer.

I grabbed my keys from the entrance hall table, rushed out of the apartment, and took the elevator to the fourth floor, where there was a lounge area overlooking the building's lobby. I could see a single ambulance and a police car stationed in the circular drive, their rotating lights flashing and pulsating silently. A small knot of people gathered in the hall down below, and the murmur of their voices rose as the emergency medics raced through the lobby rolling a stretcher.

"There's no hurry," I whispered.

I thought of going down to join the crowd, except that I'd feel compelled to tell them what had happened to the senator, and, for Mary's sake, I knew I shouldn't say anything. In addition, I also had a feeling that Paul Hammer's family, not to mention the state of Florida, might not want the location of his death shouted from the newspaper announcements.

I went back to my apartment and began to grate the Gruyère, Montrachet, and Carayac cheeses into a heaping mound. From time to time, I nibbled a larger chunk that resisted the grater. The kitchen was large, floored in black and white squares of linoleum, with countertops of black granite. The old glass-fronted cabinets, painted white, still lined the butler's pantry, and the new cabinets were matched to them, also painted white. One huge window centered over the sink let in lots of light. It was a grand kitchen for cooking, and I was looking forward to the next two days of preparing food for the party. As the cheese fell into little mountains, I forgot about the heavy-breathing messages on my phone. Cooking could lull me into a strange nowhere land where my mind blanked out and thoughts disappeared. I didn't even listen to music while I cooked. Just little ol' me and piles of cheese.

I stirred the cheese slowly over the double boiler, watching it melt, and I remembered everything that was going on. In the moment of remembering, the phone rang. I froze. I'd forgotten to attach my cordless, hands-free phone to my belt, my usual practice when I got into major cooking mode. I grabbed the regular phone with my left hand, while continuing to stir with my right.

Quietly, I said, "Go blow." I pushed the button to disconnect and placed the phone down on the countertop.

It rang again immediately.

This time, before I could utter a word, scatological or otherwise, I heard Mary's voice yelling, "It's me; don't hang up!" Because the words were already spewing from my lips and I couldn't stop them, I said, "Go blow," followed by, "Sorry, I know it's you now."

"What is *wrong* with you, woman?" Mary said.

"I'll tell you later," I said. "How's it going?"

"They got him out of here, and I'm just doing a little tidying up; then I can leave, too."

"Oh, my God, *tidying up,*" I said. "Mary, you can't be expected to clean the aftereffects of *death*."

"Wanna bet?"

"Yes!" I stirred the cheese like a maniac. "The family can hire specialists for a job like that."

"I have my pride."

"What's that supposed to mean?"

"It means I worked five years for the senator, and when I leave this apartment, I'm leaving it clean."

"You certainly do have integrity," I said. "Misplaced integrity, but nevertheless."

"I have a favor to ask," Mary said.

"Yes."

"You don't know what it is."

"Doesn't matter," I said, "the answer is yes."

"I'd like to come by your place after I'm done here and have a drink."

"Great idea—then I can tell you my own bit of nerve-racking news."

Mary said dryly, "Maybe this has to do with why you answer the phone by saying, 'Go blow'?"

"What's your drink of choice?" I said.

"Today, I'm not picky."

While the melted cheese cooled, I whipped up a pitcher of martinis and placed it in the refrigerator. I popped two martini glasses into the freezer, set the oven to 350 degrees, then slowly stirred sour cream into the melted cheese, making sure it didn't curdle. Cayenne pepper, several other spices, and a smidgen of baking powder were folded in at the end. I buttered two large cookie sheets and dropped spoonfuls of the cheese mixture at regular intervals. The first batch would bake for ten minutes.

I checked the hall bathroom and decided the toilet needed a quick scrub. Only after I'd finished did I realize that this echoed Mary's unpleasant chore.

The dinger on the timer sounded, and I tore through the apartment to get to the cheese puffs. From long experience, I knew they fell flat and turned crisp if they baked too long. I lined them up on wax paper, like little yellow suns, scrubbed the cookie sheets, rebuttered them, and started all over again for the second batch. I popped one of the freshly baked puffs into my mouth and said a silent thank-you to my grandmother as the cheese melted in my mouth.

My grandmother, a wealthy grande dame, would be horrified that I had invited Mary to my apartment for drinks. I'd grown up in Savannah, Georgia, visiting Grandmother for Sunday dinner every week. She'd died twenty years ago, and there had been many moments since then when I had gotten a real kick out of imagining her displeasure, particularly the moment my son, Andrew, had announced he was gay.

My own parents, Andrew's grandparents, had coped well with his announcement. He'd chosen Christmas Eve three years ago so that he could make an elegant connection between the birth of the son of God with his own birth as a gay man. Though Peter and I were distinctly antireligious, and Andrew was a nonbeliever, the association between Jesus Christ and himself had galvanized the entire family. Perhaps it also helped my parents that they'd retired overseas, to the coastal town of Antibes in the south of France. Or, for all I knew, maybe they harbored secret thoughts that Andrew would grow out of it. I didn't believe he'd ever change, which didn't mean I was totally sanguine about it, either. Mostly, I didn't want my son to get AIDS. And, after all, the story of Jesus Christ hadn't ended happily.

After I put the second batch of cheese puffs in the oven, I wandered through the living room, shaking the down pillows on the couch and straightening several picture frames. In all the excitement, I realized that I hadn't written my parents their weekly e-mail, something I tried to do every Monday night. If I didn't get to it by tonight, they would call in the morning, which I definitely wanted to avoid. They had many ideas for how I ought to be spending my time, from teaching English as a Second Language classes to importing antiques they'd ship over while I served as the go-between with dealers and designers.

The doorbell chimed.

"I made a pitcher of martinis," I said as soon as I opened the door.

Mary screamed at the sight of me, and I realized that she hadn't seen my haircut.

I grabbed her arm and pulled her inside. "What do you think?"

She mock-hyperventilated, with her hands fluttering around her chest and her bosom heaving. "You look tre-men-dous."

"Gee, thanks."

In the living room, she collapsed into a corner of the couch. Just then, I heard the timer in the kitchen.

"Those are my cheese puffs," I said. "Take off your shoes, relax, and I'll be right back."

I was transferring the puffs onto the wax paper when she came shuffling into the kitchen in her sock feet.

"Sorry," I said, "but if I don't get these off right away, they keep cooking."

She nodded and moved to look out the kitchen window. "Have you ever seen anyone dead?"

I thought for a minute. "I don't think so," I said finally.

"Maybe it's one of those experiences that, in hindsight, seems like it was educational, but right now—"

I interrupted, "Right now, you don't see its value."

"Exactly." She turned around. "Hey, do you mind if I call home real quick, tell my son I'll be late?"

"There's the phone." I gestured to the cordless next to the oven, where I'd put it down after talking to her earlier.

She stayed in the kitchen while she telephoned, which made me feel good. Seemed like she trusted me to overhear the conversation, and also, I *wanted* to overhear the conversation.

"Patrick, this is your mother," she said imperiously into the phone.

And she thought people weren't scared of her.

"Listen to me," she said. "I left the slow cooker on this morning with some chicken."

Pause.

"Right, I'm glad it smells so good." She rolled her eyes at me and I smiled. "I'm gonna be late because I found Senator Hammer dead in his apartment today." Another pause.

I had to fight the urge to laugh. When I glanced at Mary again, I could see she was fighting it, too. Quickly, I opened the freezer door and hid behind it while bringing out the martini glasses.

"I'll tell you all about it when I get home. For now, you just need to know the following: Your father will be home at five o'clock wanting his dinner. You make the microwave rice and ladle the chicken over it, okay? Tell him I'll be home soon as I can. Get going on your homework."

"What's your husband do, anyway?" I removed the pitcher of martinis from the refrigerator and began stirring with the long glass spoon.

"Insurance claims adjuster."

"So he really does travel."

She raised her eyebrows. "Pays well, and it's steady."

Somehow I had the impression that Mary wasn't as easygoing about her husband's *traveling* as she made out to be, even if she traveled a bit herself, but I decided now wasn't the time to say anything.

I poured two martinis and picked them up. "You'd better take a couple of cheese puffs, too," I said. "These are powerful."

Instinctively, she pulled open the correct drawer and found a napkin, onto which she placed three cheese puffs.

"Take one more—I'm going to need a little sustenance myself."

After we'd gotten ourselves situated, we reached for the martinis. I held mine up for a toast. "Here's to life," I said.

"Don't you mean death?"

"No, I mean *life*."

We clinked glasses and took healthy slurps. Mary smacked her lips together and closed her eyes.

"Now that hits it," she whispered.

I nodded and grabbed a cheese puff. "You ready to describe all the gory details?"

"In a minute—first tell me why you were answering the phone with 'Go blow.' "

So I told her about the phone calls the night before, how I disconnected the telephone, and only remembered to reconnect it in the early afternoon, when I found twenty-three messages of heavy breathing.

"You save 'em?" Mary asked.

"Yup." I nodded vigorously.

"Let me hear one."

I took another generous gulp of martini and went across the room to get the phone for her.

When I stood in front of her with the phone, she said, "Thank you for your hospitality. I really do appreciate it."

I waved her words away, got the voice mail going, and handed her the phone. "Press the number seven to keep hearing them."

She listened for about two minutes, then disconnected. "Sort of silly-sounding, huh?"

"I know what you mean. At first, when I called you right after finding them, I was scared just by the number of them. But there's something ersatz about the whole thing, like it's a joke."

"Who's really got time to leave twenty-three messages of heavy breathing?"

"A kid?"

"Possibly—or someone who's playing around because they're bored."

"I will say this, though." I took a smaller sip of martini. "Something strange is going on in this building. I don't know what it is, and I wouldn't go so far as to say it has anything to do with the voice in my head, but I definitely think there's been suspicious stuff."

She nodded. "Even the senator dying on the john."

Startled, I stared at her. "He died of old age, right?"

"Could be." Mary chewed on her first cheese puff. "Yummy."

"Oh, come on," I said. "Senator Hammer was at least eighty years old."

"Eighty-two, to be precise." She washed down the cheese puff with martini. "I'm not saying it wasn't old age—I'm saying that the whole thing made me uneasy." She shivered and pointed to the gas fire. "Can we put that on?"

I jumped up and grabbed the remote control. "How much flame do you want?" I asked, making it grow more and more fiery.

"That's good."

"Was he still on the toilet when you found him?"

"You think a dead man can stay upright on a toilet?" she demanded.

"Don't get your panties in a twist," I said.

Mary shouted, "Don't get my *what* in a twist?"

I started to giggle. "Haven't you ever heard that saying, 'Don't get your panties in a twist'?" I said. "It means not to—"

She interrupted, laughing, "I know what the hell it means—I just can't believe you said it."

Obviously, the martinis were doing their job.

"I've been meaning to ask you something," I said.

"What?" She tried to make it sound intimidating, but I was on to her now.

"Is this Jerome guy you travel with white or black?"

Mary threw back her head and guffawed. "Oh, my God, oh, my God," she yelled.

I laughed myself, but persevered. "There is nothing at all funny about my question."

She pointed at me, howling. "Yes, there is."

"Well, what's so damn funny about it?"

"You're really asking whether you can be my friend," she said, swiping at her eyes with the napkin.

"I am not!"

"You figure if I've got a white boyfriend then I could have a white girlfriend."

I grinned. "So, Mary, what do you think of white people?"

"They're fine." She slurped her martini. "Jerome is black, though."

I stood up. "I'm getting us more cheese puffs."

"We keep eating those puffs, there won't be any left for the party."

I returned with small plate of them, plus the last of the martini mix. The glass spoon clanged like a bell as I stirred and then poured.

Mary said, "Oh, no more for me, no more," while simultaneously holding out her glass.

"I'm not throwing this stuff down the sink." I emptied the pitcher, giving us each about a quarter of a glass full.

We had a moment of contemplative silence as we sipped.

I prodded gently. "So, he'd fallen off the toilet?"

"He slipped sideways, and the wall's right there. He was sort of lodged, all higgledy-piggledy, in that tiny space."

"Doesn't sound too comfy."

"I think he was beyond feeling whether or not it was comfy."

"That's good, anyway."

Mary nodded. "He was A-okay. I liked him."

I stared at her for a second, building up my courage to ask the next question. "How come you clean people's apartments?"

"You mean why don't I do something better with myself?"

"No, I really mean *why* do you clean people's apartments?"

She threw another cheese puff in her mouth. "It's com-plicated," she drawled.

"You don't want to talk about it?"

"It's been a long enough day—and this drink is doing a number on me. I don't want to ruin the effect." With a heavy sigh, she struggled briefly to sit up straighter. "I probably ought to head home."

I nodded. "Ummm."

Then something happened that was every bit as astonishing as hearing that voice in my head. Simultaneously, we both slid lower and tilted our heads back against the pillows. We fell asleep.

I woke up first, an hour later. Mary had slumped to the left, and her head was resting on a sofa pillow. Her snores were like something out of a fairy tale, a monster's crashing footsteps in the deep, dark forest. I tiptoed into the bathroom, peed, brushed my teeth, and stared at my suddenly aging face. I still couldn't accept that I was fifty years old. More like seventy. With both hands I fluffed my darling haircut, which remained darling despite the martinis. Finally, I shook out two aspirin and gulped them down with a glass of water.

I took two more aspirin with me to the kitchen, filled a tall glass with ice and water, then returned to Mary in the living room. I stared at her peacefully sleeping, and debated. It was five o'clock, and the Metro ride all the way to Shady Grove was at least an hour, probably longer with the rush-hour crowd.

"Hey, Mary," I whispered.

Her lips parted, and she groaned something indecipherable.

"I think you'd better wake up." I thought I was over being scared of her, but it was always prudent to be careful when you woke someone from a martini-induced sleep, particularly someone you didn't know all that well yet.

Mary murmured, "No, thank you."

She sure had good manners.

I put the glass of water down on the coffee table, then touched her shoulder. "Mary, come on; your son will wonder what happened to you."

One eye opened, and she glared at me. I jumped away with a little shriek. Now both eyes flew open and blinked wildly.

"Where am I, if you please?" she said.

"You're at Anne's apartment. I'm Anne." I smiled gently, feeling like an idiot. "Remember, Senator Hammer died on the john, and you had to clean everything up; then you came here, and we drank martinis?"

Big brown eyes searched the coffee table and landed on the martini glass. Hers, unlike mine, had about a quarter of an inch of liquid left in the deep well of the glass. Suddenly she sat up in a rush, reached for the glass, and drained it.

I offered, "There's some aspirin and a glass of water, if you're so inclined."

She threw herself backward and said, "I am inclined—get it, *inclined*?"

"You are one weird drunk," I said.

"Everyone tells me that—I never remember, so I have no other way of knowing."

I picked up the aspirin and held them out. "Here, I think these would be a good idea."

She tossed them into her mouth like they were candy, chomped on them, and swallowed. I grimaced.

"I can't taste bitter or sour," she said.

"That's impossible."

"Happens to be true."

"It must be some kind of psychological thing," I said. "Like you refuse to experience anything negative."

"Nothing to do with it." Mary heaved herself straighter in the couch. "I got tested."

"And?" I sat down, reached for the fire's remote control, and lowered the flame.

Mary looked at me like she finally understood how dense I was. "And I can't taste anything bitter or sour. Missing crucial cells on my tongue." She smiled and blushed. "My only claim to fame."

I leaned forward. "Lemme see."

She slid to the edge of her chair and stuck her tongue out at me. I moved in close and examined her rather impressive-looking tongue.

Mary spoke while her mouth remained open, so the words were thick. I watched the tongue move like some kind of beached sea animal. "I'm abnormal and proud of it."

Not to feel left out, I extended my own tongue and wagged it around.

"Now, *your* tongue is normal," she said, still talking so that her words were mushy.

I said, "I want a tongue that can't taste bitter or sour."

"You've got the voice. Be grateful."

Mary stretched, making her bosom explode even more dramatically from her chest. Then she heaved herself to a standing position, where she rocked for a few seconds. "Mind if I use the facilities?"

"I scrubbed the toilet before you came."

She shook her head. "You really have issues."

I went into the kitchen and peered at the remainder of the cheese-puff mixture. There was probably another cookie sheet's worth, but I wasn't sure whether they'd turn out well now. I picked up the wooden spoon and gave the batter a couple of vigorous stirs.

Mary, coming up behind me, said, "They'll be okay."

I glanced at her. "You think so?"

"Trust me."

I smiled and began to butter the cookie sheet.

"Maybe I can stop by tomorrow afternoon, after my Thursday, and give you a hand," Mary said.

"I'll be okay."

"I'm an exceptional cook."

"Somehow that doesn't surprise me."

She nudged me with her elbow and laughed. "You could clean while I cook—that toilet looked great."

After Mary left and the last batch of cheese puffs were cooling, I wrote a long e-mail to my parents in the south of France. I didn't tell them that their grandaughter had hooked up with a college senior; I didn't tell them I was making a friend who happened to clean apartments for a living; I didn't tell them that I'd heard a voice in my head asking me to prevent a murder; I didn't tell them that a Russian hunk had declared his love and had, in the name of love, refused to sleep with me.

Instead, I told them I was having a party. I told them I'd cut off all my hair and it looked great. I told them about the weather. I told them their grandaughter was coming home for the weekend to help me with the party because I suspected she had a small case of homesickness. So, in essence, I told them nothing much.

One boring job down, I contemplated the next one. Dinner. Go out? Stay in? Go out for takeout and stay in to eat it? I turned to the window, to check whether going out was even an option. If it looked the least bit like rain, I would opt for the leftover fettucine alfredo.

The doorbell rang.

I checked that I was fully clothed, and was halfway there when I slowed my steps. The door, lost in the dark shadows of the unlit entrance to my apartment, exuded anxiety. My own, of course. An apartment door couldn't, in and of itself, be anxious.

There weren't all that many choices of who could be ringing my doorbell, and the most likely was Ivan. Without turning on the lights near the door, I tiptoed forward and put my eye to the peephole. I made out nothing at all until my eye dropped about a foot and I saw Miss Dora. Quickly, I turned on the lights and threw open the door.

She was dressed, head to foot, in golden lamé. In the dim hallway, she shone like a beacon. Even her walker was festooned with looping garlands of gold, remnants of Christmas-tree decorations. Miss Dora cocked her head up and said, "Am I too late for the party?"

"Oh, Miss Dora, please come in."

"*You* don't look very festive," she grumbled as she moved through my doorway. Then she stopped. "The party's over?"

I leaned close to her head and shouted, "You're early, not late! The party's not for another two days!"

"Ah, shoot!" She looked down at her outfit. "Don't know if I can do this again in another two days—it took forever."

I yelled, "Please come in and visit for a while!"

"Just a few minutes," she said. "I need to sit down and rest before I head home."

Resolute, she clumped forward with the walker. The gold garlands swayed. In the living room, she stopped to get her breath and look around. "Pretty."

I couldn't believe she'd actually said something nice. "Like you!"

When she'd managed to sit down in one of my armchairs, I said, "Would you like a cup of tea?"

"How about a sherry?"

I debated over the sweet or dry sherry, and went with the sweet.

She loved it, smacking her lips with pleasure.

"So, Miss Dora, I guess you know about Senator Hammer?" I said.

She nodded without any apparent grief. "I was hoping he'd marry me."

I blinked, then saw the amusement in her face. A joke! So I laughed heartily, and she joined in.

"Ever since the murder, people just keep on dying," she said. "I have a theory that death is contagious. That's why I put all this on and hotfooted it to your party." She looked around, obviously still surprised that there was no party. "I also have a theory that you can fool death." She thrust out her meager, gold-lamé-covered chest. "Death wouldn't dare touch me!"

I leaned forward and raised my voice, even though it seemed like she was hearing better when she sat down and could concentrate. "Tell me about the murder."

"Well, that Nicholas Appleby was an idiot! He might've been handsome, but he should have known better than to pay for sex."

I found it difficult to believe that Miss Dora was talking about paying for sex.

She continued, "I know people have their appetites—you can't live to my age without understanding the appetite of a human being, and I know it's hard to deal with it when you're young, but Nick was sixty-five years old. He should have turned on *Saturday Night Live,* indulged in a big bowl of ice cream, and given it a rest."

"You mean sex?"

She nodded and sipped her sherry.

I considered trying to get her to backtrack and fill me in on all the details, in chronological order. But a glance at that glittering lamé changed my mind. Best to let her give full expression to herself, howsoever she wished. I took a sip of sherry and waited, though not for long.

"I've always figured sex is like a terrible itch," Miss Dora said. "Have you ever suffered from poison ivy?"

"Yes, it's—"

She interrupted, "Sex can be like that when you're young, an unbearable itch. You gotta scratch or die!"

Her face, all loose wrinkles and folds of white skin, trembled.

I figured she was upset, so I thought about trying to change the subject. But then I realized she wasn't upset. She was passionate. Her lips, moist from the sweet sherry, opened and closed twice.

She said, "So, my question to Nicholas Appleby in the hereafter is this: did he really need a pineapple finial stuck up his ass? Did that scratch his itch unto death?"

My eyes bugged. A pineapple finial?

Miss Dora finished her sherry and began to gather herself together, ready to launch from sitting to standing.

"Was the murder ever solved?" I said.

She stared at me as if I'd spewed nonsense.

"First of all, Nick actually died of a heart attack, but they theorized it was the finial that caused the heart attack. Anyway, they caught the murderer in Nick's Rolls-Royce as he drove out of the garage. Poor child. Underage, of course. I'd imagine he completed serving his time several years ago."

Miss Dora rose from the chair and grasped her walker with firm hands.

"I hope you'll make the effort to come by again Friday night," I said.

"Oh, I'll be here. I don't plan to die for at least another twenty years," she said.

I escorted her out my door and pressed the brass button to call the elevator. Just as the elevator doors closed, she said, "Nice haircut."

By this time, I was close to starving. Much too hungry to go out or to take the time to prepare a whole new meal. I sprayed a frying pan with olive oil and dumped in the congealed fettucine alfredo. With a nonstick spoon, I poked the mass of pasta until it started to sizzle around the edges. I turned down the heat and went to set a single place mat on the dining room table, where I also turned on the electric fireplace and lit the candles in my grandmother's silver candlesticks. It looked so grand and romantic that I felt strangely buoyed up.

I stared into the fake flames of the electric fire while I ate, and then shifted my gaze to the candles. Quietly, I reassessed everything. I still thought the breathing noises left on my voice mail weren't truly threatening. Since they'd come after I talked to Louis the doorman, Michael the manager, and Ivan the Russian stud about the German guy lurking in the laundry room, I had to assume they were meant to discourage the line of questioning I'd begun. If Mr. Lucas Bower was really a security guard, why would my questioning elicit scary phone messages of heavy breathing? And, really, why *had* Ivan acted so bizarre? In my mind, I replayed the encounter at the swimming pool the evening before. I concluded that my question had bothered Ivan. He was guilty about something, and I was going to have to find out what it was. Perhaps it was time to pay him a surprise visit.

Then there was Senator Hammer's death on the toilet, which kept waving at me from the back of my mind, as if to get my attention. Everything pointed to his having died of old age, but I wondered how long Mary had been down in the laundry room. I jumped up, grabbed the cordless phone, then sat back down at the dining room table.

"Hi, Mary? It's me."

She moaned. "Are you going to be one of those girlfriends who *hounds* me?"

"I'm very independent, but we are in the midst of a serious investigation, and I had a question for you."

"What?"

"Do you think you could be a little more gracious?"

Her voice dripped with sugar. "What, baby cakes?"

"Much better." I paused to take a quick bite of pasta. "How long were you in the laundry room during the time when the senator must have died?"

"About thirty minutes," Mary said. "But the police obviously thought his heart gave out."

"You said yourself that you weren't sure."

"That's 'cause there's something going on. I can feel it just like you do."

"I thought you were putting your faith in *my* feelings."

"I've been meaning to explain, but those martinis kind of took all the words out of me. The thing is, I probably never entertained the idea that you were crazy, because you were saying what I was already feeling."

"Back to Senator Hammer, then," I said. "Thirty minutes is a reasonable length of time. Someone could have killed him."

"Dubious."

"Why?"

"Mostly because he didn't look like anyone had killed him—to be perfectly honest, he looked like he was taking a dump and then died."

"Did he have a surprised expression on his face?"

"I don't know!"

"Was he smiling?"

"Honey, do *you* smile when you take a dump?"

"That's private information."

"Well, it's not private to me—let me announce to the world that I do not smile when I take a dump!" Mary practically shouted.

"You know, I'm just trying to prevent a murder—"

She interrupted, "If Senator Hammer was murdered, then you've already failed; plus it means your voice got it wrong and the murder occurred early."

I whirled the last strand of fettucine around my fork. "That's true—I hadn't thought of that."

"Huh." She snorted.

"You're pretty smart," I said.

"Don't need to tell me."

"Okay, see you after you finish your Thursday."

I took my plate into the kitchen and washed all the dishes. I'd tried to use the dishwasher when I'd first moved in, but I couldn't stand waiting a whole week just to fill it up enough to warrant running a cycle. So now I washed and dried the dishes by hand, another opportunity to daydream.

Finished, I investigated the freezer for the possibility of ice cream. *Nada.* Typical single woman: no ice cream under the mistaken belief that I would somehow avoid eating too many calories if I didn't keep ice cream in the house. Ah, well. I opened the pantry closet door and stared knowingly at the shelves of food. There would be something here that satisfied my sweet tooth if I just kept looking. To use Mary's lingo, I *felt* it.

Sure enough, I saw the wooden box of French, chocolate-covered apricots that my parents had sent to me when I moved into the apartment. I'd shoved them back, nearly out of sight, on the topmost shelf, but now I stepped up on the handy stool I kept in there and reached for them. My salivary glands shot sparks inside my mouth as I wrestled to get the box open. Using a screwdriver and some swear words, I managed it. I placed two plump apricots, covered in rich French chocolate, on a dessert plate and carried it into the dining room, where I pulled out my chair to ceremoniously seat myself. Delicate, careful, I nibbled at the first apricot.

Yikes. That was a shockingly magnificent taste. The chocolate clung to the sticky apricot, which in turn stuck to my teeth. One bite required serious probing into the hidden crevices of my mouth.

After I'd finished the second apricot, with my taste buds still firing overtime, I reviewed the conversation I'd had with Miss Dora about the murder of Nicholas Appleby. She'd said the murderer, who'd been a kid at the time, was probably out of prison. Perhaps this kid, now a man, had returned to hang around the building in some capacity, eager to take revenge on the person or persons who'd nailed him leaving the garage after he'd murdered Nicholas Appleby.

On my to-do list, then, besides preparing for a large cocktail party and seducing Ivan, was to figure out whether the Kennedy had recently taken on any new male employees. I knew everyone in the obvious positions—doorman, receptionist, manager, parking garage attendant, housekeeper. But there were many more behind the scenes, like electricians, heating and cooling people, custodian, landscaper, and most of those jobs tended to be filled by men. A visit to Angela in the morning would be a start.

As I showered, I wished I hadn't eaten quite such a large dinner, not to mention those apricots, which now struck me as repulsive. I placed both hands on my distended stomach and took solace in imagining the zaftig Russian women Ivan was used to. Of course, I knew there were willowy beauties in Russia. I just chose not to dwell on them. I rubbed the towel hard over my short hair, having already learned that it looked best when I messed it up. Then I ladled on the body cream.

I questioned what to wear. Since Ivan was gorgeous, I figured plenty of younger women were always seducing him with revealing cleavage and tight butts. I couldn't compete with that, so I had to go with my strengths. What, one might wonder, were the strengths of a fifty-year-old woman? I sat on the edge of my bed, feeling the smooth satin of the bedspread beneath my bare bottom. There had to be something, I thought, trying not to despair. Unfortunately, the two halves of my robust bottom reminded me of those apricots. And I already mentioned that their memory was a bit sickening. I rocked back and forth, from one half to another, feeling them squish together and then apart.

Maybe fifty-year-old women had no strengths, relative to younger women. Okay, so I was losing my nerve. I'm not ashamed to admit it. For the first time in days, I wanted to hear the voice again. Should I have sex with a man solely for the sake of the investigation? Was that immoral? And would it even provide me with relevant information?

The truth was that I hadn't had sex with anyone (never mind making love) for six months. The last time had been with a man I'd met at the library, of all places. He was sixty years old, cultivated, and quite attractive. Also, as it turned out, one of those married men who didn't wear a wedding ring. As Miss Dora so aptly pointed out, the desire for sex was an itch caused by exposure to something toxic, like poison ivy. With age, one's immunity built up. Or ideally it did. This wasn't a uniform process, of course. With poison ivy, in fact, the more exposure you had over the course of a lifetime, the worse your suffering. Still, I persisted in believing that aging did bring gifts. My "itch" was barely there most of the time. Other times, admittedly, it could get pretty damn itchy. But it was never terrible. I didn't suffer.

I wanted to go to bed with Ivan.

But . . .

I wanted to go to bed with Ivan and then be able to turn back the clock and pretend it had never happened. Suddenly, in one of those moments of overwhelming insightfulness, I wondered *why*. Why couldn't I be comfortable with my own desire? So I had a little itch that needed a little scratching. Nothing wrong with that. Like most moments of insight, at least for me, I only got as far as the question. I wasn't so hot with the answer.

I scooched off the bed and went over to my bureau to find my oldest and dearest pair of blue jeans. I'd had them for twenty-five years, since the early Chicago days of my marriage to Peter. I'd be surprised if I wore them even once a year. I treated them like some kind of precious talisman, particularly since I was secretly thrilled that I could still fit into them. They were men's jeans, with a button fly and a magical faded-blue color. I pulled them on over black underpants. Then a skimpy black bra and a tight black T-shirt. On my feet, my black embroidered chinese slippers. In the bathroom, I stared for a minute at my reflection, debating. Then, in a fit of bravado, I carefully applied only a pale neutral lipstick. My fingers ruffled my hair. I saw my face go still.

We rarely really look at ourselves. Usually we're putting on a face, literally or figuratively, when we look into a mirror. We *think* we're looking at ourselves, but really, we're not. It's almost unbearable if you simply stare into your own eyes, without expression, without thought, without an agenda. Simply unbearable. I dare you to try it.

Ivan lived in a wing distant from my apartment. Before the recent addition, the Kennedy was in the shape of a cross, and Ivan's place was at the top of the cross. Mine was at the intersection of the vertical and horizontal lines. As I wended my way down the long, dimly lit halls, I realized I'd never actually been in this part of the building. I was no longer nervous. Staring into the mirror had done the trick. Nothing could be so intimidating as my own naked face. And naked was where I was going, make no mistake. I was going to get naked and scratch my itch. And, oh, yeah, check whether Ivan had any pertinent information about a murder occurring at the Kennedy within approximately twenty-five days.

In front of his door, I stood still and listened. Not a sound, but old buildings were constructed to be quiet. I knew he could be inside having a raucous time with someone closer to his age. Unlike my apartment, there was no doorbell, just a small knocker mounted around the peephole. I let the knocker fall three times. The door flew open almost immediately, surprising me.

Ivan was robed. That's the only way to put it. He was wearing a black velour robe that fell all the way to his ankles. His wide, handsome face exploded out of the top of the robe, framed by its hood.

"You look like a monk," I said.

He grinned. "I am not *quite* a monk." He took a step backward and gestured for me to come in.

"You were rude last night at the pool." I marched past him, my hands thrust deep into both pockets of the jeans. "I thought I'd give you the opportunity to apologize."

Briefly, it flashed through my mind that I'd suddenly figured out the strength of a fifty-year-old woman. Assurance. Self-confidence. Insouciance.

He lived in a studio apartment, where he'd made no attempt to hide the bed. It was front and center.

"Would you like a beer?" he said.

"Sorry, I hate beer."

The bed was covered in a furry brown comforter of some kind. I thought I'd seen it in the Pottery Barn catalog, because I'd briefly considered purchasing it for my guest room. There was a small love seat tucked under the windows, which was where I sat down.

Ivan stretched one arm along the doorjamb leading into the kitchen, then folded it back to wrap around his head. Very cozy. "I also have vodka."

"Do you keep it in the freezer?"

He smiled and gave his head a quick nod.

"I'll have some vodka, straight, no ice."

When he disappeared into the kitchen, I let out a big sigh. I had to admit that he wasn't merely good-looking. He had something. Charm. And, yes, for a young man, an enviable amount of . . . assurance, self-confidence, insouciance.

He crossed the room holding two small shot glasses of icy clear liquid. After he gave me mine, he patted my knee, as if to say, *Please move over*. I moved over, and he sat down next to me. In the silence of our sipping, I heard the sound, despite its low volume, of bombastic music.

"Is that Borodin?" I said.

Ivan blushed. "I wasn't expecting company."

"What's wrong with listening to Borodin?"

"So *Russian*—it's embarrassing."

"Could you turn it up?"

He shook his head no.

"But I'd like to hear it more clearly, and, you know, with these fifty-year-old ears, I need some help." I tapped my right ear, the one closer to him.

He leaned toward me, his lips a breath away from my ear. "Can you hear this?" he whispered.

A thrilling tingle rushed over my body. And, at the same time, a cry of despair, anger, pain, joy burbled out of my mouth. It had been so long. I had forgotten the exquisite beauty of desire. Tears filled my eyes. Mortified, I blinked quickly, trying to wick them away.

He carried me to his bed. He removed every piece of clothing with ease. He didn't laugh. He didn't frown. When he threw off his robe and his naked body stretched over mine, I did. I laughed, I frowned. I was one noisy, demonstrative person. I'm pretty sure he liked every minute of it.

Several hours later, during a lull, I said, "You claimed you wouldn't make love to me."

Ivan was lying on his back, both hands folded winglike under his head. "I said I loved you."

"So—exactly."

"If I *love* you, then I must be willing to give you what you need. Correct? That is love."

"You didn't want to make love?" I teased.

His eyes slid sideways to look at me. "I did not wish to make love, no."

Stunned, I stared at him.

"Truly," he whispered. "Now you may never love me as I love you, but I had no choice."

My right hand formed a fist and I beat him on the chest. "You're ridiculous—I'm insulted."

"Oh, you American women!" He rolled to face me. "I tell you I love you, and what do you reply? That you are insulted by me!"

"Because it's insulting to say you love someone you don't even know."

"I don't know you?" One hand ran down my body.

"That doesn't count."

His hand moved again. "This doesn't count?"

I swatted him away. "No, what your hand touches has nothing at all to do with loving a person. That's sex."

"I don't wish to argue," he said. "We'll see who's right eventually."

We made love again. I think it was the fourth time, but I wouldn't want to swear to it. I've never been the type to keep count, because, as I now realized, there'd never really been a reason to count beyond three. Three was three. Anything more than three simply became stupendous.

We dozed for a while, but at four o'clock in the morning, I woke up. A few seconds later, I had the sense that he, too, was awake.

"Are you hungry?" he whispered.

"Starving."

With a great heaving of the bedclothes, he rolled out of bed. I felt the vibrations of his footsteps as he walked into the kitchen. He was a big guy. He'd never closed the blinds over his windows, and the deflected light of Washington swam through the room. I vaguely wanted to go back to my place, but only vaguely. The temperature of the apartment had dropped through the night, and it was cozy underneath the furry comforter.

"Ivan?" I called.

"Yes?"

"Why did you react so oddly when I asked about Lucas Bower?"

"I didn't!"

He appeared briefly, framed in the kitchen doorway. "Cheese and crackers okay?"

"Sure."

I sat up in bed, punching the pillows behind me and then fixing his, too. He handed me the plate of cheese and crackers.

"One minute." He trotted back to the kitchen and returned with two tall glasses.

"What's in there?" I asked.

"American Coca-Cola."

"Why not Russian Coca-Cola?"

"Very funny." He put the glasses of cola down on a side table, climbed into bed, then helped himself to crackers and cheese.

We chomped in silence.

After a while, we both gulped down the Coke.

"You're keeping a secret from me," I said, lying back on the pillows.

He didn't answer.

"You are—I can tell." I ran a hand down his muscled arm. "Are you a double agent or something?"

He chuckled. "You don't even know what a double agent *is*."

Genuinely insulted, I said, "Of course I know what it is!"

"I am not involved in any kind of subterfuge," Ivan said. "You are placing your own secrets onto me, that's all."

"I don't have any secrets!" Maybe because of all the sex, I momentarily fooled myself with the lie. I was convinced I was on the up-and-up.

"Shall we not argue?" he said.

It occurred to me that we were sitting up in bed, at least a foot away from each other, and that he wasn't touching me. I'd stroked his arm just moments before, but he hadn't reciprocated. "I call it a discussion, not an argument."

"Semantics." His voice was rough.

"We could argue about that," I said, light and joking.

He rolled on top of me with no warning, crushing the plate

with its leftover crackers and cheese into the fur of the comforter. "Ivan, you're making a mess!"

In a flash he was making love to me again, and in my ear he murmured, "Semantics. Americans and their semantics."

An hour later, I heard the first bird sing. I threw off the covers and got out of bed. When I came back from using the bathroom, I pulled on my clothes.

"What are you—"

"I want to get to my place before everyone wakes up."

"Why?"

"This is private."

"Oh, sure." He smiled and stretched.

I gave him a serious look. "Really, Ivan, I'd prefer that this remain our secret."

"See, you're into secrets."

Since he was right, I didn't answer. I kissed him good-bye on the cheek. "My daughter will be home for the weekend and to help me with the party tomorrow night," I said. "I *definitely* want this to be a secret from her."

"I am gentleman." He closed his eyes and nestled into the pillow.

"You're going to have a hard time working today."

"I am strong." He opened one eye. "Right?"

"You betcha." I shut his door quietly, felt in the back pocket of my jeans for the key to my apartment, and pulled it out so that I was ready to let myself in the door right away.

Ivan probably was a strong young man, and he'd make it through the day reasonably well on so little sleep. But I couldn't imagine how I'd be able to concentrate on cooking unless I caught up on my missed sleep. I took a hot shower, pulled on a flannel nightgown, and literally crawled under the covers of my own sweet bed.

* * *

I woke up to hear the doorbell pealing. I had no idea where I was, much less who I was. My eyelids weighed a ton, but the sound of the doorbell was so excruciating that I jumped out of bed and stumbled toward the entrance hall of the apartment. By the time I was peering through the peephole, I'd nailed down my identity and location. Horrified, I saw Mary standing outside and remembered that we'd agreed that she'd come by after work Thursday to help me cook. So, I thought, it must be about three thirty in the afternoon. I looked down at my nightgown and debated. Then I opened the door.

She stepped inside and stared at me.

"This is a surprise," she said. "Are you sick?"

"You told me I needed a boyfriend."

"And you're telling me you got a boyfriend looking like that?"

I dropped my head forward. "Please, I beg of you, can you make the coffee?"

Mary started to laugh. She tossed an arm around my shoulder and gave me a squeeze. "You gotta tell me *everything*."

I nodded.

She brought the coffee into the library, where I was sitting comatose on the green velvet couch. After I'd taken two gulps, she said, "Begin at the beginning and don't leave out a single detail. I love sex stories."

"I'm not going to tell you every little thing—that's disgusting."

Her eyebrows arched high. "Ex-cuse me?"

I reached over and touched one of the eyebrows. "Is this real?"

"No, I draw it on."

"Okay." I drank more coffee.

"Who's the lucky guy?" she said in a gentle voice.

"You're trying to trick me into telling you everything by pretending to be all innocent and nice."

She batted her eyelashes. "I know," she said so quietly that I almost didn't hear her.

"It's Ivan Chernislava—he lives on the fourth floor."

"Oh, my God." She started to bounce on the couch.

I held my coffee high. "Hey!"

Her big wide grin encouraged the ham in me. Or maybe I started to come alive from the long sleep and the hot coffee. Anyway, I told her absolutely everything.

At the end, when I finished talking, she clasped her hands beneath her chin. "What a great story," she said.

"Yeah, except it was for real, and now I have to deal with him."

"Most men I know are fine with one-night stands." She grinned at me. "This *was* a one-night stand, wasn't it?"

I swatted her on the arm. "You got your choice of cleaning shrimp or . . . cleaning shrimp."

"I'm not cleaning shrimp," Mary said.

"I guess I'm cleaning the shrimp." I headed for the kitchen, with Mary right on my tail.

"I'll cut up the veggies," she said matter-of-factly.

I pulled open a drawer, took out a small knife, and handed it to her. "This is the best paring knife in the world."

"What are you going to use for the shrimp?"

"The second-best paring knife in the world."

We got to work, Mary to the left of the sink cutting celery, cucumbers, carrots, cauliflower, and green peppers into the most beautiful shapes and sizes I'd ever seen. I labored to the right of the sink, with the water coming in a steady trickle out of the faucet so I could keep washing the goop and shell off the shrimp.

After we'd settled into the routine, I said, "Your turn to tell me about *your* boyfriend."

"I figured we were coming to that."

I nodded.

"I got to know Jerome two years ago, when my son had him for freshman English."

I waved the knife at her. "Bad girl."

"I didn't say I slept with him then," Mary said, "just got to know him because he called me in to discuss my boy, Patrick."

She handed me a carrot stick, which I ate in two bites.

"Patrick's in the gifted program, but Jerome said he had exceptional talent as a writer, and he wanted to make sure we were doing all the things to encourage him, like getting him to read good books, suggesting he enter writing contests, offering to read his work, that kind of stuff."

"Sounds exciting."

"I always knew Patrick was smart, but the writing thing did kind of thrill me and my husband—"

I interrupted, "You've never told me your husband's name."

"Jacob."

"A lot like Jerome."

She shook a long stalk of celery at me. "Jacob and Jerome start with the same letter—that's the *only* similarity, so cut the crap."

I giggled and pulled out the thin string of shrimp poop, which I dangled from the tip of the knife and thrust in her general direction.

"You want to hear this story or don't you?" she said, trying to appear above my childish maneuvers.

I washed the poop away. "Please continue."

"Anyway, one thing led to another."

"Wait a second," I said. "I don't see how one meeting at the beginning of the school year led to you guys becoming lovers."

"We started communicating with e-mail—Jerome would send me the titles of some books I should get out of the library and leave next to Patrick's bed, or he'd let me know there was an assignment due the following week that I ought to read in its first-draft form. And I'd respond." Mary gave me a sneaky look. "E-mail is ba-aa-d. The Lord invented e-mail to encourage our sins; I'm sure of that."

"That means you think it's a sin to be with Jerome." I hoped I didn't sound triumphant, since I was trying not to judge her behavior.

She nodded vigorously, almost too happy. "Especially since Jerome is married."

"So are you—"

"I know, I know."

"His being married seems worse to you?"

"I know Jacob *travels,* so it's fair that I *travel,* too." She popped a piece of cauliflower in her mouth.

"Give me one of those," I said.

She handed me a big hunk of cauliflower.

"But Jerome's wife definitely doesn't travel."

"Maybe you're wrong about that—I wouldn't have pegged you for a traveler."

"She's a minister. There's no way she fools around."

We were quiet for a minute.

"Do you feel guilty about what you're doing to her?" I said finally.

Mary nodded her head. "I do, and so does Jerome."

"But you can't stop?"

"Nope, we can't seem to stop."

I stared out the window for a moment, taking a second to figure out why Mary's tone was in direct opposition to what she was actually *saying.* She seemed gleeful about being out of control. Maybe most people enjoyed losing control, and maybe that was something I needed to learn about. I'd been a bit out of control the night before with Ivan, but not completely. I'd never let go to the extent that I did something I truly believed was wrong.

Whoops, yes, I had.

I'd slept with Ivan in order to determine whether I should be suspicious that he could be a murderer. It had had nothing to do with actually wanting to connect with him in an honest way. Still, Mary was driven by passion, and I'd been driven by the opposite. Call it manipulation.

I jump-started the conversation again. "Do you want to divorce Jacob and marry Jerome?"

"I wouldn't do that to Patrick."

I struggled to explain. "I mean if your son was grown-up, or didn't even exist, would you want to marry Jerome?" She wouldn't turn to look at me, so I stared at her profile, so full and rich, like she was an ancient Ethiopian queen.

Instead of actually answering my question, she said, "Do you ever think that we do bad things on purpose so we get to the right ones eventually?" She looked at me and saw my confusion. "Like, when you make a wrong turn on the way to your destination, and it takes you the hell and gone out of your way, except you end up having a flat tire right smack in front of a service station, and if you'd gone the right way, you'd be in the middle of nowhere on some superhighway—"

"Or you might not have gotten the flat tire at all, if you'd gone the right way to begin with."

Mary sighed. "I guess so."

"Sorry for being grumpy. I haven't eaten anything since those cheese and crackers at four A.M."

"You better stop and get something."

"A quick peanut-butter-and-jelly sandwich should do it." I tossed the last shrimp onto the pile.

"Make me one, too. That way I'll stay through dinner and get some of this cooking done—can I steam the shrimp?"

I felt a flutter of anxiety. "Do you know how to make them really—"

"Watch me, baby."

She was clearly teasing, because when my back was turned, while I made our sandwiches, she disappeared into the pantry and then added a secret ingredient to the shrimp water. It was so secret that despite my trying to withhold food from her, she still wouldn't tell me what it was. Of course, the shrimp were fantastic, with a piquant flavoring that I couldn't identify.

Unable to control ourselves, we ate two shrimp each, then hogged down the PB-and-J sandwiches.

"Want some milk?" I said.

"Um, yeah."

After the shrimp had cooled completely, we whipped out plastic baggies to seal up all the veggies and the shrimp.

"What else do we have on the menu?" Mary said.

"Let's see, cheese puffs, shrimp, cold veggies, and dip. I'll buy the cheese and crackers tomorrow."

"Don't forget the weenies for me to pass."

I grinned. "Oh, and I was going to make this concoction, an old family recipe. You hard-boil a bunch of eggs, chop 'em up, and form them into a round, low shape, like a single-layer cake pan turned upside down; then you spread a layer of sour cream, and over that, another layer of caviar."

Mary screwed up her face. "Weird."

"People smear it on crackers and they love it, I can assure you."

"That's fine, but I don't really think you need it."

"Maybe I won't bother then."

She picked up her purse, getting ready to leave.

"Thank you for your help," I said.

"You don't always have to be thanking me so much," Mary said. "Remember, Jacob will bartend. Just get all the liquor and glasses together. Oh, and ice. You always need more ice than you think."

We were standing in the entrance hall of my apartment when I brought up a tricky subject "Mary, I'm paying you and Jacob."

"Nope."

"Yes, I have to," I argued. "It's not right."

She put on her most intimidating face. "Are we friends?"

"Of course, but you're not coming to the party as a friend." I sighed. "Maybe you should."

"This is the best way to scope out suspicious goings-on. Consider me your undercover friend."

As she went out the door, she turned back, smiling mischieviously. "You think Ivan will call you tonight?"

"I hope not," I said. "I have to clean this apartment tonight."

I remembered what it was like to hope the phone would ring and that it would be Peter speaking in a deep, sexy voice. I remembered the rush and thrill of loving only him. I did remember. But I honestly didn't believe I would ever again experience such delicious feelings of complete desire. The desire to have the phone ring. So simple.

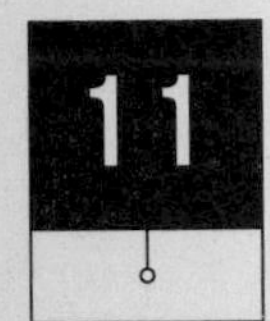

Exactly three minutes after Mary left, the phone rang. Glaring with my best evil eye, I willed it *not* to be Ivan.

"Hey, Mom," Laura said.

"Hi, sweetie—what's up?"

Her voice whined ever so slightly. "I've been waiting to hear whether you cut your hair. Did you get my warnings in time?"

"No, I didn't." I tried not to sound too happy about that.

"Oh, my God, how much did you take off?"

"Mmmm, let's see, how to put this?"

"Mom . . ." she moaned.

"All of it."

Silence.

"You shaved your head?"

When I didn't answer, I heard her screaming to her roommates, "My mother shaved her head!"

"I didn't *shave* it," I said. "I received a fabulous, very short haircut from Lagos at Elizabeth Arden."

Shrieks and yells were echoing through the phone as the other girls commiserated with Laura over the perfidy of mothers who didn't listen to their daughters' advice. Weakly, I said, "It looks really nice—everyone says so."

"Mom, I'm so freaked," Laura said. "I don't know if I'll even be able to *look* at you—"

I blurted out, "I have a lover who's twenty years younger than I am—does that prove to you the haircut looks good?"

Laura yelled to her suite mates, "My mother has a lover who's, like, thirty years old!"

To my amazement, cheers erupted in the faraway Juilliard dorm room.

"That is so cool," Laura said. "Who is he?"

"A Russian god—he lives in the building."

"I saw him!" she screamed. "He was totally, totally hot!"

You're telling me, I thought.

"I saw the guy this summer, before school started," she yelled to the other girls. "He's a hunk."

Back on the phone to me, Laura said, "They all want to meet you, Mom. They think you sound so great."

Well, good grief.

Trying to reclaim my older-woman decorum, I said, "Are you still coming to help out?"

"Of course—especially since now I'll be able to meet him."

"And your father's bringing someone."

"Yeah, he told me," she said. "Her name's Ann, too; isn't that so *obvious?*"

Obvious of what? I wanted to know, but didn't ask.

"Gotta run," Laura said. "I'll see you tomorrow."

By the time I'd cleaned both bedrooms and bathrooms, it was midnight. It was too exhausting to consider cleaning the living room, dining room, library, and kitchen that night, so I left it for the morning. Naturally, as soon as I officially quit cleaning, my energy surged and I wasn't in the mood to go to bed. Of course, I'd slept most of the day, making up for my night of manipulative passion.

I checked my e-mail and had a nice reply from my parents, wishing me well with the party and letting me know that they'd arranged for a massive flower arrangement, intended for the center of the dining room table, to be delivered Friday. Then I clicked on an e-mail from Peter, telling me that he'd arranged for a massive flower arrangement, intended for the dining room table, to be delivered Friday. My parents and Peter had always meshed well. In fact, they'd advised me not to divorce him.

If you've ever made an unpopular or misunderstood life change, and then watched as your family reacted with distrust, even with out-and-out hostility, you could probably imagine my parents' reaction. People tended to dislike change, in themselves as much as in others close to them. So, first, you had to make the huge, painful decision to get divorced, which was hard enough, and then you had to deal with everyone's resistance to that decision.

I was of the opinion that life shouldn't be so hard. Obviously, I didn't know what we could do about making it less diabolically difficult, especially since I didn't truck with talk of God or the devil. I preferred to keep things at the prosaic level. It was hard to change, and the people closest to you made it even harder. How come? The real kicker was people's short attention spans, since, in the end, they were apt to adjust to change with equanimity. My parents had now adjusted until, sometime in the future, I made another decision they didn't like, which they'd probably fight just as vociferously.

I replied to both e-mails, and sent a quick e-mail to Andrew at Swarthmore, telling him about the party and that Laura would be home for the weekend. I kept my big fat mouth shut about *why* she needed to be with her mother.

One o'clock in the morning, and I was wide awake. I decided to do my laundry. I wanted fresh towels in the kitchen and bathrooms, but I could admit that I had an ulterior motive. Despite the lovemaking with Ivan, and all the cooking and prep work for the cocktail party, I felt like I was getting nowhere fast in preventing a murder. A visit to the laundry room seemed like something to do.

As if to honor Senator Paul Hammer's prediction, the laundry room was hopping with young people, even at one in the morning. Nobody was actually screwing, but there was a singles-bar feeling, enough so that I felt immediately out of place and embarrassed. I figured it must have something to do with Thursday night, and preparing for the weekend. I quickly tossed the towels into a washing machine, and was about to run back upstairs when I heard Ivan's voice coming from a far corner.

I ducked low and whirled around to look. His back was to me, as was the back of the man with whom he was speaking, and they were talking in Russian. I'd never seen the other man. Suddenly Ivan turned and headed for the closest dryer. He started pulling out a huge pile of clothes and dumping them, unfolded, into a laundry basket. Then, as if I wore a radio-controlled tracking device around my neck, Ivan's head rose and he looked directly at me. I gave him a little nonchalant wave. He crooked his index finger and made the universal gesture for "come here." I wondered why I had to go to him, until I realized that one of his arms still overflowed with a pile of clean clothes.

I sauntered across the room, dodging the young people who were somehow under the misperception that doing laundry was fun, and stopped about two feet from him. He dumped the load of clothes.

"Anne, this is my friend and fellow countryman, Thomas."

Thomas and I shook hands, and I noticed that he was probably much closer to my age than Ivan was.

"How are you?" Ivan peered at me closely.

"Terrific." I smiled my brightest fake smile. I wondered why Ivan was doing his laundry so late, considering how little sleep he'd gotten the night before. I glanced at Thomas, whose lidded eyes and smirk had been giving me the creeps before I'd even been conscious of anything other than *not* wanting to run into Ivan.

Or *wanting* to run into Ivan.

I'm not adept at playing the sex game. I don't seem to have the requisite flexibility. Indeed, I felt like I was in the hands of an iron-worker who first thrust me into hot flames so that I became malleable, pounded me with a hammer into the desired shape and form, then, equally shocking, plunged me into ice-cold water, where I hissed and steamed, only for him to discover that something had gone wrong—I was misshapen, off balance, *wrong*. And so I was again relegated to the flames. I'd never played the game well, ever.

Ivan said, "Thomas arrived this afternoon, and, as you can see, he brought as many dirty clothes as he could fit into two enormous suitcases."

"He's welcome to come to my party," I said.

"He doesn't speak English very well, but some other Russians in the building plan to attend." He tipped his head to me. "So if you're sure . . ."

"The more the merrier." I turned away. "See you later."

In the elevator going back up to the ninth floor, I kept swearing under my breath, though I had no idea why. I threw myself on the couch in the living room, seriously disgruntled. How long was this Thomas planning to stay with Ivan? And so what? Did I really want a relationship with a man twenty years younger than me? I marched into the bathroom and glared into the mirror. I spoke out loud. "When you're seventy, he'll be fifty—when you're eighty, he'll be sixty."

Okay, so I didn't want an actual relationship with Ivan. But maybe I wanted to date him for a couple of weeks, just long enough to make Peter's eyes pop out of their sockets and to bask in my daughter's admiration.

I returned to the couch, curled up in the corner, and wished that I hadn't put the towels in for a wash, because otherwise I could go to bed. Something was eating at me, and it took only a second to figure it out. Maybe it was the extreme quiet in the living room, reminding me of hearing the voice, but what I felt was guilt. I had the terrible sense that I was doing everything *wrong,* somehow exactly the opposite from what the voice had expected. I'd listened to Mary's advice about having a party, but I couldn't remember why it had seemed like a good idea. In fact, I remembered that at the time it hadn't seemed like a good idea at all. I'd resisted her, and she'd somehow bulldozed me into it. I didn't blame Mary. She wasn't the one who'd heard the voice.

A murder will be committed in thirty days. Prevent it.

I couldn't remember what the voice had sounded like. The memory slipped sideways, as if it were a vapor escaping from my ears, spiraling up and out of sight. I'd imagined it. No voice spoke in my head. How absurd, after all. I wasn't crazy, exactly, just susceptible. The words kept stringing together in my head, singing a song. *Creative, sensitive, imaginative, ingenious, childish, inventive.*

The phone rang. I jumped straight into the air, my arms flung out like I was on a roller coaster. I figured it was Ivan, calling to apologize for . . . what? I know! Calling to apologize for not having called! Wasn't the man supposed to call the next day? No, maybe not. I'd never been any good with the rules twenty-five years ago, so what made me think I'd have a clue about the rules nowadays? Still, I thought it was Ivan, phoning to tell me that he couldn't stand it. He had to come over for a quickie right away. No, I could not say no. I could not protest. He was on his way, and if I didn't let him in immediately, he would begin shouting my name and pounding on the door.

I chose a low, sexy hello.

The voice definitely didn't belong to Ivan, though it had a foreign accent. Whoever it was tried to disguise its thick timbre and deep nature by pitching it high. He said, "You should be ashamed of yourself, you dirty little girl."

I laughed straight into the phone. I thought it was such a *stupid* thing to say. I mean, okay, I knew he meant to be threatening and scary. But, please.

There was a shocked silence.

"Sir," I said, still giggling, "you simply can't call me a little girl and expect me to take you seriously."

"Mind your own business." Now the voice was guttural and angry.

I hung up the phone immediately. You're never supposed to speak to prank callers at all, much less laugh and patronize them.

Funny, though I hadn't actually *heard* the voice in my head, I felt as though I had. For no sooner did I doubt myself than I received this phone call that very clearly said, *You are* not *imagining it.*

I tingled with excitement. Okay, I had to review the sequence of events. I'd come up from the laundry room, where I'd talked to Ivan and met his mysterious friend, Thomas. I replayed the phone call in my mind, trying to determine whether it might have been Ivan's voice. No, I was positive not. But there was Thomas. Was it a Russian accent I'd heard? Again, no, I didn't think so. But I had only Ivan's word that Thomas *was* Russian. Perhaps he *spoke* Russian, but that didn't mean he wasn't actually from another country. It seemed too coincidental not to be meaningful. I felt sure that the phone call was linked to Ivan and Thomas.

I toyed with the idea of calling Ivan myself. But what would I say? Should I ask whether Thomas, at his instigation, had just completed a threatening phone call to me?

Suddenly I grabbed the phone and hit *69. It was a long shot, but worth the try. The recording came on telling me that the last number that had called my line could not be identified.

Still excited, I returned to the laundry room to put my towels into the dryer. The place was quieter, with only an Asian couple folding their clothes together in a distant corner. They nodded to me, and I waved back. After the dryer started, I went into the library and began looking at the books. Soon enough, the couple left, lugging a huge basket between them. It appeared to be at least a month's worth of dirty clothes. Took me aback.

Quickly, I dashed back to the laundry room. All the lights were on, and the sound of my dryer gave a happy thump and thrum to the place. I scouted up and down the rows of washers, then dryers. That was when I realized that my dryer was keeping company with another. I peered into its porthole, trying to deduce something from the nature of the clothes, but all I could see were an inordinate number of pink towels. Quite sickening. One pink towel, okay. More than one was nauseatingly pink.

The two long clotheslines were loaded with several tablecloths and bedsheets, also rather lurid in design. I pushed between them, heading for the area where I'd seen the security guard emerge several nights ago. It was much darker, especially with the long hanging items on the line blocking a lot of the light. I waited for my eyes to adjust and wondered whether I ought to pull the stuff from the line.

I blinked and made out the back wall of the laundry room. No doors, nothing. I stepped forward and ran my hand along the crumbling plaster, thinking that the Kennedy needed to do some renovating down here. I followed the wall all the way to its right corner, where it intersected with the wall of windows overlooking the park.

Then I retraced my steps and continued all the way to the left, where that tall wardrobe was wedged tightly into the corner. Nothing smelled very good back there, and I wanted to forget about any more searching, but I was alone and, given the hour, stood a good chance of remaining alone. Plus, I'd been intending to explore the wardrobe, though I didn't expect it to magically open to a fantasy world as it did in the Narnia books.

Maybe there was something hidden in the cupboard. Stolen artifacts, or money, or drugs, though it would be a lot easier to hide something in an apartment rather than in plain view down in the public laundry room. I tried the handle of the cupboard, and the door creaked open with admirable noise and hesitation. There was nothing inside, and it was dirty. Plus, it smelled like some cats had once decided it was their private litter box. I started to slam the door shut and then stopped.

I stepped up into the wardrobe and ran both hands along its back wall. Given how dark it was, and the yucky smell, this took courage. I expected to feel my hands begin to coat with dirt, but slowly I realized that I hadn't touched even the slightest veneer of dust, much less anything raunchier. I reached higher, sliding along the smooth wood, until I felt it: a thin line running vertically, like a straight and true vein. Excited, I stood on tiptoe and followed it all the way up, close to the top, where it made a sharp left-hand turn. It ran straight along the top edge until reaching the cupboard's left corner, where it made another sharp turn downward.

After I hit the bottom, I returned to the center and pushed. Nothing happened. I pushed harder, while simultaneously moving all over the place. No give. Suddenly I realized that I hadn't explored across the bottom. Crouching, I followed the final vein to the right, until my hand hit some kind of metal lever. Fooling with it, I managed to yank it backward, where it clicked in place.

Again, I pushed. The left half of the wardrobe's back wall gave slightly, separating, but the right half didn't move. Frustrated, I sighed and sat down on the floor of the cupboard. The cat-litter smell wafted around me, and I debated getting out of there. It was dark and creepy, and I was nervous about what I'd discover if I did succeed at opening the back of the wardrobe. Then I remembered the voice warning me, and I thought about the possibility of someone being killed. My hands, almost on their own, began patting along the vein to the right of the lever. And there it was, a second lever, which I quickly snapped backward.

Rising to my knees, I pushed hard. The entire back of the wardrobe lifted from the bottom on some kind of silent mechanism. It moved slowly and required no other help from me. When it was wide open, I was staring into an empty bay of the parking garage. Faint light from an overhead fixture drifted through the chilly metallic air.

I stepped into the garage. Worried that I might get locked out, I patted my pockets nervously, to check that I had the security card to let me back into the building, then moved forward to look around. Where exactly was I? The parking spot was tucked into a corner, protected on either side by walls. Turning around, I looked directly into the wardrobe. I returned to it and reached up to pull down the wardrobe's back wall. When it was about to click into place, I checked it out from this new perspective. To my amazement, I saw that it had been faux-painted to resemble a concrete wall in a perfect match to the other walls.

I swallowed. No doubt about it: This was truly weird. So weird, in fact, that I got good and scared. I lifted the fake wall, hopped into the wardrobe, and pulled it closed behind me, making sure it clicked solidly. I emerged from the wardrobe, shut the door, and began fielding my way through the hanging items on the clothesline. They felt like cold, icy slaps against my cheeks. And, okay, they scared me, too.

Everything scared me.

I nearly fainted. Instead, I crouched down and then sat back on my bottom. I leaned forward to plunge my head between my knees. I panted quietly and told myself not to pass out. I didn't get aggressive about it because I didn't respond well to aggression, even if it came from me. Slowly I began to feel better. I raised my head and blinked. When I was ready, I stood up, staggered to a nearby dryer, and propped myself against it. I hadn't come so close to fainting in years. Even during the last period of my marriage, which had certainly been stressful, I'd never had an episode like this.

At that moment, Lucas Bower walked into the laundry room. His physical presence was overwhelmingly huge. He breathed heavily, so that he sounded like an animal. By the time I focused on his face, I had actually convinced myself that I was going to die. And with that conviction, to my astonishment, came peace. True, I didn't want to be hurt, to feel pain, but I realized then that what usually caused pain was the fear. I figured he'd strangle or stab me, and if I didn't resist or fight back, he'd succeed very quickly. It probably wouldn't hurt more than stubbing my toe.

So now I knew. The murder I was meant to prevent was my own. I felt a flash of indignation at having failed. And, boom, I changed my mind—no death for me, thank you very much. I'd believed from the start that there was a *reason* the voice chose me, and I had to admit I'd felt quite special at having been chosen.

Lucas Bower grinned at me. "Good evening, madam."

What was the 'madam' stuff?

"Good evening, Mr. Bower." I almost said *Herr* Bower, but stopped myself in time. I headed for my dryer, opened the door, and felt the towels. Still damp, but under the circumstances, I decided they could air-dry on the towel racks in my apartment. I started whipping them out and doing the three-way fold.

I called over my shoulder, "How long have you worked here?"

"One year." He was walking slowly down a line of washers behind me.

"Do you have a day job, too?"

"You are a questioning lady, aren't you?"

That shut me up. I thought of several retorts, but finally decided that silence would be the most effective. He reached the end of the row, and from my peripheral vision I saw him lean close to the window, peering into the dark woods. The silence was nerve-racking, and I had to consciously keep myself from saying something. He turned around in slow motion and ambled back. I literally clenched my teeth together in an effort not to break the silence.

When he drew alongside me, he spoke again. "*Aren't* you a questioning lady?" he repeated.

I remembered reading *The Gift of Fear,* by Gavin de Becker, which suggested that on an unconscious level we always know when we're in danger. If we don't allow the constraints of good manners, or being unwilling to risk hurting someone's feelings, to get in the way, we are much more likely to protect ourselves. On a gut level, we always know the truth. I glanced at him, keenly aware that his repetition of the question was intended as an attack. My gut had been screaming about this guy from the first time I saw him, and now the second time.

I spoke in an icy tone. "I don't appreciate your attitude. I plan to speak to the manager first thing in the morning, when I will register a complaint."

He literally took a step backward, which I claimed as a small victory. Both hands went up in mock surrender. Even better. "Just making conversation," he said.

I picked up my basket, filled with folded damp towels, and walked steadily out of the laundry room. Balancing the basket on my hip, I pressed the button for the elevator, and the door opened immediately. By the time I'd closed my apartment door behind me, even turning the double lock, my knees were about to give out. I dropped the basket in the bathroom, then sat down carefully on the toilet. I could hear the faint trickle of water in the pipes. This was an old building, after all. Then I picked up on the more distant sound of the gigantic trees that surrounded my apartment rustling in the autumn wind.

I stood, leaned over the bathtub to plop the rubber plug in the drain, and turned on the hot-water faucet. I waited until I could see steam coming, when I added the cold water to it. I was calm as I lowered myself into the big tub, but I certainly didn't feel peaceful or at ease. I leaned back in the water, slowly sinking all the way so that the water lapped at my neck. I didn't have a shadow of a doubt that something very bad was going on at the Kennedy.

It was, amazingly enough, up to me. I began to strategize how we would work my party the next night, and one of the first things I realized I had to do was tell Laura and Peter about the voice. I didn't care if they thought I was crazy or if they worried about me. Nothing mattered except preventing this murder.

12

Since I knew I wouldn't have any time alone with either Laura or Peter before the party, I hopped out of the bath, dried off quickly, and threw on my emerald-green terry-cloth robe. I sat down at my desk and began to write a long, careful e-mail. In the end, I also sent it to my son, Andrew. They all needed to know what was going on. I revised extensively, searching for the right language, and particularly the right tone. I hoped to minimize their alarm for my state of mind, naturally, because the more straightforward they could be, the more likely they'd be helpful. I also explained that my new friend, Mary, would be working undercover at the party as a waitress and kitchen helper. But, I wrote, although she worked as a domestic for other people in the building, I wasn't paying her to work at the party because she was my friend.

It was three thirty in the morning when I finally clicked send. The relief sweeping over me was so intense that I lay awake in bed, trembling. Finally, almost as if my body had separated from my mind, I collapsed into sleep.

I'd set the alarm for seven A.M. As soon as it started to ring, I sat straight up in bed, threw back the covers, and shot to the computer. Sure enough, there were three e-mails waiting for me.

> Dear Anne,
>
> No wonder you haven't seemed quite yourself . . . what an extraordinary event. I must tell you this, just to relieve your mind: There has never been a saner person than you. If you heard a voice in your

head, then you heard a voice in your head. Now we have a murder to prevent. Count on me.
Your ex, Peter

Dear Mom,
This is amazing news. I'm so glad to be coming home and able to help you.
See you soon.
Love, Laura

Mom,
How frighteningly cool. You know I'm a physicist and that I positively must debate the possibility that a voice could speak in your head (that is, a voice *not* attached to *its* own head). Quite surreal. I am also your son, and I know that if you say it happened, then shit, it happened. I love you and I believe you, even though I don't see how, scientifically, this could be. Rather paradoxical and all the more interesting, therefore. I expect a full accounting of the party. Keep me posted.
Love, Andrew

I swiped at tears. Then, getting down to business, I made a pot of coffee, jumped into sweat clothes, and started cleaning. I carried the mug of coffee with me while I dusted the living room, library, and dining room. By noon, I'd finished all the cleaning. I changed into jeans and a sweatshirt, grabbed my last-minute shopping list, and headed down in the elevator. I stopped in the management office.

"Hi, Angela, you coming to my party?"

"I can't wait." She howled with laughter, over what I couldn't imagine.

"Is Michael in?"

"Not right now—he's up on the fifth floor, settling some dispute."

Since Michael wasn't around, I decided to try to milk her. "Sweetie, have there been any new employees added in the last couple of months, especially a young man in his late twenties?"

She screwed up her nose. The endearment I'd used clearly pleased her, so she wasn't inclined to wonder why I was asking. "Nope, nobody. The Kennedy prides itself on not having a lot of turnover," she parroted.

"Okay, well, could you give Michael a very important message for me?"

"Of course." Angela picked up her pen, ready to write.

"Tell him I find Mr. Lucas Bower a distinctly uncomfortable presence in the building. I would like to register an official complaint. He's rude, scary, and peculiar."

"Oh," she said, scribbling like mad. "I will certainly tell him." However, she looked puzzled.

"Gotta run—see you later."

It was one thirty in the afternoon by the time I hauled my butt back to the apartment, wheeling my hand cart full of cheese, crackers, ice, cocktail napkins, swizzle sticks, twenty-five-watt lightbulbs, and weenies. Since I was about to keel over, I realized that I hadn't eaten anything all day. Quickly, feeling more and more as if I were a windup toy gone beserk, I slapped together a peanut-butter-and-jelly sandwich, which I ate while tearing all over the place.

First, I unscrewed all the lightbulbs in the three main rooms of the apartment and replaced them with the lower-wattage bulbs. Then I pulled out the glasses and liquor bottles and piled them on the bar in the living room. It wasn't really a bar, per se, but an eighteenth-century mahogany server with a brown marble top. It didn't have the storage available for a full bar setup, so I had to bring in the extras from the butler's pantry.

Mary arrived at exactly three o'clock, raring to go. She started tidying the bar while I moved around the living room, putting new candles in all the candlesticks. The doorbell rang, and the two flower arrangements arrived at the same time.

"Glory hallelujah," Mary said.

I handed her the slightly larger one. "This goes in the center of the dining room table."

"What about that one?" she asked, skeptical.

I started moving around the three rooms, trying it in various spots. She kept shaking her head, nope, nope, nope. "Well, shit," I said, "it's gotta go *somewhere.*"

Mary started to giggle, triggering my own. I didn't know why we always found everything so funny. I tried the arrangement on the bar.

"Jacob won't be able to maneuver," she said.

"What if I unplugged the lamp on my desk and put it there? I don't need the light."

"Not bad." She ambled over and began untangling all the wires so that she could get rid of the lamp.

The flowers finally in place, and the lamp hidden in a closet, we went into the kitchen, and I had some time to update Mary on the phone call I'd had the night before, the wardrobe's mysteries, and my run-in with Lucas Bower. "I left a message for Michael this morning, an official complaint about him."

She started slicing lemons. "Maybe he's the bad guy and you'll get him fired. Story ends happily."

"What about how the back of the wardrobe is a secret entrance from the garage into the laundry room?"

"Umm—that's a puzzle."

"It really scared me. When I got back into the laundry room, and before the Lucas guy appeared, I almost passed out."

"You have to stay cool," Mary said, rolling a single eyeball in my direction. I'd had no idea that an eyeball could move like that, especially separated from its mate.

"Someone's going to be *killed* and you're telling me to stay *cool*?"

"You ever heard about the Dalai Lama?"

"Yeah, sure."

"He says to stay cool."

"Those are his words?"

"No, they're not his *exact* words, but that's the general idea."

"I thought you were a Christian." I picked up a dishrag and wiped the kitchen counters.

"Jesus Christ was *very* cool," she said.

"Says who?"

"Jerome's wife, the minister."

We both grinned at the nonsensical nature of the discussion. Then I said, "So, now that I'm cooled down, I have to let you know that my daughter and my ex reacted very positively when I told them about the voice and the possible murder and stuff."

"Hey, your *ex* is coming to the party?" she yelled.

"We're friends. He's bringing a date, so don't get—"

"—your panties in twist," Mary said.

"Right." I opened the freezer. "The weenies are in here. Should I defrost them?"

"No, they go straight from the freezer into the oven. Makes them all plump and yummy."

"What else do I have to worry about?" I said.

"You really want to know?"

"Spit it out."

"You look terrible."

"I was going to take a shower later, after I finish all the dirty work."

"Why don't you do it now, before your daughter gets here?"

She displayed the lemons on a glass plate in a perfect little circular design.

"Bossy, bossy," I muttered.

"And so right, right," she said.

My new haircut significantly lowered the amount of time it took to shower and thoroughly beautify myself. Nervous, I put on the outfit from Neiman's. I had this peculiar feeling that sleeping with Ivan might have affected my sense of style. Like maybe now I would rather be wearing a tight, sexy dress. But after I made up my eyes, something I hadn't done since I'd cut my hair, I was pleased with the result. With lipstick and a quick swath of blush, I felt . . . interesting.

I opened the door from my bedroom and heard voices.

"Laura?" I yelled.

"Laura *and* Andrew," Mary yelled back.

I rushed into the living room and found both kids. They took one look at me and screamed. I pretended to be a fashion model, turning this way and that. "What do you think?"

Andrew swept me into a hug, making me feel like an elf in the arms of a giant. "Looks great," he said. "Now can we talk about this voice? I have a million questions."

Laura kissed me. "I really hate to say it," she began, "but you were right and I was wrong about the haircut."

"You met Mary?" I turned and caught a glimpse of her face.

"We took care of all that," she said.

"What did the voice sound like?" Andrew said. "Please be specific."

"It was the Lord," Mary said, grinning.

"The who?" he asked.

Mary and I started to laugh.

"Actually, we're tending to think it might be the lady Lord," she added.

"What's this *we* stuff?" I said. "I never once said it was the Lord."

"Oh, you mean *God*." Laura turned to her brother. "The Lord is *God*."

"Did it *sound* like God, Mom?"

Andrew's intellectual curiosity had always been somewhat out of control. I realized that I had to get things organized or he'd have us pitched into an endless debate.

I clapped my hands authoritatively. "It is now four o'clock. You must take your belongings"—I eyed their bulging backpacks—"to the studio apartment I reserved for Laura. Did you bring something appropriate to wear?"

Laura said, "What's wrong with your guest room? Andrew can have that and I'll sleep with you."

"This is a housewarming," I said. "Everyone's going to be poking around, checking me out. I can't deal with your usual mess."

"Moi?" Laura grinned.

"You're a total slob," Andrew said helpfully.

"Before you go and get ready, I need to update you on what else has been happening—"

Laura interrupted, "I told Andrew about the Russian god."

Mary snorted.

"That is so unladylike," I said to her. "Please, everyone, sit down. You, too, Mary."

Mary complained, "I have work to do."

I gave her a look and she sank into the nearest armchair.

"This party is *not* a party, so don't even think about having a good time," I announced.

Laura rolled her eyes, and Andrew said, "You know I hate parties."

"I adore parties, and I plan to have a good time," Mary blurted out.

"You're the one having to work, so I guess that makes some kind of convoluted sense," Laura said.

I waved my hand at Mary. "Now listen; we have to figure out a logistical game plan."

"You don't know who's coming," Mary said helpfully, "so how are you going to do that?"

I stared at her. Suddenly everything went blank inside my head. "Pretty good point," I muttered.

"You know what I think?" Laura said.

We all looked at her expectantly.

"Everyone should have a fabulous time at this party, while also keeping a careful awareness, a catalog, of every conversation, every interaction, every *everything* that goes on."

"Right," Mary said, grinning, "but spare the help—that's me and my husband, the bartender—from your eagle eye."

"Maybe you're the murderer," Andrew said.

I peered at Mary's face and smiled. "I never thought of that."

"That would make me the murderess, not the murderer."

"Listen, did you guys notice that Senator Hammer died?" I asked.

"Yeah, I read a little bit of his obituary," Andrew said.

"He died two days ago, when Mary was cleaning his apartment."

Mary held up two hands of denial. "Oh, please, don't you go making fun of that nice man."

"Did you kill him?" Laura's eyes danced.

I knew Mary and I were both thinking about *where* he died, and we started to laugh.

"Tell us," Laura said.

But by then we were laughing too hard to speak. I kept imagining Mary opening the door to the bathroom and finding him on the john, and Mary, as if to perfectly fulfill what I was thinking about, started to mimic how aghast she'd been. She clasped her bosom theatrically and made gasping noises that were part laughter and part horror.

Laura and Andrew, oblivious to what was making us laugh, still found it catching. Pretty soon we were all hooting.

I finally managed to squeak out, "I don't think the voice meant for me to find this so damn humorous."

"Or maybe She did," Mary shouted.

"Mom, please tell me, what did the voice *sound* like?" Andrew tried to stop laughing.

"Exactly like you!" I screamed.

"Oh, come on—"

"And you," I said, pointing first to Mary and then to Laura, "and you, too!"

"We get the picture," Andrew said.

"It was a voice that wasn't a voice," I said, honestly trying to explain.

Mary stood up, "I've got to blow my nose."

"Maybe it was actually an angel," Laura said.

"I don't have a clue," I said, "but I know I heard a voice, and I fully believe that the voice's warning was on the up-and-up."

Mary returned to the living room and passed around the box of tissues. After we'd all blown our noses and wiped our eyes, I said, "Okay, I really do have other stuff to tell you."

I proceeded to describe everything else, the phone calls, the run-ins with Herr Bower, the back of the cupboard leading into the garage, the on-again/off-again behavior of Ivan, my altruistic decision to seduce Ivan in the name of furthering the investigation, the arrival of his mystery Russian friend—or *possibly* Russian friend—and, finally, my complaint to management about Lucas Bower.

To Mary, I said, "Have I forgotten anything?"

"I think that covers it." She smiled. "I find it remarkable that you share your sex life with your kids, but hey, more power to you."

"They tell me; I tell them," I said while I eyed them, wondering if they felt as philosophical about it as I did.

Laura said, "We're moving beyond the old boundaries of parent-to-child."

"Yeah, now we're child-to-child," Andrew said.

"Okay, you're in trouble," I said.

He stood up. "Perfect time to get out of here and change into party clothes." Andrew looked at Laura. "I dib the first shower."

In moments, they were gone.

"That went all right, don't you think?" I said to Mary.

"You're fishing for compliments."

"Very true."

"They're terrific."

"Your son next," I said.

Mary started polishing glasses on the bar, and I went to fill little crystal dishes with mixed nuts, which I scattered around the living room, library, and dining room.

When the doorbell rang, I got there before Mary. "That's probably Jacob," she said from behind me.

I opened the door and saw a tall, heavyset white man. "No, I don't think—"

"Hey, Jay," Mary said.

I turned and glared at her. "*This* is your husband?"

She grinned like a little girl. "He's awful white, huh?"

Jacob held out his hand politely. "How do you do?" he said, shaking mine.

"Hello, Jacob," I said.

"You can call me Jay," he said.

"I didn't know you were white," I said lamely.

His eyes twinkled. "Mary likes to tease."

"I noticed."

I couldn't believe this man *traveled*. He seemed so genial and nice. My mind was also awhirl with conjecture about the fact that Mary's husband was white and she was having an affair with a black man. I could hardly wait to have a good long discussion.

Mary took Jay around the apartment, showing him everything, and then he went into the guest bedroom to put on a bow tie. Behind the bar, he was quite a presence, with thick, unruly black hair and a tall, husky build.

"Did Mary tell you why I'm having this party?" I asked him.

"Yes," he said gravely. "She told me the Lord spoke to you."

"Actually, she keeps saying it was the Lord, but I don't think so." I decided that the time had come to be a little more forceful on this issue, probably because my kids were involved. "I don't believe in God."

He tried to keep a straight face. "Who do you think it was?"

I found my eyes snatched by the expression in his big brown eyes. "It was just a voice, that's all."

Mary spoke from behind me. "Jay brought a little notebook, and he's going to jot down anything he hears or sees that's relevant."

As if on cue, Jay pulled out a small notebook from his breast pocket, along with a pen.

Laura and Andrew burst through the front door, chattering, and we got everyone introduced. I said, "Jay has a notebook and pen, so if you have something you really want to remember, you could come tell him and he'll write it down." I turned to Jay. "Is that okay?"

"Sure thing—makes me feel important."

I clapped my hands to get everyone's attention, surprising myself.

"She's gone military on us," Andrew said brightly.

I dropped my hands to the sides of my body, embarrassed. "So, places, everyone, places," I shouted.

"Mom, this is not a theatrical production," Laura said.

"I'm just getting a little nervous," I said.

"You need a drink," Jay said. "What'll it be?"

"A vodka martini."

The doorbell rang, blending with the sound of ice rattling in the martini shaker.

Peter, my ex, and his date, Ann, arrived first. Peter was dutifully gracious about my new haircut, and I managed a quick enough glance at Ann to figure out she looked about forty years old. My party began with a flourish when Miss Dora rang the doorbell and stood there clutching her walker, which was strewn with blinking Christmas lights.

"Miss Dora, how do you do that without a plug?" I yelled at her.

She grinned at Andrew, having decided he was the youngest and handsomest male around. "I'm *charged,*" she said.

As we all laughed, the doorbell pealed again, the martini shaker shook double-time, the tall wax candles flickered, flames from the gas fire cast shadows on the ceiling, and the odor of lilies melted into the apartment's atmosphere of beauty and joy. The idea of murder drifted away.

Five minutes later, Peter took me aside. Then, as I waited for him to speak, I noticed that his face was white.

"We had an accident on the way over here." His trembling hand tightened around my arm.

"But you're not hurt?" I looked from him across the room, to the Other Ann.

"Not us."

"What about the other car?"

"The driver was rushed to the hospital. I wanted to follow the ambulance there, but the police said it would be better to just call later." He swallowed. "So I'll telephone in a little while for news."

Careful and keeping my tone neutral, I asked, "Whose fault was it?"

"Hers—she made an illegal left-hand turn right into me." His hand was still on my arm, still shaking. "One of those times when you just can't believe what's happening, like why on earth did she turn that wheel? It was insane."

"Maybe she was drunk."

"I suppose." He leaned closer to me. "I don't want to ruin your party."

For a second, I thought he was about to rest his head on my shoulder.

"Look, I don't care what the police said; just spend a little time with the kids and then go to the hospital. That'll make you feel better."

We watched Andrew and Laura in conversation with the Other Ann, over by the bar.

"I can't believe her name is Ann," I said.

Distracted, Peter blinked. "What?" Then the words registered. "Doesn't mean anything."

"Okay, listen, I have to get Miss Dora settled. Have a glass of wine and try to relax."

I squeezed his hand and walked briskly over to Miss Dora, who was gripping her walker and swaying a bit. I edged her toward a chair. "Why don't you sit down?"

"Thank you, I think I will."

Suddenly, Mary loomed beside us. "What can I get you to drink, Miss Dora?" she bellowed.

"An old-fashioned, and have the man make it strong!"

Mary made a fluttering motion with her hand, shooing me away.

I scurried off, searching for my martini, which I found beautifully full, the vodka tremulous at the lip of the glass, where I'd put it down on the entrance room table. I managed a quick gulp before the doorbell rang.

Michael, the manager, holding a bottle of wine, and Angela with a small bouquet of flowers, stood waiting. Their expressions were nervous, as if they weren't used to going to parties. I oohed and ahhed over their gifts, then pushed them in the general direction of the bar, where I seemed to push everyone. The doorbell rang again, and this time I opened the door wide, pulling it all the way back on its hinges so that it would stay flat against the wall. No more doorbells. Let the whole world come in.

I introduced myself to a clutch of young women, all of whom displayed their bellies, though said stomachs were far from flat or picturesque. Despite our national obsession with skinniness, I was pleased to see that these women showed their bodies, even if they, frankly, shouldn't have. I'm nothing if not contradictory. I managed another frantic swallow of martini when I heard the elevator ping, and soon I was welcoming a new group of people, more middle-aged and genteel this time.

Phew, I thought. Somehow, I just hadn't expected a turnout like this. In fact, I probably hadn't wanted to give a party because I figured no one would come. I felt obscurely pleased, like I'd won a popularity contest, but also somewhat overwhelmed.

I eased into the living room and stared at the controlled chaos. Mary was passing something, maybe the weenie dogs, on a silver tray. People were three-deep around the bar, where Jacob was in high style. Judging from the two-handed martini shaking going on, the martini was the drink of choice. I saw Laura talking earnestly to a strange man wearing a blue suit. I didn't like the way he was leering into her cleavage, but then I remembered that she was information gathering. This was a party with a purpose beyond mere entertainment. *Jeepers, get a grip, Anne.*

I sipped my own martini and felt everything recede, as if I had become invisible and I was watching the party on a movie screen with the sound turned off. People's mouths opened and closed with incredible violence. I noticed Peter talking closely with Andrew while the Other Ann listened. She was beautiful, but nothing at all like I'd imagined. I'd expected blond and elegant, but instead she seemed to be of East Indian background, and she had small oval glasses perched on her nose. I liked her already.

My reverie stopped when arms encircled my waist from behind. I smelled him immediately: Ivan. And, yes, despite my children and my ex-husband being in the room, I felt my stomach drop about a foot while my breathing tightened, and I leaned backward into the embrace. He kissed the nape of my neck.

There's simply nothing better than having the back of your neck kissed. I didn't know this until that moment, because, I swear, no one had ever kissed me on the neck before. Except, maybe, my mother or father when I was an infant. That's probably why it feels so good, actually. We have this visceral memory of being kissed by our parents. But there's also something secretive about it. You can't see what's happening, only feel it.

I almost moaned.

"Good evening, Anne," he whispered directly into my ear. He had all the moves down pat, without question. Those lips right at my ear sent shivers down my neck. I shuddered with pleasure even while I watched, as if in slow motion, as first Mary, then Laura, and finally Andrew and Peter, turned to stare at me. Their eyes opened wide. Laura grinned. Mary's bosom jiggled. Andrew bit his lower lip. And Peter? Peter truly looked as though he might keel over. I thought of the car accident he'd been through and decided he'd had enough shocks for one night. I stepped away from Ivan and turned to greet him with a chilly smile.

He introduced me to three men and two women, all Russian, including a reintroduction to his visiting guest, Thomas. The women had names like Petrouscha, Magdalena, and the like. I couldn't hold on to their names because I was so annoyed by their dramatic sexuality. Lord have mercy, as Mary would say. They glittered like Miss Dora, but to much better effect. Gold and diamonds, gleaming skin, robust long hair that curled and shone. They were like undulating serpents, hissing their hellos and thank-yous and vat-a-gorgeous-apartments in some kind of endless rhapsody. Horrified, I closed and opened my mouth, searching desperately for my inner serpent.

And I found her!

I grew two feet taller, my bust expanded, my voice deepened, and I said, with utter nonchalance and detachment, "Won't you please help yourself to a drink?" Then I glared at Ivan, hoping to kill him instantaneously.

As his friends turned to the bar, their hissing only moderately lessened, he moved closer to me. I stepped back, right into an older gentleman who cried out, "Whoa, there, you sassy pony!" Before I could react to this astounding remark, Ivan slipped his arms around me, but this time from the front. Expert, needless to say, Ivan dipped me backward. I felt my muscles cry out, first in agony, then ecstasy. He kissed me full on the mouth.

In my mind, the words *sassy pony, sassy pony* reverberated.

Ivan yanked me upward and, briefly, I thought I might pass out. Instead, I huskily whispered, "Martini, please."

"At your command," he whispered back.

Remember, every word the Russian god utters is spoken with a thick accent. My knees wobbled.

Faintly, I heard Miss Dora. "This is the best party I've been to in twenty-five years!"

I smiled at her.

Mary appeared and dangled a weenie dog in front of my face. "Eat this immediately," she ordered.

I didn't want to eat it. I wanted another martini. "Why?" I tried to bat it away.

"You need sustenance."

"I think I got plenty of that." I grinned at her.

She chortled, but kept on wagging the darn weenie dog right in front of my lips. "Eat."

I opened my mouth and she dropped it in.

As I was chewing, she said, "You gotta remind Andrew to circulate, circulate, circulate."

"He hates parties."

"Tough—he's got a job to do."

I whirled around and marched through the crowd, smiling benignly at everyone as I pushed them aside.

Peter, the Other Ann, and Andrew were staring at me like I'd become a monster.

I grabbed Andrew's arm. "You have to move around, talk to other people," I said. "Remember what this is about—*murder*."

"Is that Ivan?" he muttered.

"Who?"

"The gorgeous guy who kissed you!"

"Yeah, that's Ivan."

Peter said, "I guess you've been busier than I realized, Anne."

The Other Ann took a step backward. "I'm going to get another glass of wine."

"Have a martini!" I said.

When she'd been swallowed up by people, I turned to Peter. "She's perfectly lovely."

Peter didn't answer.

I grabbed Andrew's arm, but spoke to Peter. "If you'll excuse us, we have work to do. And if you want to take your mind off the accident, you could do some investigating, too."

"I forgot all about that other business," Peter said.

"This isn't about *having fun*," I said to Peter. "This is about preventing a murder."

I pushed Andrew ahead as he moved, but he squirreled around to face me. His smile stretched so wide it practically touched his earlobes. "Murder seems like the farthest thing from your mind."

"Don't get fresh with me," I scolded.

"How old is Ivan?"

"I'm not sure." I squeezed his arm tight. "I want you to talk to the Russian guy with him, the shorter, older one with acne scars. See him?"

"Okay." He sounded dubious.

"He's staying with Ivan, and there's something suspicious about him."

"You really think *Ivan* might be involved?"

"Yup."

"But you slept with him!"

"The line of duty demanded it."

"First I'm getting a drink," he said.

Ivan approached me, with two martinis held high in the air. I grabbed one. He clinked his glass to mine and said, "To a great hostess."

"Thanks." I drank a huge swallow of icy martini.

He grinned at me. "Why are you so angry?"

"I'm not at all angry."

Ivan sipped at his martini again, taking his time. "Those women who came with me, they are not interesting—they're so obvious, so shallow, so . . ." He waved his free hand around, as if searching for the right descriptive phrases.

That was when I saw a tall, thin man with white hair pause in the entrance hall of my apartment. I guessed he was about sixty years old, a more reasonable age to mine than Ivan's. He obviously hadn't expected such a hullabaloo, and he was reassessing whether he wanted to enter. He was handsome in that academic, Jewish intellectual way, a type of man I hadn't married, but had always found attractive.

"Excuse me," I said to Ivan. Holding my martini firmly, I slithered through people until I stood in front of him.

I introduced myself, then promptly took a sip of martini. At a party, you never knew when you might lose your glass. It was always best to drink fast.

He said, "How do you do? My name is Ibrahim Nahas."

We shook hands as I quickly revised *Jewish* to *Arabic*. "Please come in, get a drink, mingle," I said a little too heartily.

"Thank you." He still hesitated. "I live in the apartment below you, eight-oh-two."

"Oh, darn it, are we making too much noise?"

"No, no!" Ibrahim laughed. "I just felt you might want assurances that I *do* live in the building."

We'd managed to move into the living room. I gestured toward the bar. "Drink?"

He touched my elbow. "Please, I will fend for myself. See to your guests."

I turned away, feeling that I both wanted to talk to him and should check him out, but unsure how to remain by his side while he waited for his drink without it seeming odd.

Sure enough, Mary sidled up. "He looks secretive," she said.

"I don't know how to—"

"Circle your way back to him."

I looked around and noticed that Andrew was talking to Ivan's guest, Thomas. Peter and the Other Ann were nowhere in sight, which probably meant they were in the library or dining room. I stood on tiptoe and saw Laura talking to the old man who'd called me a sassy pony. I stared at her until she looked up, when I shook my head slightly. In a flash, she was moving away, melting into the crowd. I watched and saw her resurface next to a young man I hadn't noticed before. She was a master.

I walked up to a group of older women and introduced myself. I knew that it was unlikely they'd actually be murderesses, but they could be a good source for the building's gossip. I'd also begun to feel a faint uneasiness at not behaving in a more hostesslike manner. It would be inappropriate to have had a party where I never met half my guests.

The most elegantly dressed woman, her hair perfectly coifed into a white helmet and her fingers lined with massive rings, shook my hand graciously and intoned, "I am Mrs. Cadwallader."

"I'm delighted you chose to stop by," I said, suddenly feeling grubby and absurdly juvenile.

"Your apartment is *stunning,*" she said. "May I ask the name of your decorator?"

"I didn't use a decorator."

I thought all of them were going to drop their false teeth, which wasn't a particularly fair comment, since the success of preventive dental care in our country would suggest that they probably still had their own teeth. I guess I didn't want to admit that I was closer to their age than to Ivan's. The age difference between me and Ivan, on display to my kids, was definitely getting to me.

Mrs. Cadwallader said, "How astonishing." Then her eyes twinkled and she tapped me on the hand holding my martini, as if catching me in a joke. "You must *be* a decorator."

"No, no," I protested. "I just inherited some beautiful things, that's all."

To change the subject, I said, "Did Lagos tell you he cut off all my hair?"

She laughed. "He did, indeed! He's not one to hide his light, as you must know. It's a wonderful cut."

In the space of three minutes, I'd received more compliments than I could keep track of. I spied Ibrahim moving through the living room, holding a glass. "Ibrahim!" I called out. He switched direction and came toward us. I started to make introductions, but the women laughed and said they all knew each other.

"How long have you lived here?" I asked him.

He sipped his scotch, pursing his mouth with satisfaction. "Three years, I believe."

"Ah, so the murder was well before your time." I shot an arch look at the ladies, trying to rope them in.

A short, plump woman, whose name I'd already forgotten, piped up. "Those were the days!"

"I'm sure it was interesting," I said, "but I'd rather not have another murder occur here."

"Wait a second," Ibrahim said. "A murder literally *at* the Kennedy?"

We all automatically deferred to Mrs. Cadwallader, who told the story with efficiency but zero pizzazz.

When she'd finished, I said, "What about the detail of the pineapple finial? Is that chalked up to rumor?"

She blanched.

"Pineapple finial?" Ibrahim said.

"Apparently, the dead man was found with a—"

Mrs. Cadwallader interrupted, furious. "Utter nonsense."

Since she looked like she might bonk me on the head with the nearest heavy object, which happened to be a brass fireplace tool, I shut up. But I opened my eyes wide at Ibrahim, suggesting that if he'd find me later, I'd fill him in.

Clearly amused, he sipped more scotch.

"And what's with that scary security guard in the laundry room?" I blurted out.

They seemed to edge away from me. I was discovering that detective work didn't particularly mix with being socially acceptable. And, in fact, I felt strange in my own skin. Maybe, partly, it was the haircut and the new clothes, but maybe, also, I wasn't cut out for this stuff. Again, the perversity of life. I could make a major change, like the drama of cutting off all my hair, and it felt immediately natural. Other changes, more subtle and, therefore, one might imagine, less shocking, could be *more* challenging. I felt almost dirty by asking all these questions and artificially directing the conversation. But, after all, what was dirtier, my feelings of awkwardness as a detective or imagining a dead body? Rallying, I figuratively clutched my detective's hat and pushed on.

Ibrahim said, "I didn't know about a security guard in the laundry room, but then, I send my laundry out."

All the ladies nodded in agreement.

So, what the hay? I thought. I told them the story of my descent into the laundry room at midnight—I even explained that my motive was intense curiosity because of Senator Hammer's insinuations about all the hanky-panky going on down there. I had them mesmerized, absolutely mesmerized. When I got to the part where Lucas Bower's hulking frame emerged from the shadows, they, like Mary, let out gasps of alarm. I hammed up the rest, though there really wasn't much more to describe. I told them about my second run-in with him, and then my official complaint to Michael. Glancing around, I saw that Michael stood fairly close by.

"Michael, did you get my message about Mr. Bower?" I yelled over the voices of the party guests.

The ladies, plus Ibrahim, glared at Michael. Somehow they'd decided to throw their weight with me.

Michael's face flushed and he edged toward us. "Now, now, shouldn't mix business with pleasure."

He was right, from his point of view.

"Why on earth does the building need security in the laundry room at night?" Ibrahim demanded. "Has something happened that we, as residents, don't know about?"

"Absolutely not." Michael's mouth and lips tightened like a bow preparing to shoot an arrow. "We are simply a proactive management team."

Suddenly Ivan appeared to my right. He smiled his laziest, most ingratiating smile directly at the ladies before holding out his hand. "How do you do? My name is Ivan Chernislava."

They cooed and clucked at him, Ibrahim melted away, and Michael touched my wrist.

He whispered, "Mr. Bower is no longer with us—I apologize for the unfortunate interactions that occurred."

The power of a party.

"Thanks, Michael."

I looked at my watch and realized that the party was halfway over. It was hard to imagine another hour of this, but when I checked around the room and saw my kids, Mary, and Jacob valiantly at work, I gathered up my energies. Then I went to find Peter and the Other Ann.

They were in my bedroom, both perched on the edge of the bed as Peter talked earnestly into a cell phone. One finger was plugged into the ear without the phone. I made wide, questioning eyes at the Other Ann.

She shrugged and moved her hand like a floppy fish.

Peter spoke into the phone. "Is the family there?" After a second, he added, "Would you please give them my name and telephone number? I'd like to attend whatever services they decide to have, but I certainly wouldn't want to bother them with that right now."

Horrified, I realized the woman had died.

Peter recited and spelled his name, then gave his home telephone number.

When he'd disconnected, we all stared at one another.

"I'm so sorry, Peter," I said finally.

"Thanks."

The Other Ann reached over and took his hand. "It wasn't your fault," she said softly.

"No, not really, or technically, but . . ." His words trailed off.

"Not in any way, shape, or form," I said.

He stood up. Even though he was six feet, three inches tall, with a strong physique and a handsome, WASPy face, he seemed to have shrunk, like a gorgeous pair of silk pajamas put through the hot cycle by mistake. I thought of silk pj's because we were in the bedroom, and because silk pajamas were a bit of a fetish for him. I'd always found them off-putting, not in the least attractive or sexy. Give me nudity any day.

In the tradition of inappropriateness, to which I am partial, I began to imagine a threesome right there on my bed, with the Other Ann, the first Anne, and Peter. I didn't find the fantasy at all appealing, much less a sexual turn-on, so don't ask me why I thought of it. Probably something to do with my hormones having been so radically switched on by Ivan, as if his twist of the knob, sending power into my body, had been turned too far.

As Peter and the Other Ann began walking out of the bedroom, he said, "Are you in love with that Russian guy?" His voice was mournful, doomed, as if that, too, would be another death he had to cope with.

Since it pissed me off, given the presence of this lovely woman by his side, I spoke sharply. "No, of course not. I'm having a sexual relationship with him."

"Oh," he said.

By this time, we were passing through the living room and the bar. Peter said, "Tell the kids I'll call them tomorrow, okay?"

"Will do." I put a hand on his back, already sorry for letting myself be sharp with him. "It wasn't your fault."

He nodded.

"It was very nice to meet you," I said to the Other Ann.

"You have a beautiful apartment," she said, "and wonderful children. Thank you for having me."

Polite, even with all the confusing undercurrents in the situation. I liked that.

After they'd left, I turned around and did a quick scan of the party. The crowd hadn't thinned out at all, to my surprise. I tested my drunkenness quotient, which I do by emptying my head of all thoughts and seeing if they are replaced by any kind of swirling motion. Nope. Time for another martini. I'd only had half of two, which amounted to a single martini. And this was my party and I was working hard, so I would damn well indulge myself. I squeezed to the front of the bar, taking liberties as the hostess, and got Jacob's attention. I raised my eyebrows.

Another? he mouthed.

I nodded my head up and down like a puppet and he went right to it.

While I waited, I chatted with one of the Russian debutantes to my right.

"You have the most stunning taste," she gushed.

"Thank you, that's so kind." I was trying to sound grand and elevated, even though it was she, standing in three-inch stiletto heels, who towered over me. I hoped the heels wouldn't punch holes in my grandmother's antique carpet.

"How do you know Ivan?" I asked.

She giggled. "Old, old friend."

"Like, *friend* friend, or just a friend?"

She winked at me. "Ivan said he'd cut off our tits if we told you anything."

"Is that right?" I smiled sweetly. "Isn't that just like a man to be threatening and try to come between the natural sisterhood that exists among women?"

Jacob handed me the martini, and I took a quick sip so that it wouldn't spill. Then I scootched sideways, making room for others at the bar, but staying close enough to continue the conversation.

Her brown eyes appeared to fill with tears. "Vat a beautiful ting to say."

"We women have to stick together."

"I know Ivan really does admire you," she said carefully.

"And you know we're lovers, right?"

She swallowed. "You and Ivan?" Jacob handed her a martini and gave me a wink. She continued, "But you're at least old enough—"

"Watch out," I joked. "Sisterhood will only take you so far!"

"I mean, aren't those your kids I met earlier?"

"Yes, of course they are."

"Ivan didn't say anything about you being, umm, sexual—"

I interrupted, "Are you his lover, too?"

Her face had gone bright red, even across her forehead and shooting down her neck into her stupendous cleavage.

Then, boom, like a freak of nature, Ivan was there, smiling serenely.

I looked at him and couldn't help the surge of disappointment. Okay, I knew it was stupid of me to think that a thirty-year-old could actually be interested in me, a woman twenty years his senior and well within the age range of being his mother.

Funny, as I kept staring at him, his wide, handsome face, the deep, luscious brown eyes, the full, wide mouth, and the body—phew, the body—I couldn't wrap my mind around seeing him as a son of mine. I remembered making love, the weight of him on me, a weight so weighty that it hadn't seemed heavy at all, but more like the lightness of a balloon. Barely there because it was so welcome. I hadn't believed that he really loved me. Had I? No, not really, not completely. But I'd certainly felt desire for him. My body still craved him and, yes, even my mind wanted to sleep with him again. Partly, it was pride. It had been a good moment when I'd seen Peter's jealousy, and when I'd heard Laura's astonished thrill that he was my lover.

It's just that I didn't expect my infatuation to end quite so quickly and unceremoniously, while staring at the boobs of this woman who exuded sexuality in a way that I'd never been able to pull off and who had obviously slept with Ivan. Clothes and a new haircut had transformed me on the outside, but I was just the same on the inside. Plain old Anne.

Ivan wrapped one arm around my waist, bunching up the fabric of my silk blouse. "I'm having such a good time," he said.

"Wonderful." I extricated myself smoothly. "I must see to my other guests."

He managed to shoot me an arch look before I got away. Ivan was never perturbed by any of my brush-offs, as if he knew better. That, of course, made me think that maybe he did know better.

I headed across the living room to Miss Dora. A small plate, loaded with shrimp, cheese puffs, and weenie dogs, was next to her on the table. I sat down in the matching wing chair on the other side of the table. "May I snatch some of these goodies?" I said.

"Of course, help yourself. Your darling son brought them over without asking, and I didn't have the heart to tell him that I never eat at cocktail parties. Just drink, that's my motto."

"Doesn't that make for a viscious hangover?"

"Nope." She grinned. "I don't get hangovers. I banished them after my husband died. Just up and decided that if I had to be a widow at the foolishly young age of sixty-five, then I shouldn't have to cope with hangovers, too."

"Do you have children?"

"Had two—they died within a year of each other, about ten years ago now."

"That's terrible."

"The older you get, the more you accept death."

"But I thought you didn't accept death?" I smiled tentatively. "You told me you weren't going to die for a very long time."

"Well, sure," she snapped. "That's me. But not everyone feels like I do about it." She took a smacking gulp of alcohol.

I had a feeling one of us was going to have to make sure she got back to her apartment safely, and maybe even tuck her into bed. "It sounds like you're saying people who die *want* to die, but you know that's not true."

"Says who?"

At a momentary loss for words, I took a sip of martini.

"Anyone who dies wants to die," she said.

"Oh, come on! That's ridiculous . . . the mother who's killed in a terrible, fluke car accident and leaves behind two toddlers, you're telling me she wanted to die?"

"Yup." Miss Dora coughed. "This isn't a popular thing to say, of course, so I don't usually share my thoughts so openly." She glanced at me slyly. "I thought you'd understand."

"I've never really given that much thought to death, but I certainly wouldn't accept that those who die are always prepared—"

She interrupted, "I didn't say *prepared,* and I don't really mean that they *want* it, consciously, more that they've come to the conclusion, for reasons they don't really understand, that it's their time."

"And the reason, then, that you're still alive is because . . . ?"

"Because that's been my decision. I'm going to live to a hundred and twenty years old."

I sipped my martini.

"I admit that because I'm now ninety-five years old, this is a self-aggrandizing argument, but I still believe I'm right. Anyway, the proof is in the pudding. We'll see if I live to one hundred twenty."

"How did you decide on that age?"

Again, the sly look. "Can't tell you." She ran her tongue over her lips eagerly, then took another gulp. "Now you've done your duty by me—go on and talk to your other guests. Someone will drop into that chair because they're pooped and they figure they'll do a good deed by talking to me."

I took another sip of martini, then stood up reluctantly. This party was beginning to seem endless. I wanted nothing more than to be alone. Even the idea of a postmortem with Mary and my kids was exhausting to imagine. Of course, I knew the heart had really gone out of me when I realized that Ivan was using me, probably because he knew I was suspicious of him. But then, hadn't I used him? I'd gone to bed with him both to check out whether he might have something to do with the murder and to boost my frail, fifty-year-old ego. I wanted to believe I was sexy still.

Disgusted, I held the next sip of martini in my mouth for several seconds before swallowing, suddenly horrified by its taste. I put the glass down on the side table and walked away. In the kitchen, I grabbed a diet soda out of the refrigerator and chugged it down while gazing at the door to the walk-in pantry. I had a ridiculous temptation to walk into the pantry, close the door behind me, settle comfortably on the floor, and just stay there until the party was over. I could make myself good and sick by eating chocolate-covered apricots.

Mary marched in right at that moment. "Hey, get out there."

"I'm hitting bottom," I said.

"No can do." She grabbed the soda can from my hand. "You have to keep at it—don't give up now."

"Mary," I said wistfully.

"What?"

"Ivan slept with me for some reason, but I know it had nothing to do with any actual sexual or romantic interest in me. I think he's trying to throw me off his scent. Why, I don't know."

She shrugged, then peered more closely into my eyes.

"Hurt your feelings?"

"A little . . . I know it's stupid. . . ."

"Under the circumstances, it's not stupid, but you have to move beyond, figure out your next step. Put the hurt feelings into a box for right now, and shove them under the bed."

"Mary," I said, "you're a genius."

"I am?" she said.

But I didn't answer. I was moving down the pantry hallway as fast as I could.

In the living room, I spied Ivan talking to Laura.

"Excuse me, excuse me," I said, pushing my way across the room.

Ivan's smile was slightly tentative, especially given how he usually beamed out confidence.

"Hi," I said flirtatiously. Then I looked at Laura and rolled my eyes dramatically sideways, as if to say, *Why don't you take a hike?*

"My goodness, I need another drink," she said, disappearing right away.

"So, are you busy tomorrow night?" I asked. Laura and Andrew had decided to return to their respective colleges the next day.

His mouth turned down. "Unfortunately, I'm committed to entertaining Thomas." He leaned forward and kissed me on the lips. "What about Monday night? I put him on the plane that morning."

"Great, consider it a date."

I checked my watch. Twenty minutes to go before the ending time of nine o'clock that I'd posted on the general invitation. *Please let this be over soon,* I begged.

That was when the fire alarm went off. Not just the smoke alarm within the apartment, which could have meant either too much smoke, or that the batteries were running down. No, this was the real thing, a pealing, screaming, blistering shriek of an alarm that made the air vibrate.

For a moment, the whole party froze, everyone peering around with astonishment. This was a party, they seemed to say; why was the fire alarm sounding?

Miss Dora was the first to act. She leaped up from her chair without any apparent effort at all, grabbed that brilliantly lit walker of hers, and started for the door, while simultaneously yelling, "Fire alarm, fire alarm, everyone out!" Or, anyway, I think that's what she was yelling. You couldn't really hear much, even your own thoughts, over the din of the alarm.

Feeling somehow responsible for all these people in my apartment, I began clapping my hands and shooing them out. I rushed to both bedrooms to check for stragglers, and then pounded on the closed bathroom door. Back in the living room, I ran into Mary, who was calmly ushering people through the door with the words, "Keep your drinks, keep your drinks."

"I'm staying to make sure whoever is in the bathroom gets out," I screamed.

She nodded. "The library, dining room, and kitchen are empty."

I turned around and went back to the hall bathroom, pounding on the door a second time. It was flung open by the statuesque Russian woman who'd caused all the trouble earlier. She looked manic and odd, and it occurred to me that she might have been using the bathroom for privacy to snort some coke.

"It's a fire alarm," I yelled. "We have to get out!"

She teetered on her heels through the apartment. I grabbed my keys from the entrance hall table's drawer, slammed the door behind us, and headed for the stairs, following the last party guests. I saw that the Russian babe was pushing the elevator button. "No, you can't use the elevator; we have to walk down."

"I can't walk down nine flights in these!"

The din from the alarm was still shattering.

"Take them off!" I grabbed her arm and yanked her toward the stairs. At the top, she balanced against me while she removed the heels. Suddenly, she seemed to have shrunk five feet.

Since it was a Friday night, a good portion of the occupants of the building were home. We met many others on the staircase, and I joked with all of them, "If you'd come to my party, you'd have a martini to see you through this emergency!"

Most of them smiled, but a few looked at me like I was insane.

I didn't really expect that we were having a fire in the building, so I have to admit to enjoying the descent. My leg muscles, from all the walking and swimming, were toned, and I got a kick out of hearing the Russian debutante behind me, her breath becoming more and more ragged.

She moaned, "I am in such bad shape."

My slippered feet flew down the stairs.

With the others, we spilled through the lobby and out the main entrance. This was fun, I thought, and quite like an extension of the party, except that it was no longer *my* party, and I didn't have to feel responsible for any of it. We milled around outside, at first energized by the cold night air, then, abruptly, realizing that those of us without coats, which was all the partygoers, would get uncomfortably cold very fast.

I spotted Mary and Jacob standing close to Laura and Andrew, so I headed in their direction.

"Hey, I hope they let us back in soon—it's chilly out here."

Andrew said, "I heard people in the new wing smelled and saw smoke—it could be a real fire."

He introduced me to his source for this information, a handsome older man, who I guessed was gay.

"Why didn't you come to my party?" I demanded.

"I wish I had," he said, smiling.

I felt the first waves of shivering shake my body. Andrew

wrapped an arm around my shoulders and pulled me close against his long, bony frame. Though he was tall, like his father, he hadn't filled out yet. I knew his shoulders would broaden and his muscles grow thicker in the next couple of years. Child to man, still unfinished. Grateful, I grabbed some of his warmth. He put his other arm around Laura.

We watched for a minute without speaking as six firemen, in full regalia and carrying big axes, ran into the building with loud, clomping footsteps.

Mary said, "What happened to Miss Dora?"

"Oh, my God, I forgot about her!" I said.

"She was one of the first out, and we hustled her onto the elevator before it stopped working," Laura said. "She's sitting on the bench over there, and someone wrapped a blanket around her."

I shook my head. "This is unbelievable."

In a quiet voice, Jacob said, "I see flames." He pointed to the new wing.

I stared up and down at the windows until I, too, just made out a flickering light on the top floor.

"Maybe there was something wrong in the wiring of the recent construction," Laura said.

The alarm system still shrieked, but it was less deafening now that we were outside. We watched as lights in the new wing went off, then on, and finally off again.

"I hope this has nothing to do with the warning about a murder," I said. When no one answered me, I continued, "A person could die up there, an old person like Miss Dora."

"That would be a tragedy, not a murder," Mary said.

"Unless someone set the fire, like arson," Jacob said.

I shivered.

"I don't think this is what you were being warned about," Andrew said, "but I do find it suspicious even so."

"It's almost like it was deliberately meant to interrupt your party, Mom," Laura said.

"Probaby just a coincidence," Jacob said.

"No such thing as coincidence," Mary announced.

I could see the irritation on Jacob's face, but he didn't answer her. It occurred to me that he was probably scared of her. Maybe that was why he *traveled*.

Mary did have a rather forceful way of expressing herself. That, plus her imposing figure, could certainly intimidate. More strongly than I meant to, I said, "Coincidence has a scientific explanation, doesn't it, Andrew?"

"Sure," he said, grinning, "just like there's scientific strictures against the possibility of hearing a voice in your head."

I poked him with my elbow. "Thanks," I grumbled.

"Science doesn't pretend to have all the answers," Mary said.

"You're right." Andrew smiled gently.

"Hey, look!" Kate said.

A slew of firemen poured out the entrance of the building.

"I didn't see that many go in," I said.

"They probably used other entrances, just in case," Jacob said.

A burly fireman picked up a megaphone and started speaking. "Ladies and gentlemen," he yelled, "we encountered a small fire in the garbage chute on the top floor of the new wing. It's completely extinguished. You may safely return to your apartments. Thank you for your quick and orderly evacuation. Good night!"

We held back, waiting until the first influx of people had made their way through the front doors.

"I hope no one expects the party to continue," I said. "I'm exhausted."

"They have to return your glasses," Mary said.

I groaned.

"I'll stand by the door with a tray, and Mary can stand on the other side with another tray. We'll collect the glasses and say goodnight in a very decisive tone of voice," Laura said.

We decided to walk up the nine flights, since the elevator was so crammed. I was less thrilled with my performance going up. The muscles in my thighs burned, and since I was foolishly trying to keep up with Laura and Andrew, I quickly grew short of breath. We left Mary and Jacob far behind. Outside my locked apartment door, a small cluster of glasses had been left, all of them empty. I opened the door and we started to bring them in. I gazed at the mess and sighed for my beautiful, orderly apartment.

"We'll get it all cleaned up," Andrew said. They knew me well.

"You know what?" I gave a big stretch. "Let's just forget it. We'll clear up anything that looks destructive, like it might be leaving a stain or something; then let's go out and have a great dinner."

When Mary rang the doorbell, I greeted her with the admonition: "We're doing a fast tidy; then I'm taking everyone out to dinner."

Mary bulldozed into the apartment. "I'm cleaning this place up!"

"I mean it, Mary. You've done more than enough already."

"Where do these go?" Jacob said, his arms already full of bottles.

I gave in.

Thirty minutes later, the place was perfect.

"Just a quick vacuum and dusting, you'll be back to new," Mary said.

"And I'm not doing that until tomorrow!"

"Okay, okay." She plopped into the living room wing chair. "I think we need to compare notes real quick; then Jay and I'll take off."

"You don't want to come to dinner with us?"

"It's been a long day," Mary said. "I'm excited about going home and having a hot bath."

Laura said, "Mary, can I get you a drink?"

I grinned at her. "Who raised you so good?"

She smiled, tolerating me.

"I'll have a scotch on the rocks. Jay's not drinking because he's the designated driver."

I glanced at Jacob, wondering again about their marriage and relationship.

When everyone was comfortable and settled, and the leftovers were placed together on the coffee table, Andrew spoke first. "Ivan's guest, Thomas, is Russian, for sure. He said he was just a regular tourist, had known Ivan for about ten years, and figured that when he was recently laid off, and Ivan offered to pay his airfare, he'd finally see America."

We were quiet for a minute.

Andrew continued, "I don't believe a single word he said."

I was surprised, because Andrew had sounded so matter-of-fact when he delivered this information. Plus, as a scientist, he'd never exactly trusted in his own—or anyone else's—gut reactions.

"Really," he said.

"You sound serious," I said.

"I'm so serious that I'm going to have to extract a promise from you, Mom."

"Ooo-oooh," Mary said.

"You can't have anything else to do with either of those guys." He glared at me. I'd never seen such a solemn expression on his face, and it surprised me enough that I considered following his orders.

"I'm disappointed that you would sleep with that lowlife—" he continued.

"Andrew, don't be ridiculous," interrupted Laura. "You as much as anyone should be able to appreciate a gorgeous man, and poor Mom hasn't gotten any action for—"

"Wait a second!" I held up two hands like a double stop sign. "We're not going to analyze my formerly paltry sex life."

Jacob burst out laughing, and Mary's bosom did its jiggling Jell-O action, indicating that a laugh was about to burst out. Sure enough, seconds later, there it was.

Andrew tried to remain serious, but no one in the face of Mary's laughter could remain unmoved. He smiled and then laughed silently.

"This makes it even more important for me to carry through on the date I have with Ivan for Monday night," I said.

"A date's okay," he said, still smiling.

"What exactly is a date?" Mary said, winking.

I said, "A date is, I must confess in the interest of complete disclosure, a date is—"

"Oh, God." Andrew groaned, hiding his face in both hands. "A date is—"

"Mom, please don't tell us—we're too young for this," screamed Laura. But she was laughing and mock covering her ears, like they were actually two big flaps expressly designed to catch the least little nuance of what I might say.

"A date is sex."

Dead silence. I opened my hands from where they were folded in my lap. "Sorry, we can't mess around here. This is serious, I don't need to tell you."

"Exactly why I started out by saying that you *cannot* have anything more to do with them," Andrew said.

"Andrew, baby, first of all, Thomas is leaving town on Monday morning."

Andrew exploded, "No, he's not! You see! He told *me* that he would be here all week!"

"He did?"

"Yes, he did."

"That's interesting, very, very interesting."

"What if she went on a double date with him?" Mary said.

I looked at her like she'd lost her mind. "Who would join me and Ivan on a double date?"

"Let's think about this," Mary said.

"How about Dad?" Laura said, all excited.

"Not a bad idea," Andrew said. "He's the one other person, besides everyone in the room right now, who knows about the voice. I could trust him to be smart and to protect you."

"I'm not going on a double date with my ex-husband—-that's ridiculous!" I said.

Laura said, "Why'd Dad leave so early anyway?"

I took a few minutes to tell them about the car accident he'd had on the way to the party, and how he'd discovered that the woman driving the other car had died.

"May God bless her soul," Mary murmured.

"Poor Dad," Laura said. "It wasn't his fault, right?"

"Not at all, but he seemed pretty shaken up by it. I sincerely doubt that he'll be in the mood to go on a double date with me."

"Maybe it'll be just what he needs," Andrew said. "Take his mind off one death by helping to prevent another."

"Smart boy," Mary said.

"I am not—" I started to say.

"Then you're also not seeing Ivan again," Andrew interrupted, "because I have a lousy feeling about both of those guys."

I was quiet. Even though I respected Andrew's perception about Thomas, and, yes, I accepted that Ivan really wasn't interested in me because he was just busy deflecting my sleuthing, I still found it difficult to believe he was truly dangerous. Though all signs pointed to the realization that the voice had led me to an involvement with Ivan for a good reason, I simply couldn't work up any fear of him.

Maybe that was the danger of sleeping with someone, especially if the sex happened to be good. I found it unacceptable that I could have terrific sex with a murderer. Then again, a great orgasm was sometimes called a *little death*. Murder most orgasmic. Since orgasms were so fruitful for me, I'd never really bothered to analyze them.

"You can be the one to ask your father if he wants to go on a double date with me," I said finally. "It's a ridiculous idea, and I'm sure he'll agree."

"We could go with you," Jacob said, "except Ivan would think it was suspicious that you were going out with the help."

"Yeah, we're out of the picture," Mary said.

"I'm sick and tired of you being the help," I blurted out.

Calmly, she said, "Oh, don't get your—"

"Panties in a twist!" I screamed.

The others started to laugh, and shortly thereafter Mary and Jacob left to drive home.

I took the kids to the Irish pub, Nanny O'Brien's, a couple of blocks away, and we were able to snag a table because, at nine thirty, the evening was still young. Young for those who were young. I felt dazed with fatigue.

Andrew snapped his fingers in my face. "Time for a second wind."

"I'll try," I muttered.

"Get her another martini," Laura said.

"Absolutely not—I'll have club soda."

We ordered hamburgers, and Andrew got a Guinness, since he'd turned twenty-one over the summer.

"It's unbelievable that I can't have a beer," Laura said. "This country is so backward—we can vote and drive, but we can't drink."

"Order a Guinness, Mom, and let Laura drink it," Andrew suggested.

"Nope." I smiled to take away the sting of my refusal.

"You're being inconsistent," Laura argued. "You let me drink at home."

"Yeah, I know."

Laura rolled her eyes.

I wasn't sure whether I should mention Laura's disasterous hookup in front of Andrew, but apparently they'd discussed it on the train from Philly to Washington, because Laura brought up the subject herself.

She blurted out, "I guess I'm supposed to have learned my lesson with that jerk last weekend, but what about *passion*?"

"Passion works for me," Andrew said dryly.

"Have you ever had a significant relationship *begin* with passion?" I asked Andrew.

I genuinely wanted to know. My predilection had always been for positive relationships beginning with an intellectual or emotional connection. Since sleeping with Ivan, however, I was suddenly more open to other possibilities.

"Of course," Andrew said.

Laura shook her head. "I'm scared."

"A little fear is healthy," I piped up.

Our burgers arrived and we dug in, eating like we'd been fasting for a week. An Irish tenor stepped to the microphone on a small stage in the center of the room and began to tune his guitar.

Andrew spoke through a mouthful of burger. "Fear is *not* healthy."

I swallowed my own hefty bite. "Fear can keep you safe."

"Short-term." Andrew took another bite of burger.

Laura looked from one to the other like we were a tennis match. When I didn't say anything, she finally spoke to Andrew. "What do you mean?"

"Even though your experience was very painful, you shouldn't regret it." He lifted the burger to his mouth, then paused. "You may not know what you learned from it, but you learned *something.*"

"Yeah, to avoid random hookups with glib, charming seniors." I mimicked Andrew's dry tone.

"Mom, you're being overprotective," Laura said. Then she picked up Andrew's Guinness, gave me a defiant look, and gulped a nice mouthful.

I ate a french fry and kept my overprotective mouth shut. The tenor began to sing an old ballad, with a recurring refrain of "Her red hair flows like the blood of Ireland." It was beautiful, despite the absurd lyric. Andrew and Laura continued to talk over the singing, but I didn't listen too carefully. For the first time since I'd heard the voice's warning, I simply let go. I replaced its memory with the voices of my children and the singer. They seemed every bit as meaningful as that voice in my head.

Soon after, I left them to their brother-sister bonding and walked back to the apartment, where I tumbled into bed, as hungry for sleep as I'd been for that hamburger.

The next day, Andrew and Laura went to their father's for brunch. I lazed around, reading the morning papers and staying in my flannel nightgown. They called on their way to the train station to let me know that Peter and the Other Ann had agreed to double-date with Ivan and me on Monday night.

"What am I going to say to Ivan?" I whined. "A double date with my ex-husband is so peculiar."

"You're good at making a joke out of things," Andrew said.

I sighed as loudly as I could.

He let out a guffaw. "It's so great to boss my mother around!"

"Let me talk to Laura."

"Hey, Mom," Laura said.

"Don't you think this is a silly plan?"

She was quiet for long enough that I knew she was torn between my point of view and Andrew's. And since I understood whose side she was obligated to take, I made clucking noises and added, "I guess I'll tell him I had some kind of brain fart when I asked Peter, only then I'll probably have to explain what the word *fart* means, and the whole thing will get even more humiliating—"

"Call or e-mail us about how it goes, okay?"

I spent the next hour (or two) in a grand sulk. Double-dating with Peter was absurd, and I was confused about whether or not I should have given into Andrew's insistence. When I sulk, I clean. So I stomped around the apartment with the vacuum cleaner at full throttle, which turned out to be gratifying, because, looking closely, I could see all kinds of junk from the party littering my Oriental rugs. The vacuum made a high, clicking, rattling noise over its usual growl, like an old man clearing his throat while simultaneously yelling swear words. My nightgown dampened with my sweat, while bits of hair, flecks of shrimp, and cracker crumbs clung to the flannel. After I'd put away the vacuum, I stripped off the nightgown and crammed it into my dirty-clothes hamper.

I was downright hot from all that vacuuming, and, still naked, I went back into the living room to admire my work. Inspired, I loaded a CD of Strauss waltzes, flicked on the gas fire, and began to waltz around the room. Stark naked. I passed the gold mirror on the wall at the end of the living room and saw myself, the breasts that usually drooped now raised because my arms were held high, my long, bare neck, and my small waist. I danced until I was breathless and my feet ached. In the kitchen, I drank a long glass of water and decided I would take a quick shower, and then go to an early-evening movie at the Cleveland Park cinema. After the movie, I grabbed dinner at the Parthenon, a local Greek restaurant.

On Sunday, I successfully avoided the swimming pool, laundry room, and all other public spaces. I retreated into the cocoon of my apartment by reading every page of the Sunday paper, writing a long e-mail to my parents in France, and finally, beginning to read a huge work of nonfiction by Bill Bryson called *A Short History of Nearly Everything.*

I avoided Ivan, most of all, and I tried not to think about how hard it had been *not* seeing his handsome face since Friday night. Just before I fell asleep, I asked for the voice to come and explain to me why I so desired the number one culprit in this pre-murder investigation. No voice came.

15

I snored.

Although I no longer had Peter to poke me and make me turn over, I sometimes woke myself up with a good loud snort. I always laughed because the sound of a snore is so absurd, like a person has become an animal. Even though Peter had originally agreed to the double-date idea, I wasn't surprised to be woken Monday morning by a ringing phone *and* my own snoring. I reached for the phone, still half-asleep.

"Snort!" I garrumphed.

"Anne, are you all right?" Peter said.

"Sorry, I was snoring." I yawned loudly into the receiver. No niceties for a former husband. "Are you chickening out?"

He was aggrieved. "It's more complicated than that."

I threw off my comforter and padded through the bedroom.

I heard him sigh. "Are you making the coffee?"

"I'm making the coffee for *me*."

In the kitchen, I kept the phone cradled against my shoulder and pulled out the coffee beans from the freezer. "What's going on?"

"I'll wait until you grind them."

"Can I call you back? I'll attach the phone that—"

"Fine. I'm at home."

I checked the clock on the stove. Eight A.M. and Peter was at home?

I ground the beans and got the coffeemaker going. Then I filled a mug with water and popped it into the microwave so that it would be all warmed up. I had to have a warmed-up mug. One of those things.

I clipped the phone to the waistband of my pajamas, attached the earpiece, and dialed his number. I wasn't concerned about him, beyond the fact that I knew he was leaving me high and dry for the date with Ivan that night. Fine by me. Andrew was back at Swarthmore, and I wanted to be free to take the investigation where it needed to go. Maybe into Ivan's bed?

"I've quit," Peter said.

I poured the coffee into the hot mug, not understanding. "What did you quit?"

"I quit my job."

I slammed the carafe back onto the plate. Coffee sloshed around like tidal waves.

"You're a senior partner—what are you talking about?"

"I'm starting fresh, a new life," he said. "I'm going to be a teacher."

"You couldn't be a teacher if it were the last job on earth."

"I'll be a great teacher, and you know it."

"Peter, what the hell is this about?"

"The car accident, that woman dying, your party, seeing you being kissed by that Russian stud, the way I was unfaithful to you, it's all come together into one big, decisive, cosmic moment."

"Peter, I forgave you long ago for that!" I bit my lip, as I'd done so many times over the last several years, to keep from telling him the truth about *why* he'd been unfaithful. I knew I should probably confess and ask for his forgiveness, but hey, I've never pretended to be a good person.

"It's about forgiving myself—don't you see? I *kill* women. Nothing short of radical change will matter."

"You don't kill women—that car accident wasn't even your fault—"

Peter interrupted, "What if I told you it was?"

"The Other Ann agreed with you that it wasn't your fault; plus, by the way, the police said it wasn't either."

"I've already turned in my resignation. I hope to get a job teaching history at the National Cathedral School, giving back to women, or girls, actually."

I immediately flashed to a vision of handsome Peter striding up and down a classroom, with a bunch of nymphomaniac sixteen-year-olds gazing at him in total adoration and budding sexuality. Disaster.

"You need to see a shrink right away. Call Dr. Armstrong—he knows all about you through me, so you won't have to waste any time filling him in on your past history."

"What a great suggestion," Peter said dryly.

"Dr. Armstrong is the best in D.C.—you said so yourself when I started seeing him."

"Don't you think he might have some preconceived negative ideas about me?"

I moved the mouth of the receiver to the side and hurriedly slurped some coffee. "If you think you're so bad that you kill women, any of his perceptions should be okay with you."

"I don't need to see a shrink."

"Oh, right, you're just making a spur-of-the-moment decision to utterly and completely change your life because you believe you *kill* women, but, no, you have no need for counseling."

"I'm not finished," he said with uncharacteristic patience.

I moaned and drank some more coffee. I'd walked into the library while we'd been talking, and now I collapsed onto the green velvet sofa.

"I'm going to teach history at the National Cathedral School, *and* I'm going to win you back."

"We're divorced. I don't want you back."

That was the understatement of the century. I imagined Peter in this apartment, marching around and taking control. I could never waft in my white nightgowns with him here, much less waltz around naked. Plus, I had a sneaking suspicion that I wouldn't be able to go to bed with Ivan, either.

Sweetness oozed in Peter's voice. "Of course you don't want me back. That makes perfect sense. I don't expect this to be easy. It's not supposed to be easy."

"I'm hanging up now," I said.

"Please don't—"

I disconnected the phone, then yanked off the headpiece and the part clipped to my waist. I dropped them on the rose marble coffee table. I picked up the mug and started to drink, then put it back down again. I turned to look at the trees gathered like sentinels, crowding close.

"Trees," I said, "that man is in serious trouble, but how come it's up to me to save him?"

It was a beautiful late-October morning. Sun slanted through their branches, illuminating the red and gold leaves. Suddenly the wind picked up and the branches bent forward, waving to me. I waved back. Maybe the voice was warning me about Peter. "Is it Peter's death I'm supposed to prevent? Can you tell me, trees?"

The phone rang, but I ignored it. Or I tried to. People always pretended that they could ignore a ringing phone, but in actuality, you couldn't. Every shrill ring sent shivers up and down my body. I counted to twenty after it finished, then clipped the whole business on again to check for a message.

"Anne, this is Ivan, calling to confirm our date tonight. I have something special planned. About eight o'clock at my place?"

That man's voice gave me ants in the pants.

I knew I should see Peter tonight, to try to convince him to go to a therapist of some kind. I owed it to my kids to help him. But . . . I . . . didn't . . . want . . . to.

I called Mary on her cell phone.

"Can you talk?" I said.

"I'm cleaning Mrs. Cadwallader's place, and she's out at some meeting, so yeah."

I told her about Peter.

"Did he ever act like this before?"

"First time."

"I don't get why it's your responsibility. Couldn't you ask Andrew to call him?"

"You think that's fair to Andrew?"

"He's his son—you're just an ex-wife."

"Okay, maybe I'll send Andrew an e-mail."

"That's good."

"How was the rest of your weekend?" I said.

"Kind of on a par with yours."

"What?"

There was a long silence.

"Jay wants us to go see a marriage counselor," she finally muttered.

"You're kidding me." Secretly, I wondered whether the cocktail party had somehow influenced Jacob. And I wasn't altogether sorry if it had.

Mary exploded, "I'm not going to see a marriage counselor."

"What's wrong with getting some help?"

"I'd have to admit that I'm having an affair with a black man," she said.

"You don't have to admit to anything—"

She interrupted, "If you're not honest, what's the point in going?"

"Calm down," I said. "Do you want to stop by here to eat your lunch?"

"I can't—I've got two jobs today."

"You sound mad."

"I am mad."

"I mean, you sound mad at me."

"I'm mad at the world."

"Maybe you can not take it out on me?"

"Okay," she said grudgingly. "I could stop by on my way home tomorrow."

"Good—then I'll be able to tell you about my date with Ivan tonight."

"Are you going by yourself?"

"Yes, and I've got a plan all figured out. I'm going to have fabulous sex with him, and then, when he's asleep, I'll do some investigating."

"What if he wakes up?"

"I could just pretend that—"

"Maybe you should put something in his drink, you know, a sleeping pill."

"That makes me a little nervous—"

She interrupted, "One sleeping pill isn't going to hurt him."

I started to laugh. "What if he goes to sleep before he manages to, you know . . ."

"You're just after his body—admit it."

"That's not absolutely and completely true. Semitrue."

"I think you should drop a sleeping pill into his drink. Andrew's opinion kind of freaked me out, and that way it'll be less likely he can hurt you."

After we hung up, I sent a quick e-mail to Andrew, explaining that I thought his father could use some counseling, and maybe he'd accept the advice of his brilliant son better than his ex-wife's. I spent the morning paying bills and taking care of other desk work. Then I went to do my laps in the pool, certain that at noon on Monday I wouldn't run into Ivan.

When I came out of the hot shower, the beautiful day had dramatically changed. The trees bent in the wind like slender grass stems, and the sky had grown dark as night. I switched on the Weather Channel and discovered that there was a hurricane watch for downtown D.C. I went to turn off the computer, so I didn't end up frying the thing in a storm, but naturally I had to check my e-mail first.

From Peter:

> My Anne,
> I understand why you hung up the phone this morning. If you feel it's so important that I see a health care professional (when you enlist Andrew, I know you mean business), then I will. I've got an appointment this evening with Dr. Armstrong. I assume, as does Andrew, that you've canceled the date with Ivan.
> Love, Peter

From Andrew:

> Hi, Mom,
> I talked to Dad . . . you were right, no surprise. He's gonna get some counseling. I know you won't be seeing Ivan tonight, but I also know that you're not going to give up on your quest.
> Maybe you heard a voice, okay, but maybe the voice came from your own mind. I'm not saying you're mentally ill or anything, so don't get all riled up. You have to admit that with Dad flying off the wall, and you hearing a voice in your head saying that you're supposed to prevent some murder, well . . .? Laura and I are a little worried.
> But there's an obvious reason for this.
> You and Dad should never have divorced. Apart, you're losing your bearings. Maybe together you'd calm down. So I'm urging you to see

Dr. Armstrong yourself. It makes sense. If Dad needs a therapist, then so do you. Please do this for your kids. And give some serious thought to at least experimenting with renewing your marriage to Dad.

Love, Andrew

Furious, I switched off the computer and slammed down the lid of the laptop. I ranted inside my head while I watched the trees sway, the leaves tumble and fly on currents of air, and the sky disappear into dark clouds. The trouble was . . . the trouble was . . . the trouble was . . . I sputtered over and over again.

The trouble was . . . he was right. I'd heard a voice in my head, and I was firmly convinced that a murder would be committed *because* of what the voice had said. How crazy was that? Pretty damn crazy. In addition, I had a close relationship with a good doctor, one who knew me very well. By seeing Dr. Armstrong, I wouldn't be risking an opinion that was based *solely* on my hearing a voice once. He'd have context. He'd understand I wasn't normally the type of person to whom this would happen.

Only I didn't want to. I felt like a small child, stamping around the apartment. *I don't wanna! I don't wanna!* I even spoke the words out loud. "I don't wanna!" Actually, by the time I'd finished circling through the whole apartment three times, I'd begun to feel better. I knew I didn't want Dr. Armstrong, much as I respected him, to take the voice away from me. I didn't want anyone to take away my independence. Most of all, I didn't want to return to marriage with a man who'd hurt me, even though I knew there was a reasonable chance that with Peter's current crisis, and if he saw a decent shrink, he wouldn't hurt me again.

I threw myself across my bed and snuggled my face into the familiar-smelling comforter. Bed made me think of sex. Sex made me think of Ivan. *My turn to have fun,* I thought. *My turn.* I wouldn't go see Dr. Armstrong; I wouldn't give marriage to Peter another chance, and that was final. I knew, in a way that I couldn't express to anyone, that I was healing myself. I'd been unhappy my whole life because I thought I was undisciplined, boring, and plain. Not anymore. I was falling in love with myself, and nothing was going to stop me. Nothing. If Andrew didn't like it, I'd accept the consequences. My turn to be me.

My turn. I rolled over onto my back, arms and legs spread-eagled. My whole body pulsed with a gentle tremble. My toes and fingers tingled. Utter joy. I was going to put myself first, and I was going to start by having sex with Ivan, Russian stud.

16

Restless, I threw on some sweats and went skulking around the building. First stop, one floor down. I lingered outside the apartment of Ibrahim, even daring to put my ear to his door for a quick listen. Unfortunately, the complex had been built like a brick shithouse, and it was very difficult to determine whether or not anyone was home, much less the possibility that a murder was being committed. And I had to admit that Ivan was a more likely candidate than Ibrahim. I probably just wanted to shift blame elsewhere so I didn't feel guilty about sleeping with Ivan. On the other hand, Ibrahim had been attractive. I thought I could sleep with him, too.

All of a sudden, I wanted to jump into bed with any available man.

Next stop, the laundry room. Not a soul was there, but I wandered around for a while anyway. Someone had left a huge load of clothes in a dryer. I found myself circling back to them, staring. It bugged me. They were going to get so darn wrinkled. Finally, unable to control myself, I opened the dryer door, pulled out all the clothes, and dumped them in a pile on one of the long folding tables.

Then, yes, I started to fold them.

They were a man's clothing, a rather large man, truth be told. He didn't have very good taste, either. In fact, the underwear was made of a slippery fabric that didn't look like it had been bought in this country. I checked the tags. Yup, made in Romania. It occurred to me that Romania was awfully close to Russia. Or I thought it was. I got to the giant blue jeans, and without consciously thinking about it, I checked the pockets. There were four pairs, in varying shades of fading. Deep inside one of the pockets, my fingers touched something small and round. I pulled it out and saw a red dot, a little dirty and crumpled, but perfectly matching the red dot I'd seen on the mailbox. I pinched the dot between two fingers and put it in my own pocket. I finished folding all the clothes and left them in several neat piles.

I made my way directly to the mailboxes on the lobby level, where I loitered deliberately. I decided it didn't matter if my constant presence alerted suspicions. Even that level of attention might prevent a murder. I didn't need to figure out the reason for a murder in order to prevent it. I stuck my right hand in my pocket and fingered the red dot. Then I grasped the bottom rim of the mailbox front and yanked on it. Locked solid, it only rattled in place. I peered at Ivan's apartment number, printed on the front of the individual mailboxes, and tried his box. Naturally, it didn't open.

Still, I hung around. I greeted Max, the doorman, and didn't mind that he must have noticed how aimless I was. I felt his eyes following me as I wandered into the huge, empty living room. In there, I plumped up pillows and even pushed armchairs to a more attractive positioning. Exiting from another door, into the long, wide hallway, I said hello to Sally on reception-desk duty and glanced through the glass door that led to the management offices. I could see Angela's back as she worked at the computer. I stood still, quite deliberately, and waited until she sensed my presence and turned around to glance curiously at me. I flapped my hand in an idle wave and continued to stand there for a few seconds.

Back to the mailboxes, where I got lucky. The postman arrived, this time an older man who wore a neatly trimmed white beard. He fiddled with all the keys and kept trying different ones, none of which worked.

"Looks like you've got a problem," I said cheerily.

He shook his head.

"Would you like me to get the key from management?"

"Thank you, I'd appreciate that." He began unloading bundles of mail and placing them strategically along the counter.

I practically skipped into the office. "Hey, Angela, the postman's a substitute and he doesn't have the right key. Can I take it to him?"

She hopped up and disappeared into a walk-in closet. I saw what looked like hundreds of keys dangling from hooks. She handed me the key with a distracted smile. "Thanks, Anne."

I left the office slowly, just long enough to hear her speak into the phone. She sounded on the verge of tears as she said, "But you promised that *He's Just Not That into You* had nothing to do with why you haven't called!" I knew she wouldn't remember she'd given me the key. After the postman opened the mailboxes, I reclaimed the key and headed down the hall, in the general direction of the office. But I walked right by and leaped onto an elevator further away from my apartment.

Hurry up, hurry up, I pleaded with the elevator. On my floor, I broke into a run down the hall and into my apartment, where I grabbed my wallet. Using the service elevator this time, I rode to the basement, then walked up the sloping driveway to the sidewalk that ran in front of the Kennedy. Keeping to the same side of the street, I trotted down Connecticut Avenue, the wild wind tearing at my clothes, to the shoe repair shop. With a high-pitched squealing noise that made me think I might go deaf, they copied the key. Everything in reverse, I dashed back to the Kennedy and entered at the basement level. I returned the key to Angela, who barely acknowledged me because she was screaming into her cell phone.

If I were the manager of the Kennedy, I'd fire her.

Back in my apartment, I went into the kitchen and pulled out three cans of kidney beans. Probably Ivan's surprise for that evening included dinner, but when a hurricane was brewing, it was good to have chili or some other comfort food in the slow cooker. It added to the stormy ambience.

Though it didn't seem possible, the sky kept darkening, and the fallen leaves in Rock Creek Park swam in circular eddies in the air.

The phone rang.

"Hey, Mom," Laura yelled.

"Why are you shouting?"

"'Cause we're getting a hurricane—isn't it exciting?"

"When's it supposed to hit you guys?"

"Sometime tonight!"

I opened the refrigerator and pulled out three massive yellow onions.

"How are your classes going?" I peeled away the thick outer skins of the onions. Their sharp scent dashed up my nostrils, and I sniffled.

Laura, always sensitive, said, "Are you okay?"

"Sure—why do you ask?"

"I thought you were crying."

"I'm making a pot of chili, and I just started on the onions."

Pause. I knew she was contemplating how to bring up her father's cosmic moment. Or cosmic moments, plural. Never one to torment my well-meaning daughter, I said, "I guess you heard about my e-mail correspondence with Andrew?"

"Dad's gone off the deep end!" she exploded. "I mean, how much does a teacher at Cathedral *make,* anyway?"

"Not much."

Light dawned. I continued, "But you don't have to worry about your tuition or anything, honey. He's got money saved for your education in a special fund; plus, if worse came to worst, I have more than enough."

She sounded both relieved and insulted. "I wasn't worried about *that,* Mom."

Right.

"Laura, the trees look like they're going to snap in two!"

"I hope a tree doesn't fall into your apartment—maybe you should go to Dad's house."

"He's got as many trees around him as I do."

"Yeah, but—"

"Sweetie, I am very happy to be independent and on my own now. Dad is going through an interesting growth spurt, but it doesn't mean I should get back together with him."

"I know."

"Are you sure you know?"

"You could at least consider it."

"Nope."

"Okay, well, I gotta run—I'm meeting someone for coffee."

"A significant someone?" I teased, trying to lighten the mood.

Her voice had returned to normal when she sputtered, "I don't know! Jeez, Mom, it's just coffee."

Funny how no one knows anything.

I had the idea that *not* knowing was moving in the right direction. Don't ask me why. It made no sense if you thought about it too hard. On the other hand, for a person who'd heard a voice in her head predicting a murder in one month's time, not knowing had begun to seem as appropriate as knowing.

Like, knowing that I was having a hot date with Ivan, yet making the possibly fatal mistake of chopping up two smelly onions and an entire head of garlic. My hands were going to *reek*. I'd smell like a mother, not a lover. Quickly, I threw everything into the slow cooker and set it on the lowest setting.

It was four o'clock in the afternoon, which meant I had exactly four hours to eradicate the odor. I squeezed five fresh lemons into a flat pie plate. Then I placed both hands in the liquid. A small cut on my pinkie finger stung like I'd been stabbed by a thousand knives. I winced, but kept my hands in the liquid. I tried turning them so the tops were submerged, but that was an almost impossible maneuver. I turned them back with the palms soaking and stood still, staring out the window at the gathering storm.

After twenty minutes, I dumped out the lemon juice, washed up the utensils, cutting board, paring knife, and pie pan, and went to begin my beauty routine.

In my long bathtub dalliance, I decided to get dressed up. After all, Ivan had said he'd arranged something special. The only complication was finding something sexy with pockets, since I would have to keep the single sleeping pill secreted in a pocket. I worried about when and how to drop it into his drink, but I finally decided that I would simply have to see what opportunities came along and be ready to act, no matter what. I remembered an old black dress, made of stretchy material, that kind of swooped helter-skelter to the floor. I dug it out of the guest room closet and put it on over black lingerie given to me by Peter at least ten years earlier, which I'd never worn. The dress made me feel quite grand. It clung to my body in all the right places, but let go in all the right places, too. I twirled in front of the mirror and thought about the young Russian woman with the stiletto heels at the party.

Let's see how you *look in twenty years.*

The phone rang. I checked my watch. Twenty to eight. Then I eyed the phone as it rang a second time. Should I answer it? What if it was Andrew, calling to double-check that I was staying home? Or, could Peter have had an early-evening appointment with Dr. Armstrong, and now he wanted to discuss every little facet of the session?

I snatched up the phone and barked, "Hello?"

"What a lovely greeting," Mary said.

"Wow, am I ever glad it's you."

"I'm calling to tell you not to go tonight—I've got a bad feeling about this."

"Oh, come on, it's just the hurricane making you nervous."

"Okay, I'm not one to stop a woman from fulfilling her bodily needs, but you should be careful and alert."

"You're right." Suddenly suspicious of how relaxed she sounded, even though she was warning me to be careful, I said, "Did you happen to see Jerome after work today?"

"Oh, yeah."

"You are *bad*."

"I had to discuss the state of my marriage with him."

"How come you sound so happy? And shouldn't you be more careful talking on the phone?"

"I'm alone in the house, and I'm happy because that man *makes* me happy."

"Do you have sex with Jacob?"

"From time to time."

"And?"

"It's okay."

I glanced at my watch again. Five to eight. "We need a good long talk," I said, "but right now I'm due to—"

She interrupted, hooting, "*Over*due—you're overdue, like a library book. You're, like, twenty years overdue."

"Listen, sweetie, there are things you don't know about my sexuality, so don't be so damn cocky."

She stopped laughing and got real curious. "Like what?"

"Tell you tomorrow—Super sleuth needs to get going."

"Don't forget the sleeping pill."

"It's in my pocket as we speak."

"Call me in the morning—I'm doing a gentleman's apartment who works."

I dashed into the bathroom and ran my hands through my hair, making it look like a bird's nest. It gave me a rambunctious appearance that I enjoyed. Since I had a thing about being late, I practically ran to Ivan's apartment. In front of his door, I took a couple of deep breaths, not too disturbed by the fact that a little run would make my cheeks pink. Pink cheeks are an unacknowledged beauty perk, because they make you look happy, and it's my theory that happiness in a woman is the biggest aphrodesiac there is. If a man believes you're happy, then you've got him halfway in love with you right away.

Just ask me, the love expert.

Ivan was dressed in silk pajamas, the color of aging red wine stored for twenty years. Now, you may remember what I said about Peter and his fetish for silk pajamas. It wasn't a fetish I appreciated, in him. However, silk pajamas on Ivan was a whole different kettle of fish. He looked both adorable and ferocious at the same time. This was why a divorced person couldn't be totally rational as she ventured into the dating world. What you objected to in an ex-spouse suddenly became scrumptious in a new partner. That was life at its most contradictory.

Ivan reached for my hand and pulled me through the doorway. I glimpsed candles everywhere before he buried me in his arms. No kiss, just a giant bear hug. My head tucked perfectly into his shoulder, turned sideways. My arms tried to reach around his neck, but I had to stand on tiptoe.

What man knows to light a million candles and then to give a hug? Nothing more than a hug? It was perfect.

When he let me go, he growled, again like a bear, "Anne, you're luscious."

"So are you," I said brightly. I'd noticed lots of little dainty eatables on a tray, and I suddenly realized that I hadn't had anything to eat for a long time.

"Martini?" he asked.

"Only if you're having one, too." Earlier in the day, I'd figured out that it would be easier to drop the pill into his drink if we drank the same thing. For example, if I had limited opportunities, I could pick up my glass—only it would be *his* glass—and take it into the bathroom with me. Good thinking, yes? I was proud of myself before I'd even begun.

"I love these American martinis," Ivan said, disappearing into the kitchen.

I sat down on his couch and rapidly snarfed down four baby carrots and smeared some cheese onto a cracker. I was just popping the cracker into my mouth and trying to chew faster when Ivan came into the room while vigorously shaking the martinis. He clutched two glasses in the other hand, which he placed on the coffee table. They were fogged and condensed with ice from the freezer. I rubbed my hands together in anticipation and immediately regretted it. Too much like a kid, not enough like a sophisticated lover.

He tipped the shaker over the glasses, and the slow dribble of frozen vodka streamed out. "So, I spoke for a little with your ex-husband." He raised an eyebrow at me.

"Umm?" I grabbed another carrot.

"Handsome man. Why did you split up?"

"He had trouble—" I stopped talking long enough to grab a piece of celery from another plate, which I held up in the air. "He had trouble keeping his you-know-what in his pants. I found, after twenty-five years, that I was tired of it."

He handed me the martini and held his own high, clearly ready for a toast. Before he could say anything, I blurted out, "I know it's different in Europe. Americans are very old-fashioned about things like fidelity."

"To beautiful Anne," he said, "who deserves love."

"He did love me."

I knew I wasn't making much sense, but being clear was impossible when you tried to summarize a long marriage. Peter had loved me as well as I'd allowed him to. Or as well as I'd loved myself. If you ever wonder, really wonder, what you think of yourself, just look at how other people treat you. It's like looking into a mirror. I've learned this very late in life.

"Do you like all my candles?" Ivan circled around the coffee table and sat down on the couch next to me.

"It's beautiful."

We sipped our martinis quietly. In the silence, I remembered the sleeping pill and began to plot when and how I would be able to drop it in his drink. It was a gel cap that I planned to pry open, so I wouldn't have to wait too long for it to dissolve.

We heard the wind howling, and the rain suddenly began in a torrent. Even sealed away in Ivan's apartment, you could smell the storm.

He twisted around to look out the dark window. "Isn't this exciting?"

I nodded.

"I've never been in an American hurricane."

He leaned toward the window with both hands cupped around his eyes so that he could see into the black night.

"How about a Russian hurricane?"

"No, only a bad storm when I was a little boy."

Something about the way he said those words, *a little boy,* caught me. Deliberately, I moved closer to him. He stopped looking out the window, put his arm around me, and drew me close.

"Tell me a story about when you were a little boy," I said.

"Not so long ago," he teased.

I hit his chest.

"When I was a little boy growing up in Moscow, I lived with my entire family in a room about the size of this one."

"What did you mother and father do?"

"They were atomic scientists."

My heart began to race with nervousness.

Maybe Ivan was a spy, here to try to get secrets about bombs. Okay, that was stupid. The Russians, along with everyone else in the world, knew how to make nuclear weapons.

Still, I sat up and took another sip of martini. "This is very good," I said.

"Vodka from the motherland," he said, smiling.

"So?" I prompted.

He patted his chest lightly with one beefy hand. "I don't tell stories unless your head is here."

That was no hardship. I could put my head on his chest very easily.

So I did. It was quite snuggly, and just before he began to talk I heard his heart beating. *Thump, thump, thump.* Rhythmical and strong.

"I was a puny and sickly kid," he said.

"You weren't!"

He carried his glass to his lips for a sip without dislodging me. "I was a premature baby for my mother."

"How early were you?"

I could tell he was pursing his lips even though my eyes were riveted to the flame of the candle displayed on the coffee table. It flickered and danced, in time with the sounds of rain and wind outdoors.

"Several months."

His large hand moved in slow motion until I felt him cupping the back of my head. "I like this haircut," he said.

"No, you don't."

I sipped my martini and shot him a look.

He cocked his head sideways. "Why do you say that?"

"Because I think you're lying."

Ivan's large mouth curved into a languid smile. "I never lie."

"Umm," I murmured.

"Perhaps you'll notice that I didn't say I liked it *better* than your long hair."

"Ah, semantics again."

His hand was withdrawn. "I have some prep work to do in the kitchen—if you'll excuse me?"

I nodded my head. The minute he'd disappeared into the kitchen and I heard the squeak of the oven door being opened, I slammed my right hand into my pocket and pulled out the pill. Then, getting nervous that he might reappear, I picked up his drink and dashed into the bathroom. Holding the pill over the glass, I pried it open and dumped the white crystalline powder into the vodka. It floated to the bottom of the glass, looking as if it planned to take a long time to dissolve. I grabbed Ivan's toothbrush and gingerly lowered it backward into the alcohol, stirring gently. In just a few seconds, the pill had dissolved completely.

When I came out of the bathroom, he was putting a big iron pot in the middle of the dining room table. Steam billowed out in enormous clouds.

"My mother's stew," he announced proudly.

I picked up my martini glass and carried both glasses to the table, where I put his down on one place mat, and mine at another.

"It smells wonderful, Ivan."

"Can you come help me with the salad and bread?" he asked.

The kitchen, to my surprise, was spotless. "You're a neat and tidy cook," I said.

He looked around, surprised. "I always clean up as I go along."

Suddenly it occurred to me that Ivan probably hadn't cooked

any of this meal. I imagined the Russian babe in stilettos teetering around the kitchen, naked except for a cute apron tied around her waist. I picked up the salad bowl. "Anything else?"

He opened the oven and pulled out a loaf of bread that was split open and dribbling melting butter onto the cookie sheet. "All set."

I sat down in the spot where I'd put my martini, glancing at it just to double-check that it was mine. Actually, I thought, it looked exactly like his. The liquid was at the same level, and I couldn't see any signs of the sleeping pill in the bottom of his. Relieved, I watched as Ivan dished out a huge bowl of stew.

I took a small spoonful and blew to cool it. He stared at me anxiously, waiting for me to try it. Well, maybe I was wrong about the Russian babe. I opened my mouth and slurped it in. "This is scrumptious."

Ivan beamed and bent over his own bowl to begin eating in earnest. I paused to watch him. He shoveled in the stew and seemed to swallow without chewing.

For a few minutes, we ate steadily. Without a word, he handed me a hunk of bread, and I copied him by dunking it in the broth of the stew, then slurping it up while bending over the bowl. I took a breather when I'd finished. Sitting back in my chair, I picked up my martini and sipped.

"Have some salad," Ivan said.

"In a minute."

I drank more martini, thinking about him. Was Ivan evil or good? That was the question bedeviling me. One minute I thought evil, the next, good. I couldn't seem to settle about this guy, and that, of course, was odd. But maybe it had nothing to do with Ivan. Maybe it was my own ambivalence about feeling so attracted to him. It wasn't impossible that I needed to find something wrong with him, to believe he was after me for . . . I dunno . . . my money, or whatever. And Andrew's suspicions about him could obviously be chalked up to a son's horror at seeing his mother being French-kissed, for the first time, by a man other than his father.

In the midst of all this bounty, the steaming stew, hot, yeasty bread, flickering candlelight, sleek vodka, the raging storm outside, and the presence of a gorgeous man who knew how to make love, I gulped the martini. And when I reached the bottom of the glass, having tipped it unceremoniously so as to relish every drop, I knew that I'd given myself the sleeping pill.

On Tuesday afternoon, Mary sashayed her big body into my apartment. I followed in her wake, pulled along by her energy. "You look like shit," she said by way of greeting.

"I feel like shit," I said.

She whirled around. "What happened?"

"Mary," I said.

Her eyes narrowed and she leaned forward, staring into my face.

"Do you promise not to laugh?" I whispered.

Her luscious lips plumped out even more, and I saw her red tongue flick the edges of her white teeth. I could tell she was already primed to laugh, and I hadn't said anything.

"Promise?"

She shook her head back and forth, slow and ponderous. I swear I could see the laughter creating waves as it rose and swelled, rose and swelled, across her mighty bosom.

Personally, I hovered close to tears.

Mary's big brown eyes snapped with amusement. No pity for me, then.

I jumped out of it. "Okay, shit, I'll tell you."

"You betcha," she said, "but first I need a cup of coffee."

She turned and headed to the kitchen. "Smells good in here."

"Oh, my God, the chili!" I tried to dash around her, but the kitchen wasn't wide enough.

"I'd love some chili," she said amiably.

"It's been in the slow cooker for twenty-four hours!" I yelled.

Mary leaped forward and yanked out the plug on the slow cooker.

We both stared at it, nervous. Finally, Mary said, "I'm making the coffee—you can check out the chili."

I grabbed a pot holder and lifted the lid so that the steam drifted away from my face. I peered into the pot. The whole thing had cooked down to a quarter of what had been in there. I picked up the wooden spoon I'd left on a plate next to it and started poking at the contents. "This may be okay," I said.

Mary had finished grinding the coffee beans, and the water was rushing into the coffee carafe. "I'm assuming you want some coffee?"

"Oh, yeah."

She glanced at me. "I'm further assuming you only just got back to your apartment from the date with Ivan?"

"Right." I stirred the spoon vigorously. "Want some chili?"

"Lemme see."

She grabbed the spoon away from me and lifted up a pile of chili. Then she nibbled at it. "Not bad."

I opened the refrigerator. "Sour cream will help if it's a little potent."

"Okay," Mary said, "this is going to be a nice little meal."

We set the table in the dining room and I turned on the electric fire. Suddenly, I remembered the storm.

"Hey, how was the hurricane—did we get hit?"

Mary was pulling out her dining room chair. "Now I'm getting the feeling that you've been dead for twenty-four hours."

I grimaced.

"Does this have something to do with the hints you gave about your sex life?" she said.

We sat down and began to eat. "Right, I have sex and die. Then I come back to life."

"Cool. Can you teach me?"

I pointed my spoon at her. "You have to be nice to me."

"No, I don't," she said. "I don't do nice."

"That's true, isn't it?"

"Yup." She chewed vigorously.

The phone rang and I ran into the library for it.

"Anne, where have you been?" Peter said. "I've left six messages *and* sent you several e-mails. The kids and I have been so worried—"

I returned to the dining room, carrying the phone. Looking right at Mary but speaking into the phone, I said, "I've been asleep for almost twenty-four hours."

Her eyes widened. She'd just started in on a huge spoonful of chili and now she began to choke.

"Oh, God, are you sick?" Peter said.

"No, I'm not sick. I had trouble sleeping last night, so I took a pill."

He sounded suspicious. "They don't last twenty-four hours."

"This one did; take my word for it."

Mary was coughing and gasping.

"Peter, Mary's here and it's impolite to keep talking to you—"

"Please call me right after she leaves," Peter said. "I need to talk to you."

"Okay," I agreed reluctantly.

Mary grinned. "You drank the martini with the sleeping pill, didn't you?"

Against all odds, I started to laugh, and then I nodded. We finished eating our chili before I spoke. "Let's take our coffee in the library."

I turned on a dim standing lamp in the corner; then we settled onto the velvet couch.

The phone rang again, and this time I had to run back into the dining room to find it. After I'd said "Hello?" there was a long pause. I'd returned to the library and Mary stared at me, curious. I said hello again. The breathing was heavy and deep, somehow harsher than in earlier messages.

"Gimme that!" Mary lunged for the phone and grabbed it out of my hand. "Who's there?" she said into the receiver. Then, "We're onto you, mister, so watch out. We're pulling you in, sure as shit!"

She disconnected and tossed the phone onto the coffee table.

"Did he say anything to you?" I asked.

"He said, and I quote, 'Mind your own business,' end quote."

"You sure let him have it." I was full of admiration. I continued, "Do you think the phone calls have something to do with the voice?"

"Yup."

"They might be two separate things."

"Does it matter?"

"I guess not."

"So were you too knocked out to do the dirty deed with Ivan?" Mary asked.

"Can you believe it?"

I closed my eyes and conjured up images from the previous evening, speaking out loud to Mary as they flowed. The way I'd tried to leave right after dinner, in order to get back to my apartment before the sleeping pill hit me, and how Ivan hadn't understood at all. He'd stroked my hair and lured me to the bed. I'd fallen backward, with him heavily on top of me. And then my head lolled to the side, and I was gone, gone, gone. I stored sleeping pills in my medicine cabinet because you never knew when a guest might have the need, but I, myself, had such a profound reaction to sleeping pills that I never took them.

I had no memory of anything else until I woke up, alone in Ivan's apartment, and saw that it was four o'clock in the afternoon of the next day. My bladder was bursting, so I tore to his bathroom, immediately taking note that my clothes were still in place. When I came out, I fixed myself a tall glass of water. The kitchen was immaculate. There was a note propped up next to the coffeemaker.

> Anne,
>
> I hope you are not ill? I thought it best to let you sleep. If you press the on button, coffee will come out.
>
> Your friend, Ivan

I continued telling Mary, "Even though I was pretty wiped out when I woke up, I poked around Ivan's apartment."

She sat up, excited. "Did you find anything suspicious?"

"First, I have something else to show you." I went into the living room and opened the center drawer of my desk and took out the crumpled red dot I'd discovered in the pocket of the man's blue jeans that I'd folded from the dryer. I displayed it in the palm of my hand and told Mary where I'd found it.

"Okay . . ." she said.

I dug into my pocket and extracted another red dot. "I found this in Ivan's trash can, way at the bottom."

Mary screwed up her nose in disgust. "You dug through his trash?"

"Uh-huh." Then I told her how I'd made a copy of the key to the mailboxes. "I'm planning to open it up at about three A.M. tonight."

She nodded her head thoughtfully and muttered, "Wonder what they mean."

"I think it must be some kind of signal."

Mary looked at her watch. "I gotta get home. Jay said he'd be late, and I have to do something about Patrick's dinner."

"Do you think Jacob's with someone?"

"I don't know and I don't care!" She snapped her fingers. "Hey, what's with the sex thing you were going to tell me about?"

"I'm just ultraorgasmic." I shrugged. "It's a nice perk."

"So am I!" Mary beamed at me.

Sisters in the world of the big O.

We were heading through the living room when she said, "I mean it—I've had enough. I think I'm going to get divorced like you, when Patrick graduates."

"Shouldn't you at least try the counseling idea?"

Mary pulled on the bright red cape she'd been wearing when she came in. It swirled around her body.

I continued, "You don't really think Jerome will ever leave his wife, do you?"

She grinned, a big, delicious smile. "He might."

"You shouldn't end a marriage because you're *hoping* to marry someone else."

"We'll see; we'll see."

She started out the door. "You have to call the police and report those phone calls," she said.

"Right away, your highness."

18

I did call the police right away, who were magnificently unhelpful. When I told them that the *69 feature on my phone hadn't worked, they suggested contacting the phone company. They also made it clear that in the realm of threatening activity, a bunch of phone calls with heavy breathing and a few nasty words was nothing to be concerned about. A woman at the phone company, with a drawl from the deep South, was more sympathetic. She promised to do a search of all my calls for the past five days, and she made some suggestions about how to handle any new ones that might come in. Like, hang up immediately and report it to them.

I tottered around, vaguely cleaning up the kitchen and dining room from our truncated meal, when I heard my doorbell ring. Thinking about the phone calls, I froze, then tiptoed to my door. I peered through the security peephole. Peter's handsome lips practically leaped out and bit me. I swore under my breath. I was in no mood to deal with his whoop-de-do.

I threw open the door and glared at him. "Did you ever hear of calling first?"

"I was worried." He smiled disarmingly. "And judging by the way you look, for good reason."

I started to shut the door in his face. "I don't appreciate that comment."

He stopped it with his hand. "I meant you look troubled."

"What do you want, Peter?"

"I would really appreciate talking to you about my session with Dr. Armstrong."

"Right now?"

His face grew serious and he nodded.

I opened the door and let him in, against my better judgment, but then, that had been the story of our life together. I was always opening the door to him, figuratively and literally, against my better judgment. Which was why, finally, I had the sense to close the door by divorcing him. Yet here I was, opening the damn door.

He sniffed appreciatively as we passed the entrance to the kitchen. "Is that chili?"

"Do you want some?"

"I'm starving."

I turned into the pantry, with Peter on my heels.

The chili in the slow cooker was still hot, so I spooned out two more bowls. I was at least two meals short for the last twenty-four hours. I set the table in the dining room again and turned on the electric fire. I plopped spoonfuls of sour cream into each bowl of chili, then brought out two glasses of ice water. We sat down.

"Thank you," Peter said.

"You're welcome."

"You have certainly made a beautiful apartment here, but I can't say I'm surprised."

"Thank you, again."

We ate in silence.

Peter said, "This is a great bowl of chili. The meat is so tender, it falls apart in your mouth before you even have to chew."

I wasn't about to tell him that I'd been asleep at Ivan's and the chili had cooked for twenty-four hours. I was, however, considering an anonymous letter to "Dear Heloise", offering a chili-cooking tip to the general public.

"Just one of those things."

We ate quietly for a minute.

"So, how did it go with Dr. Armstrong?" I asked, hoping to get our conversation over with.

"I retracted my resignation from the firm, for the moment, anyway."

I nodded. "Your decision making about that was a little quick."

"However, I've also officially applied for a teaching position at Cathedral."

I kept my expression blank.

"I told Dr. Armstrong about the voice you heard in your head."

I should have expected it, of course. And he was entitled to tell a shrink anything he wanted, but I was furious. That was what I got for sending him to my own psychiatrist. Though, if he'd seen anyone other than Dr. Armstrong, I might be running the risk of a family intervention and being carted off to the local mental hospital. I felt my face flushing red, and dots of sweat prickled my hairline.

Peter reassured me. "He doesn't think you're crazy."

"I never thought he would." My tone was icy. I felt like throwing my uneaten chili across the table so that it landed with a splat right in his face.

Suddenly I knew Peter was bullshitting me. Dr. Armstrong was far too professional to have expressed his point of view about me to Peter.

The anger and fight drained out of me. "I happen to know that Dr. Armstrong would never give you an opinion like that, whether it was about me or you."

Peter blinked and hurriedly took a bite of chili. When he'd swallowed, he said, "He did tell me that I should retract my resignation."

"I don't think so."

Angry, Peter pointed his spoon at me. "I was there—are you telling me I don't know what he said?"

I nodded, serene. "I'm telling you that he didn't give his opinion. If you stop for a minute and go back over the meeting very carefully, you'll see I'm right." I stood up. "While you're doing that, I'll get us a piece of fruit."

In the kitchen, I grabbed two ripe pears from the fruit bowl, and peeled and sliced them into thin, long pieces. Then I dribbled some kirsch over them. I balanced two dessert forks on each plate and headed back into the dining room. Silent, I cleared the chili bowls and put the pears down at our places.

When I'd pulled out my chair and sat down, Peter opened his mouth. Then he closed it.

Finally, words came out. "You're right—he didn't tell me that I should retract my resignation. He didn't even tell me he thought it was a good idea."

His face looked so puzzled, I took pity on him.

"That's how therapy works. It's actually kind of amazing. They get us to know what we think is best. It can take a while, but it really makes a difference. The doctor is like another part of you, and you're talking to yourself."

"But why does that work?" Peter said. "Why would I think of Dr. Armstrong as myself? He's fat and bald, for Chrissakes!"

"It's mystifying to me, too." I speared a piece of pear and savored it in my mouth. "Probably one of the reasons people are so mistrustful of therapy is they don't understand it."

Peter continued, "I talked to Dr. Armstrong about wanting to convince you to give our marriage another chance."

"And I bet he didn't have anything to say about that either."

"Right." Peter grinned. "But you know I'm irrepressible."

"Well, maybe it would be useful for me to be one hundred percent straight with you?"

"Good idea." Peter actually pointed his fork at me. "What do you have to say for yourself?"

"Number one, if you ever again try to enlist the aid of our children in this quest of yours"—I pointed my fork at him now—"then our relationship will seriously deteriorate."

Peter's fork slowly drifted to the table. All the air went out of him. "You're right," he said, "I shouldn't have done that."

"Number two, I want to make something clear."

"Okay."

"I am extremely happy to be exploring new relationships with other men."

We were quiet. I speared my final slice of pear and popped it into my mouth.

Peter stood up abruptly. "So," he said. "I'll think of something."

"You could give up this nonsense."

"I'm seeing Dr. Armstrong again tomorrow night."

I knew he meant that he would have to explore the subject with his shrink. I had no quarrel with that. Dr. Armstrong was on the side of peace, not irrational, aggressive quests, of that I was sure.

After Peter had gone, I once again cleaned up the kitchen. Then I went through the tedious job of going through the phone messages and e-mails that had accumulated during the twenty-four hours when I'd virtually disappeared. Finally, I ran a deep bath into which I sank my weary body.

I expected to hop out of the bath, pronto, and then read until the wee hours of the morning, when I could use the key to the mailboxes. Instead, the hot water so relaxed me that I started to get sleepy all over again. I sat up in the bath, sloshing water, and concentrated on vigorous soaping. I'd slept too much over the last twenty-four hours. After my bath, I put on comfortable sweats and hustled into the living room. It was nine o'clock in the evening and I couldn't seem to come more fully awake. Desperate, I went into the kitchen and began grinding the beans for my perfect-cup-of-coffee ritual.

When the coffee was ready, I carried it to my desk, where I sat down at the laptop and pulled up an empty Word document. I started to write down everything, from the moment I'd heard the voice. I sipped at the coffee and finished the whole cup without really being aware of it. I wrote and wrote, even going back to revise and improve sentences. I corrected mispellings and finally reformatted it to be double-spaced before saving it and then sending the document to be printed. In a daze, I collapsed into the corner of the couch and reread it. Somehow the written statement clarified my thinking.

I walked over to the windows that looked out to Rock Creek Park. I'd forgotten to pull the drapes, so when I stood close I could see the dark mass of trees. The branches had lost a lot of leaves from the storm, and the view was stark. Winter was coming. As I tried to understand what was happening at the Kennedy, my analysis was like the trees losing their leaves. While their trunks and branches were revealed, it was still a thick, crowded forest, with no discernible shape or focus.

I checked the time on my computer and was amazed to see that it was already two o'clock in the morning. I decided that there wasn't anything special about three A.M. versus two A.M. I pulled out a small drawer in the mahogany server, where we'd set up the bar for the party, and grabbed the key. In my bedroom, I put on my black Chinese slippers.

With the key to the mailboxes in my right pocket, and the key to my apartment in the left pocket, I slowly opened the door leading into the hallway. I walked quietly to the staircase and began the long journey down nine flights. I didn't want to encourage my nervousness, so I kept my pace slow and gave myself a lecture about how there was no reason to hurry.

At the lobby level, I paused in front of the heavy door that opened to the long hallway and strained my ears to hear the slightest noise. Nothing. I pushed open the door, wincing at the sounds the door's hinges emitted. I turned and gently closed the door until I heard the latch click. My armpits felt like wet sea creatures. The hanging hall lights blazed, which I thought was unfortunate, given what I intended to do. It was also a waste of electricity. I walked quietly down the hall, on my way to check on the whereabouts of the doorman, while my mind went on a rant about all the changes I'd make at the Kennedy if I were in charge. Number one, dim the lights at two o'clock in the morning, for goodness' sake.

I passed the mailboxes and, at the hall's end, peered around the corner into the entrance hall. A doorman sat on a high chair, his back to me. He was utterly still. I watched him and, as if by magic, he slowly folded his arms on the desk in front of him and lowered his head to rest on the pillow he'd made. I kept watching, shifting from foot to foot and worrying about how much noise the mailboxes would make when I opened them.

A hissing noise started low, barely more than a vibration in the air, lasting a few seconds before a loud crash sounded. *Clang, clang,* it went, as if someone had picked up a hammer and begun pounding on the pipes. To my delight, the doorman didn't move. I turned around quickly, wanting to take advantage of the banging pipes, which was probably heat moving through the radiators.

I grabbed the key and plunged it into the mailbox front. I fiddled around out of nervousness, so naturally the key didn't work right. I took a deep breath and flapped my arms in a futile attempt to dry out my damp armpits. Then I reinserted the key, turned it briskly to the left, and felt the lock turn. I swung open the entire mailbox door.

"Hey, what's going on?" the doorman's voice boomed.

I practically jumped out of my sweatpants. My mind raced with no thoughts about what I could say as an explanation, which

I knew was really poor planning. Why hadn't I prepared myself with some kind of logical reason for opening the mailboxes? And, unfortunately, I didn't know any of the late-night doormen. This one's face was not only strange to me, but also dramatic. He looked like a movie star. Young. Gorgeous. Huge blue eyes and pure blond hair. I was stunned into further and even deeper silence. So I decided to go with all that I had. I opened my eyes wide, though they were already round as quarters. Then I stuck one hip out.

I spoke with a huge grin. "Who are *you*?"

"The doorman, John."

"John, you are one handsome man—are you an actor?"

He shook his head, a little shy and sheepish.

"You should be!" I took a half step toward him. "People must've told you that before."

John shrugged and smiled.

"My best friend from college is a big talent agent in L.A.—could I have her call you?"

"I've never done any acting."

"From what I understand, it's all in how the camera captures you." I shifted my weight to the opposite hip. "Worth a shot?"

"Sure. Thanks."

"Can you write down your full name, address, phone number, and e-mail for me?"

He disappeared, and I whirled back to the mailboxes. I saw them immediately, this time two red dots. I stepped closer, leaned forward, and squinted at the apartment number written above the red dots. Sure enough, it was Ivan's mailbox. I touched the dots, curious. Then I swung the mailbox shut, dropped the key into my pocket, and headed toward the entrance hall. I ran into John as he barreled around the corner.

He held out a scrap of paper, practically waving it. I was glad, seeing his excitement, that I really did have a college buddy in the movie business. I plucked the paper from his fingers.

Ah, those fingers. His hands were blunt and thick, the hands of a man who could build something.

"I'll e-mail her tomorrow," I said. "Meanwhile, you might want to get some portraits done by a professional photographer."

"Okay."

I took the elevator back to my floor. After I'd changed into my flannel nightgown, brushed my teeth, and turned off all the lights in the apartment, I finally managed to stop imagining John as a major movie star, discovered by yours truly. I climbed into bed and jerked my mind back to contemplating the two red dots. One dot, now two. Clearly a signal of some sort. Logically, it suggested a delivery, since the mailboxes were a delivery system. My eyelids grew heavy, and I blinked rapidly to keep myself from plunging into sleep. I saw the wardrobe in the basement laundry room. I pretended I was climbing into it and unlatching the bottom before pushing the back open. It lifted slowly. I walked through.

Boom. I slept.

19

I slept late the next morning, then frittered the day away on writing e-mails, cooking a magnificent meal straight out of Julia Child, eating only a smidgen of it, and finally, watching an old romantic comedy on television. I was in my nightgown all day and never left the apartment, even to check my mail. It's not that I was giving up—far from it. I tried repeatedly to reach Mary, and left several messages on her voice mail, but she never called back.

Otherwise, it was a day of waiting. I wasn't sure why I knew not to push things by dashing all over the place. But I knew. It felt like making bread, when I allowed the dough to rise, then punched it down for yet another rising, until it was ready to be shaped and baked in the oven. As I exchanged a dirty nightgown for a clean one, I almost wished I'd made some fresh bread. The phone rang just as I was getting into bed.

"It's Mary."

I was on alert immediately. She sounded like a rag that had been twisted and wrung out within an inch of its life. I sat up straight in bed and said, "Are you okay?"

Now I could hear the tears. "No."

"Did something happen to your son?"

"No." Her breathing steadied. "Not that bad, but pretty bad."

"Jacob found out you're having an affair?"

"Close."

"Is this some kind of a game? Why can't you just *tell* me?"

"Sorry."

"Take a couple of deep, long breaths."

I heard them through the telephone. Finally, she said, "Jerome's wife found out. He's broken it off with me."

"The minister?"

"Yeah."

"This isn't the church you go to, is it?"

"No, but it's in my general community."

I heard her start to cry in earnest. "Where are you?" I asked.

"Sitting in Jay's car, at the Wal-Mart near our house. Jerome left me a message on my cell phone, so I haven't been able to talk to him." There was a moment of silence. "Jacob is in Memphis on business—Patrick's home."

"I'm coming out," I said. "Give me directions to your place."

"No, no," she cried. "We can't talk with my son in the house!"

"Don't you have a basement room or something?"

"Yeah, a rec room."

"What if you told Patrick that I was having a little emotional crisis and that you needed to talk to me privately? He won't be able to hear us down there; plus he'll be going to bed pretty soon—it's a school night."

She sniffed loudly. "You could spend the night."

"I'd love to, and then I could drive you into work tomorrow."

"Okay, that sounds good."

She gave me directions and I said I'd be there as soon as I could.

I yanked on blue jeans, a turtleneck, and a thick sweatshirt. Then I grabbed an ancient leather jacket, my purse, and the car keys. My car, a Chrysler PT Cruiser convertible, started right away, and I tore out of the garage. As I drove down Connecticut Avenue, heading toward 495, I realized that I hadn't been outside since I'd run for the chili ingredients before the hurricane. The air was crisp and clear. I turned the heat on low and considered putting the top down. I felt as though I'd been starved for the outdoors, as if all these shenanigans, with Ivan, with the voice, with Peter, and especially with my cocktail party, had been stultifying.

I craved the sky, the air, the trees.

Mary's neighborhood was nice middle-class. Even at night, the separate bungalows looked neat, with small welcoming lights beaming out from their friendly faces. I wasn't surprised, when Mary opened the door to me, to find her house was perfectly kept and lovely. The entry was a crisp white, with a hooked rug centered on the shining hardwood floor. I could smell fresh coffee.

A giant of a boy descended the stairs, lanky and handsome with frizzy light brown hair and a sensational grin.

"How do you do, Ms. Johnson? I'm Patrick, Mary's son."

Just in time, I remembered that I was supposed to be having an emotional crisis. So, instead of simply beaming at him, which was what I wanted to do, I kept my face somewhat serious as I said hello, adding that he had to call me Anne, not Ms. Johnson.

He turned to Mary. "I'll be going to bed soon—see you in the morning."

She gave him a kiss on the cheek. "Say your prayers."

"You, too," he teased.

Mary led me back to the kitchen, which was also painted white with shining hardwood floors and bright blue countertops.

"He knows something," she muttered.

"Oh, come on—"

"He's *never* told me to say my prayers." She gave me a sharp look as she took down two big blue coffee mugs.

"I really don't think you should worry about it—a kid that age is lost in his own world. He may sense something, but as long as you keep up appearances, he'll be okay."

"You want coffee, right?"

"Yes." I paused. "Mary, your house is adorable."

She shrugged. "Nothing to compare to yours."

"That's insulting." I took the mug of coffee and added fake sweetener.

Surprised, she said, "What do you mean?"

"Everyone has their own style, and one person's is no better than another's. This house of *full* of you, and it's got a truly wonderful feeling to it."

She stared at me. I kept my face fierce. I didn't care how upset she was; I couldn't let her start making us feel unequal. I wouldn't be able to be friends with someone under those circumstances.

Mary picked up a bowl of popcorn and led the way to the basement. Here, too, the walls were painted a crisp white color, and the carpet was a shocking deep blue. A big couch, covered in blue-and-white chintz, dominated the room and faced a huge television.

"This is so cozy." I put the mug of coffee down on a glass-topped coffee table with a base of white marble.

"I'm house-proud, I admit it," Mary said. Before sitting down on the couch, she went over to a stereo system, chose a CD, and put it on. Jazz played quietly. "Okay?" she asked.

I snuggled deeper into the couch pillows and grabbed my first handful of popcorn. "Perfect—if you weren't so upset, I'd be having the time of my life."

She arched her eyebrows at me. "Only I know this is bad," I said quickly.

Mary collapsed into the opposite corner of the couch, then dug around in her pants pocket until she unearthed her cell phone. "You want to listen to his message?"

I was, naturally, dying to hear his voice and exactly what he'd said to her. She brought the message up and then handed me the phone, telling me to press 3.

His voice was deep and masculine sounding, with a slight cadence of the Caribbean islands.

"Mary, Jenny found some of your e-mail messages to me."

He hesitated, obviously guilty.

"I thought they were safe from detection—I'm sorry. Things are really bad here, as you can imagine. I can't see you anymore. I want to save my marriage. Please do not contact me. It's over. I pray that you will forgive me. I know that we have sinned terribly. I pray that God blesses you. I—"

Again, the voice stopped for a minute, searching. I knew he'd been about to say, "I love you."

Instead, the message ended.

I faced a tricky situation with Mary, because the truth was that I was glad the affair was over. It had made me uncomfortable from the first, and I'd certainly felt sorry for Jerome's wife, whatever the reasons for the failure within the marriage, since I also knew that one person was never totally responsible for a faltering marriage. Perhaps Jenny didn't express her love well, or completely. Like someone else I knew—myself.

"Hear how he was about to say he loved me?" Mary asked.

I glanced at her before handing back the cell phone and reaching for another handful of popcorn. "Yeah," I said.

I saw the way her throat bobbed twice, and I knew she was swallowing against the thickness of tears that swelled there. "It would help me if you could back up a little," I said. "Tell me why you fell in love with Jerome."

People always wanted to talk about the beloved, even if the relationship was over.

"He's handsome," she said.

I nodded. Mary sipped at her coffee and then helped herself to popcorn.

"And you could probably tell he speaks beautifully."

"Yes, lovely. Where's he from?"

"Jamaica." She was thoughtful. "But I think what really got me was his mind." She chomped on popcorn for a minute. "I know that sounds kind of funny, coming from a cleaning lady."

I shook my head no.

I shuddered involuntarily at the term *cleaning lady,* and she must have seen me, because she said, "Well, no use denying it. That's what I am, a cleaning lady."

Suddenly aggressive, she said, "I'm gonna quit. My son's been after me for years, and now I'm going to do it."

"Mary—"

"Okay, okay." More slurping of coffee. "The problem is that I don't read all that well."

"Are you dyslexic?"

"Something, probably. I never got tested."

I chewed on popcorn and tried to act like this wasn't the end of the world. I could imagine Mary as a little girl, then a teenager, and no one bothering with her.

"I dropped out my senior year of high school—couldn't take it anymore. I was failing everything except math." She looked at me, obviously waiting to see how I'd react.

"Sounds like you were lost between the cracks."

She nodded. "I was, and my parents needed money, so I went to work at about the only thing I could get, and I have to tell you, at first I loved it. I made decent money and I was good at cleaning. Not everyone is, you know."

I grinned. "You're telling me?"

"Takes one to know one." Mary shrugged. "And I kept on."

"How did you meet Jacob?"

"I cleaned his apartment—one thing led to another."

"Mary—" I stopped, unsure about what I wanted to ask.

"I probably got a kick out of him being white, sure," she said in answer to my unasked question. "But that wasn't the whole thing. He was college-educated. I liked that a lot. Made me feel smart, you know?"

"I know exactly what you mean."

"Then I found out he was unfaithful. In my defense, he did it first. By that time, we had Patrick, and I wasn't about to put up a fuss. Figured I'd just lose out, all around. So I prayed to the Lord and asked for guidance. And the guidance I got was to accept it. Plenty of men play and travel. Nothing new in that."

"I understand."

"I bet you do." She gave me a look. "Everything stayed on an even keel until Jerome." She sighed and shook her head from side to side. Her breasts seemed to rise into mountains beneath her chin before she gave a final letting go and her whole body subsided. "Another educated man—made me feel smart."

"Do you have any idea why *he* needed to have an affair? What's the deal with his marriage?"

"You ever try being married to a holier-than-thou black lady minister?"

I laughed. "No."

"She's a big woman, like me, but she's got a face that'll kill you." Mary pulled her mouth down at the edges and narrowed her eyes into slits.

"I think you're exaggerating."

"No, I'm not." She grinned. "I know I'm bad, but I used to hear all the gossip from Patrick's friends who belong to her church. They made awful fun of her."

"So that's the reason—"

"She's not much for sex."

"I sometimes wondered whether Peter said that about me."

She didn't take offense. "He probably did, but I honestly think it's true in Jerome's case. He was so desperate and damn grateful every time." She giggled and then, remembering that it was over, stopped.

"If it is true, then maybe they should end their marriage."

"I sure think so!" Her face lit up at the idea.

"I hate to pop your bubble, but you're married, so that wouldn't help you."

"He'd wait for me until Patrick graduated; then we'd get married."

The trickiness of the situation was getting worse for me, because I suddenly saw the truth. Jerome, an educated man who taught high school English to gifted kids, wasn't going to marry a woman who cleaned apartments for a living and who, furthermore, didn't have a high school diploma. I wasn't saying that he didn't know she was smart. I'm sure he did, just the way I knew it. You couldn't miss Mary's intelligence.

"I'm confused about something," I said. I drank the last of my coffee and noticed that the jazz CD had finished.

Mary stood up, graceful as always despite her size, and went to put on another CD. "What?" she said to me over her shoulder.

"How is Jerome *different* from Jacob?"

With a beatific smile, just as the music began, she whirled around. "He doesn't *cheat,* Anne."

Like a shot, I exploded with the words, "Sure, he does. He cheats with you, that's all!"

The smile froze. Then her eyes blinked. "What exactly are you saying?"

I gentled my tone of voice, as much as I could. In retrospect, I should have shut the hell up. "I think you're just paying Jacob back and that Jerome is no different from your husband. He couldn't really be a loving and respectful man, because he's hurting his wife by being with you. He is, ultimately, as cruel as Jacob's been."

Mary sucked in her breath, and I thought her lips moved with a few unspoken words. Then, "You believe it's *wrong* to be unfaithful. But maybe that's a judgment you should only make about yourself. Maybe it's okay in some cases."

I knew we were both being wildly inconsistent. "Then why do you care about Jacob cheating on you?"

"I don't!" she yelled.

I clamped my mouth shut, giving Mary time to sit back down and for both of us to cool off. Finally, I said, "Anyway, I guess it's silly to talk about, since what's done is done."

"It's not done," she said forcefully. "I'm going to talk to that lady minister first thing in the morning."

I stared at her, horrified. Finally, I whispered, "You *can't* do that, Mary."

"I'm fighting for him." Her large, gracious mouth was set strong.

"What about Patrick?"

"I . . ." She paused, struggling for control. "Don't you see? I love Jerome. I can't live without him loving me back." She opened her hands wide in her lap, turned with the palms up, as if beseeching. Which I suppose she was.

I swallowed and let my mind cycle rapidly through a million different responses until I found exactly the right thing to say. "God wouldn't want you to destroy Patrick in this way—and you *will* destroy your son. At least pray to God for direction."

I somehow thought that invoking God would calm her down and get her to see reason. Hah.

Mary jumped to her feet and bellowed, "You don't even believe in God, so don't start telling me what God would want—"

I interrupted, "I said to pray to God for—"

"Get out of my house!"

My mouth dropped open. "Come on, Mary, let's talk some more."

"Now!" She pointed her arm toward the stairs. "Get out!"

I stood up and spoke very quietly. "Are you sure you want me to go? I think it's a mistake."

Dramatically, she jackknifed her arm to her chest and then whipped it back out again, still pointing to the stairs.

I walked swiftly across the basement and ran up the stairs. I grabbed my purse from where I'd left it on the kitchen table, then dashed out the front door. My hands shook as I inserted the key into the ignition. I drove the mile and a half to the entrance to Route 270, where I pulled over to the side of the road and quickly unlatched the roof of my car. I pressed the button to put the top down, then buttoned up my leather jacket all the way to the neck, with the collar flipped high. I realized that this was the first time I'd driven in my convertible with short hair. I zipped onto the highway, raised all the electric windows, and turned on the heat full-blast.

I was grateful to be back in my apartment. I threw myself on the couch and picked up the remote control to turn on the gas fire. When I checked for phone messages, there was one from Ivan, and two of heavy breathing. Ivan said, "Anne, I am concerned. Are you well?" The heavy breathing was par for the course. It was actually becoming a first-class bore.

I went into the kitchen and poured myself a bourbon on the rocks, which I carried back into the living room. I took a long sip and then I dialed Ivan's number.

"Ivan, I'm sorry about what happened."

His tone was amused, but puzzled. "I've never put a woman to sleep with quite that level of success."

"I'd taken some medication for a migraine headache before I came up to see you, and I shouldn't have had that martini. The combination just knocked me out—again, my profound apologies."

"Accepted."

I was sure he was smiling, which meant he didn't suspect me of anything.

Ivan said, "What are you doing right now?"

"Drinking bourbon."

"Bourbon? That's disgusting!"

"Then you've never had good bourbon."

"Why don't you bring down your bottle of bourbon and join me?"

It was so tempting. I thought about the possibility of sleuthing around his apartment, but the greater truth was that I was miserable over the argument with Mary. I didn't want to be alone, plain and simple.

"I've already had a busy, unpleasant evening. . . ." I trailed off without finishing, hoping he'd try to convince me.

In a sexy voice, he said, "You can tell me everything. I will kiss it and make it better."

On my way to Ivan's apartment, I decided to agressively question him after he'd tossed back a couple of bourbons. No more slithering away. When he answered the door, Ivan wore his black robe again, the one that reminded me of a monk. I held up the bottle, which he took without a word. I walked into his apartment and had to admit that it was beginning to seem familiar and comfortable. I displayed my glass, packed with ice and bourbon. "I've got plenty."

He squinted at the bottle. "Do I add soda or water, or what?"

"This is excellent bourbon. Nothing but lots of ice."

"Okay," Ivan said, obviously skeptical. He disappeared into the kitchen while I went to sit on his couch. "Do you need anything to eat? I have crackers and cheese, and some other things," he called out.

"I'm fine."

A minute later, he returned to sit down next to me. We clinked glasses.

"*Salut,*" he growled.

I waited until he'd taken a first taste. "What do you think?"

His eyes were shut, and I knew he was holding the liquor in his mouth. Then his Adam's apple bobbed. He opened his eyes and said, "Fabulous."

"You're just being polite; I can tell."

"It's not in my nature to be polite."

"Oh, come on, you're always saying pleasant, complimentary things."

"That's because I mean them, not because I'm being polite."

We both sipped more bourbon. I leaned back against the couch and gazed into space. A cozy, neither-here-nor-there kind of feeling swept over my body.

"Tell me what happened tonight." Ivan also relaxed back into the couch. Though he was very close to me, we weren't touching.

"I don't think you'd understand."

"You could try me."

"Have you noticed a black woman around the building who cleans a lot of apartments, plus she was helping me serve at my party Friday night?"

His brow furrowed. "Yes, I think I remember her."

"Her name's Mary, and she's my friend."

"That's, well, a surprise."

Defensive, I said, "She's unbelievably smart and funny. I really like her. She was only helping me at the party because—" I stopped talking. This was the moment of truth. If I really didn't believe in what the voice had told me, and if I thought Ivan was a good guy, then I could make a funny story of the whole thing. Or, I could be more circumspect. The final *or* was that I could be both funny and circumspect. If I simply told him the truth, there was a chance that he would drop his guard and be equally truthful with me. One of the best ways to get people to open up was to be completely honest with them. They were so disarmed by your apparent trust that they dropped all pretense. I read all this in a book, naturally, but the important thing was that I *remembered* it and was actually following the book's advice.

Brightly, with a sharp grin on my face, I said, "About two weeks ago, I heard a voice in my head. I mean, it sounded like a *real* voice."

Instead of looking at me like I was either insane or a stand-up comic, he said, "In Russia, we know of such things." He leaned forward and fastened his eyes to mine. Kind of rattled me, to tell the truth.

"You haven't heard what the voice *said,*" I teased him.

He kept staring at me.

Somehow, I felt reluctant to say the words the voice spoke. I took a gulp of bourbon. Finally, I continued, "The voice said, essentially, 'There will be a murder at the Kennedy in one month's time. Prevent it.' "

I peeked at Ivan, expecting the usual expression of *Huh?* Instead, I saw thunder.

He spoke in a loud voice, "A murder—here? That's absurd!"

Ivan gulped bourbon, as if to calm himself. I had to admit that his behavior was odd, reminding me suddenly of the way he'd reacted in the swimming pool when I asked him whether he knew the security guard, Lucas Bower. I edged away from him, wondering whether I ought to leave now, while the leaving was good.

Instead, I acted on a suddenly fierce hunger to know what was happening. "In the beginning, I thought it was true. That's why I became friendly with Mary. She was in the laundry room the morning after I heard the voice, and I ended up blurting it out to her. I had to tell someone, and neither my kids nor my ex-husband were likely candidates."

I stopped talking long enough to sip the last drop of bourbon in my glass and to steal a quick look at Ivan. His face was a mask of blandness, which didn't worry me. I couldn't see animosity in his expression.

Ivan reached over and took the glass out of my hand. "Allow me," he said.

"No more for me, thanks."

Suddenly his flirtatiousness returned. He leaned over and gave me a kiss on the mouth. I think he'd taken an advanced degree in the art of kissing. "Would you like a soda, or juice, or something else?" he whispered.

"Orange juice?"

He nodded and strode over to the kitchen entrance.

When he came back into the living room and handed me the glass, I immediately took a huge gulp. I'd decided what to say while he was getting it, and I was nervous.

"The thing is that Mary believed me—"

Ivan interrupted, "I do, too."

"And that's one of the reasons we became friends," I continued. "Plus, we decided to have the cocktail party so we could scope out possibilities for who might commit a murder."

Ivan made his now famous, to me anyway, eyebrow arch. His eyebrows looked like furry caterpillars hunching their way to the next lettuce leaf.

"And were you successful?" Ivan asked.

"What?"

"Were you successful at discovering who might be the alleged murderer?" His tone made it clear that he was being facetious.

"See, even you don't believe me—that's why I appreciated Mary's attitude."

He placated me. "Wherever it came from, the voice certainly matters, and it's telling you something important. Though I would be more interested in *why* I heard a voice in my head, not so much the content of *what* the voice actually said."

"Ummm." I picked up the glass of orange juice and drained it.

Ivan said, "What a thirsty girl." Then he leaned closer, put his arm around my shoulders, and kissed me hard. Despite all my other concerns, I sank into the kiss, loving the warmth of his lips. I found it impossible to believe that a man who kissed so beautifully could be dangerous.

Then he spoke again, with his lips close to mine. "You didn't tell me what happened with Mary."

"I went out to her house tonight—she was having a personal crisis, and I wanted to be there for her the way she'd been there for me. But we argued. I guess I didn't handle things very well."

My eyes filled with tears, which surprised me. "She threw me out of her house, and I should really be home in case she calls, or I might call her. In fact, that's exactly what I'll do—call her and apologize for not being more understanding."

My voice kept rattling on like I was on speed. My head lolled suddenly and dramatically to the side, which I found humiliating. I straightened it quickly, hoping he hadn't noticed. "I really must call her immediately. I'm very worried that she's going to do something indiscreet. Of course, you know, that's exactly what she's been doing for a while now—being indiscreet, that is. She's a loving woman and she's been hurt, though she refuses to admit it."

Ivan's head nodded up and down with total understanding. The only trouble was that when his head came down, his head also remained up, so that pretty soon he had several heads bobbing all over the place. It was a little disconcerting.

I continued talking, undeterred. "I'm going to help her prepare for her high school equivalency exam. When she passes, she'll be a lot stronger and in a better position to figure out whether she wishes to remain in her marriage; plus, of course, she'll get a job of some sort. I'm not sure what would suit her, but that's her decision anyway. I just want to be a source of support and encouragement. So that's why I really must go back to my apartment—"

Ivan interrupted, his face still drifting all over the place. "I'm sorry, Anne, but you're not going anywhere."

21

I woke up lying in Ivan's bed, tucked under the down comforter as if I were a little girl. My eyes opened and, for a few seconds, I pretended that I was five years old and it was Christmas morning. The sick feeling of excitement at opening all the presents under the tree swamped me. Then the sick feeling became real and I was about to puke all over the bed. I threw off the covers and ran to the bathroom, where I retched into the toilet. Nothing came up, so I didn't exactly feel better. After I peed, I tore back to the kitchen and rummaged around until I found a can of soda in a lower cupboard. I took a few tentative sips, and held on to the countertop to keep from toppling over.

In a minute, I felt so much better that I drank half the can down in long gulps. Since Ivan had left me a message by the coffeemaker before, I looked there. Nothing.

I walked slowly back into the main room. There were no messages for me anywhere. In addition, I noticed that all the phones had been taken away. I was such a fool not to have a cell phone like the rest of the human race. The alarm clock next to his bed said three o'clock. That would be three o'clock in the morning, judging by how dark it was. I ran to the door into his apartment and tried to open it. Nothing. Somehow he'd locked it from the other side. When I crossed back to the windows and looked outside, I immediately knew that I couldn't jump from the fourth floor, especially since the land fell away on this side of the building, so it was a far greater distance than four floors anyway. I tried to open every window, but they were nailed shut.

I needed a hammer.

Systematically, I began to search through all the drawers in the kitchen, bathroom, closet, and bureau. No hammer, no knives, nothing with any strength that could be used as a tool. I felt the panic begin to rise inside my body, so I took the rest of the soda and sat down on the couch. I breathed deeply. I told myself to remember all the miraculous stories of people's survival in bad situations, much worse ones than this. I told myself that if Ivan had planned to kill me, he would have done so already. I told myself that dying wasn't so bad. I could live with dying.

Trouble was, I didn't want to die. I tried the old "pray to God" stuff, but I felt too guilty. It seemed totally wrong to ask for help now, when I'd never believed in God and had never offered my help in return. I gulped soda and tried to rev myself up for a prayer. I knew it wasn't a good time to get hung up on moral questions concerning the existence, or nonexistence, of God. *Just throw yourself on his mercy. Explain you've been foolish. Take the blame. Then ask God to save you.*

I still couldn't do it.

I prowled around the kitchen and bathroom, returning to the main room of the apartment and searching for some way to either escape or call for help. Finally, it occurred to me that I could take one of Ivan's shoes and break a window. I pulled on a thick sweatshirt and allowed the sleeve to hang down over my hand, where I grasped it and made a fist around the shoe. The glass shattered in a great splatter, but the sweatshirt protected me. Quickly, I broke every pane of glass. I dropped the shoe and yanked up the sleeves of the sweatshirt so that I could detach the screen. I pushed it out and watched it float down, down, down, through the dark trees to the ground far below.

I couldn't climb out the window, because the wooden frames for the panes of glass were still in place. I picked up the shoe and tried to break the frames, but only a few chips of wood flew off. If I had hours, I might be able to keep at it, but I wasn't sure that I did have hours. Quickly, I ran to the bed and pulled off the white pillowcase from one of the pillows. Whoops, mistake. I put the pillow *back* into the pillowcase and shoved the whole pillow through one of the window squares. By pushing and pushing, inch by inch, I got the pillow outside. Using the tails of the pillowcase, I tied it to the window.

Now, once daylight came, when someone looked at this side of the building, they'd see a huge white pillow hanging there. I hoped it would look like a cry for help, but as I surveyed my handiwork, I had to admit it probably looked more like someone was airing out their bedding.

So I leaned as close against the window as I could, cuppled my hands around my mouth, and yelled, "Help me, please help me!" The wind carried my words away, as if I'd only whispered. In addition, I knew that it was too cold for anyone to have their windows open, and the Kennedy had been built so thick and fortresslike that my voice would never be heard in the building. They had no intercom system, and I knew that even loud music didn't carry from apartment to apartment. Blame the solid building construction of the olden days.

I sat on the couch again and tried to think, though first I had to control the despair that rose inside me like great waves in the ocean. I didn't seem capable of stopping the waves as they tumbled and tossed, huge and scary, along the beach of my mind. *So, okay,* I said to myself. *You've got massive waves and they're going to drown you. You have to surf.*

In my imagination, I pretended that I was in a sexy bikini and I was paddling out to sea lying on a surfboard. The sun shone from the sky. I turned the surfboard and waited for the perfect wave. I, who had never surfed in my life, except bodysurfing on Rehobeth

Beach, caught one glorious wave, the *perfect* wave, as surfers say, and I stood on the surfboard, my arms outstretched, my body poised and balanced. And I surfed that wave right into shore.

Phew. I actually felt better. The panic was gone, and my mind was like a clear stream of water. In fact, it was so clear that I got a clear idea.

I would use my mind to save me.

Taking a few deep breaths, I folded my legs up under me as if I were Gandhi doing his daily meditation. I'd never meditated, but since I'd also never surfed, I didn't let that stop me. I knew the general principles. Watch the breath, empty the mind, move into la-la land. It quickly became apparent to me that I was gifted at meditating. Unlike the complaints of people who can never quiet their minds, I went totally still. I became aware of the darkness behind my closed eyelids. I watched the darkness and saw nothing. I listened to my breath. My hands, folded in my lap, went numb. I felt myself swimming into the darkness, as if it were a long tunnel on an amusement-park ride.

I wasn't afraid. I wasn't anything. I was in la-la land. Part of me never wanted to return to real life. But I forced myself, not to return exactly, but to do what I'd come to do.

I sent a message to Mary.

Mary, please help me. I am locked in Ivan's apartment. I think I'm in great danger. Mary, Mary, Mary. Help, help, help.

I repeated the words over and over again in my mind. I couldn't seem to stop. I knew it was irrational to expect that Mary, who had plenty of heartbreak on her own mind, and who, in addition, was furious with me, would actually hear me. But that wasn't how it *felt*. It felt like I found a connection to her. It felt like she heard me.

Finally, exhausted, I stopped. My eyes opened slowly. I rubbed my hands together and took several deep breaths. I felt light-headed and peculiar. Tentatively, I stood up and shambled into the kitchen. I found a loaf of bread, deli ham, mayo, and mustard in the refrigerator. Quickly, I slapped together a makeshift sandwich, which I crammed into my mouth while still standing in the kitchen. When I was finished, I filled a glass with ice water and gulped it down.

Admittedly, it seemed strange that I could be so voraciously hungry when I was about to be murdered. I climbed into Ivan's bed, somehow ashamed that I found it so comfy. Apparently, a down comforter exudes safety and coziness no matter what the circumstances. I was sleepy again, which surprised me, until I figured that my extreme sensitivity to narcotics probably meant that I would take twice as long to fully get the drug out of my system. As I drifted toward sleep, my mind reverted to the familiar mantra.

Mary, Mary, Mary. Help, help, help.

Everything was in deep darkness. I flailed in the comforter, fighting its tangle of feathers and flannel. I felt as if I were drowning. I gasped and sucked in air. Then I woke up completely. I stared into the dark room and wondered who I was. When I'd remembered that I was Anne Johnson, I had to figure out where I was. That took longer.

At last, I knew. Ivan's apartment. I was a prisoner in Ivan's apartment. Cold air flew in an arc from the broken windowpanes, and I huddled into the comforter I'd been fighting just minutes before. Finally, I stood up and wrapped the comforter around me. I toddled over to the broken window and looked out at the dark sky. Headlights from cars and buses on Connecticut Avenue drifted through the trees. The wind had picked up, which was why the cold air was moving more forcibly into the apartment. I knew that there were no separate thermostats in the apartment, so there was nothing I could do to make it warmer. Then I remembered seeing a space heater in the bathroom. I dropped the comforter and ran to get it.

After turning on some lights, I plugged in the heater, turned it to high, and went in search of a warm wool sweater. Ivan being Ivan—that is, Russian—I found a humdinger of a sweater. I pulled on two pairs of wool socks and went to make a pot of coffee in the kitchen, where I saw that it was actually five o'clock in the morning. I was done with sleeping.

Once again, I roamed around the apartment, searching for any bright ideas. Could I beat the door down with a heavy ski boot? Dubious. But I might make such a racket that the next-door neighbors would complain. I poured myself a cup of coffee and drank some hurriedly. Then I grabbed the boot and began to bang. To be honest, it felt good. I really let the anger and fear flow through my body and into that boot. It seemed to me, at first, that it made a lot of noise. But as I continued, my certainty faltered, mostly because whenever I stopped and pressed my ear against the door, I heard nary a noise from the hallway. It seemed as if the sounds I was making with the boot were simply swallowed into oblivion. Finally, exhausted, I dropped the boot on the floor and went to finish the coffee.

I turned on the small television set and tried to concentrate on CNN's news, half expecting to discover that the city of Washington had been attacked by aliens, or Russians, for that matter. Instead, it appeared that even CNN was having trouble dredging up anything interesting or significant news-wise. Nervous, I kept glancing at the door into the apartment, hardly believing that Ivan had left me for so long. Surely he would return. Then he might kill me.

I had to think about the possibility.

So, that brought up the voice. *A murder will be committed in thirty days. Prevent it.* The voice was warning me. You *will be murdered in thirty days. Prevent it.* Maybe the voice meant *within* thirty days, not *on* day thirty.

Frustrated, I put down the coffee mug and turned off the television. I had to be prepared to protect myself when Ivan came in, and I figured the only "weapon" I had was surprise. Quickly, I moved around the apartment again, trying to figure out where I could hide. There was under the bed, in the closet, and lying in the bathtub. All pretty obvious. Then I stared at the couch and noticed that its back curved away from the wall under the windows, leaving a small space. I wiggled back there, testing. I fit! I squirmed out again and went looking for something I could use as a real weapon when, ultimately, he discovered me.

But, I thought, *but* . . .

He would come into the apartment. I imagined the door slamming behind him, and I willed myself not to panic. He would glance first into the kitchen. And that gave me an idea. I ran into the kitchen and saw, as I'd expected, that the refrigerator was the first appliance on the left-hand wall of the kitchen. When Ivan looked into the kitchen, he would assume that he'd see me. And, not seeing me, he would continue looking, first in and under the bed, then in the closet, finally in the bathroom.

Instead of hiding behind the couch, I would squeeze myself up on the countertop next to the refrigerator. *Blocked* by the refrigerator. Then I would wait patiently until he went into the bathroom. At which point, I would hop down and tear out of the apartment. I experimented by climbing onto the countertop and making myself into a tiny, tiny package. Of course, I couldn't test whether or not he could see me, but I leaned forward tentatively and tried to assess what his line of sight would be. I was about 90 percent sure that he wouldn't see me.

It was, I decided, a risk I'd have to take.

I also didn't know when he'd return. I wouldn't be able to

crouch into a small bundle for hours and hours. Still, it had already been about six hours since he'd been in the apartment. I thought it was likely that he'd be back sooner rather than later.

I ran to the bathroom for a final pee, furious with myself for indulging in that big mug of coffee. I stuffed toilet paper in my underpants, figuring I could always go in my pants if I needed to. I wasn't too crazy about the idea, obviously, but I also thought it would be stupid to get killed just because I needed to urinate so badly that I'd run to the toilet at exactly the moment when Ivan returned. I fiddled with the bathroom door, trying to figure out if there was some way to block it as he opened it, just to buy me time, but of course if I did that, I couldn't get out myself. Giving up, I ran back into the main room, where I turned off all the lights. I left the lights on in the kitchen. He'd assume that he was seeing the kitchen completely, simply because the lights were on when the rest of the apartment was in the day's shadow.

I stripped off my extra clothing to make myself smaller, including the big wool socks. The kitchen, because it had no windows and was in the front of the apartment, was warmer, but the space heater was also doing a good job of keeping the whole place at a reasonable temperature. Finally, I climbed up to my spot again. I took a few minutes to try various positions, looking for comfort as well as compactness. Then I settled in. I put my head down on my knees and I tried to meditate.

I went into la-la land pretty quickly until, yup, I fell asleep. I woke with a start because I heard a key turning in the door's lock. My stomach clenched and I had to speak sternly to myself. *You can do this. Just stay calm. Wait. When he's had time to check under the bed, then the closet, he will open the bathroom door.* My panic spoke next. *What if he locks the door behind him?* I answered, *He can't, because he's inside the apartment. The door will open for you.*

The door squeaked loudly as it opened. I heard him breathing.

It was as if I could see him as he turned his head to look into the kitchen. He didn't say a word, which I took as a good sign. He figured I was asleep on the bed.

His feet clumped into the main room. He was a heavy man, and suddenly, I was damn glad. I could hear him move. He switched on a light, which shone slightly into the small entrance hall. I figured it was midmorning by now. I imagined him pulling the down comforter around, searching for me. His footsteps marched to the closet. Door handle turned. I waited. My heart thumped painfully, as if it would explode out of my chest. I heard the final door handle turn, the bathroom.

I jumped off the counter and my legs folded beneath me. My fingertips touched the floor, balancing me, and I straightened and ran for the door. I wrenched it open and flew through. Though my legs continued to tremble, I wobbled down the long hallway. I'd forgotten to try to figure out what to do at this juncture. Should I pound on people's doors? Should I keep running?

I kept running. I didn't dare turn around and look to see if he was coming. I thought of the elevator. I thought of the stairs. He could catch me on the stairs. He could catch me as I waited for the elevator. So I started to yell, while still running, and then I began to hammer on each apartment door as I ran. I screamed, "Help me, help me, help me!" at the top of my lungs. For what seemed like a long time, nothing happened. I turned the corner to where the elevator was. I pushed the button and also pounded on the apartment door there.

I kept screaming and yelling as loudly as I could.

Nothing happened, except that I heard pounding footsteps running down the hall. Heavy, clumping feet.

I jabbed my finger on the elevator button, then turned to the apartment door again. With both hands clenched into fists, I slaughtered that door. It flew open just as the footsteps ran around the corner. A middle-aged woman I'd seen in the fitness room stood in the open doorway of her apartment, her face frozen with terror as I literally fell on top of her. "Call the police, call the police!"

From behind me, I heard a voice. At first, I honestly thought I was hallucinating.

Mary said, "It's me, Anne. Don't be afraid. It's Mary!"

I swallowed. The fear tasted so terrible, like the worst bile or rancid meat. Saliva filled my mouth, and I had an insane desire to spit and spit and spit. I turned around.

The most beautiful sight in the world, I thought. Glorious Mary, huge and strong and panting.

She took a tentative step forward, one hand held out to reassure me.

"You're safe," she said.

I turned back to the woman standing in the doorway of her apartment, with whom I appeared to be entangled. "I'm sorry." I moved backward. "I've been locked up in an apartment at the end of the hall—"

Mary interrupted, "I don't know *where* Ivan is, but I think it's time to call the police."

The woman flushed. "You mean Ivan, the Russian guy?"

I nodded.

"He's so cute." She hesitated. "Has he done something wrong?"

"The short answer must be yes," I said. I looked at Mary with a million questions in my expression. "How did you get a key to his apartment?"

"Housekeepers have their special ways." She grinned.

The woman took a step backward. "What should I do if I see him?"

I said, "Go in the opposite direction and call Michael in the management—"

Mary interrupted, "Call the police, not the management." She grabbed my arm. "Come on, I'll explain at your place. I don't like standing around in this hallway."

The woman slammed the door, and we heard several locks turning. Then her voice: "Leave me out of your love problems. You people are ridiculous!"

The elevator signal gave its dinging sound, and the doors opened. If Mary had been Ivan after all, and I'd been waiting for this slow elevator system to save me, I'd be dead. We hopped on and pressed nine. I leaned sideways until my head actually rested on Mary's shoulder. She didn't seem to mind. She just clucked her tongue and murmured, "Poor baby." I might have started to cry except I was still too scared. I felt in my pants pocket and fished out the key to my apartment.

The minute I opened the door, I knew Ivan had been there. Ivan, or someone. I stopped walking and Mary plowed into me. "Did you come in here?" I asked.

"I came to look for you here first."

"I can tell someone's been inside."

Mary walked around me and switched on the chandelier in the entrance.

When I moved into the living room, I grabbed the phone. No dial tone. "Check whether it's connected to the wall," I said to Mary.

She picked up the line and followed it. "Yeah, it's connected."

"When did you come looking for me?" I yelled, rushing into other rooms in search of dial tones on other phones. Everything was dead.

"About half an hour ago."

"He must have disconnected the telephone service where it comes into the building in the basement."

"We can't call from the management office," Mary said, "and the doorman won't understand why we're bothering him for the police when we ought to go to management."

"Don't you have your cell phone?"

She gave me a hard look and said only, "No."

I decided not to pursue the subject.

"Why can't we go down to management?"

"Something fishy—I didn't like how that Michael handled me when I was worried about you. I don't trust him."

Suddenly I whirled around. "I didn't shut the door—"

Ivan stood in the open door to my apartment, with a very tiny revolver pointed at my chest. He slammed the door shut behind him using one foot. He was smiling, and even though I was chilled through by the sight of him, I could still see his charm. Which really made me pissed off at myself.

He shook his head slowly, as if to express his disbelief at our stupidity. "Ladies, had you simply minded your own business, there would have been no problems."

Suddenly, with stunning speed, Mary's arm shot out and walloped me so hard that I fell to the ground. She dove on top of me. Ivan ran toward us, but didn't fire the gun.

"Shit, I wanted him to shoot so someone would hear," Mary muttered in my ear.

"I . . . can't . . . breathe." I couldn't breathe for two reasons. The first was because her full weight was crushing my lungs, and the second was because, at the same time, I had the insane desire to laugh. Even in a situation as dire as this—and I have to say the situation was pretty bad—Mary could make me laugh. It gave me hope, though it also made me think that I might die laughing. I wasn't sure whether that would make dying more or less acceptable. I felt a tremor from her body, and I knew that she, too, was fighting the urge to laugh.

She rolled off me and something happened. Maybe it was the fear. Maybe it was the absurdity of seeing her lying on her back on my living room floor, and maybe, too, it was Ivan's face as he stared down at us. I could see right up his hairy nostrils. Suffice it to say, I started to laugh, and, at the same moment, Mary also gasped with laughter.

Ivan's look of incredulity, spreading over his face, which we were viewing upside down, made him appear to be laughing, too. I mean, okay, this was utterly ridiculous. But it felt so good. And, secretly, even as I laughed, I knew that this was our weapon. Our fabulous, unusual, extraordinary, beautiful, surprise weapon. So much more original than a gun or a knife or even an ax.

We roared with laughter.

I poked Mary in the ribs with my elbow. And then I yelled, "One, two, three!" At *three,* we both kicked our legs directly into the superb groin (just ask me; I oughta know) of the Russian stud man, Ivan. I knew Mary's kick was far superior to mine. I was more than willing to give her full credit. Delighted to, in fact. But I got him, too.

I could now attest that kicking a man in his genitals was a heavenly experience. Not that I'd recommend it all the time, of course. Naturally, I hated violence, but if a moment should come in a woman's life where it was entirely okay to attack a man by kicking him in the groin, then I recommended it.

Ivan dropped the revolver and it fell onto Mary's stomach,

where it disappeared for a few seconds. I saw her hand delve into her clothing and emerge holding the gun. Meanwhile, Ivan was a basket case. What a wimp. He clutched his jewels as though we'd tried to rob him. This observation would end up being quite prescient of me, actually. His mouth was curled into a long snout, from which emerged small shrieks of agony. I jumped to my feet and threw my body at him, in an effort to topple him backward.

This was one of the more foolish moves I made. The man was *built,* and despite his shock and pain, he didn't even wobble. I turned and stretched out my hand to Mary, quickly helping to haul her to her feet. She pointed the revolver at Ivan with admirable calm.

Then she said, "You're under arrest."

I whipped my head around and stared at her. "You can't arrest—"

"Citizen's arrest." Her eyes narrowed to slits, and when you have eyes as big as lollipops, that was pretty impressive.

I nodded virtuously. "Oh, that's right, *citizen's arrest*."

It was clear that Ivan was beginning to recover slightly. "What are you talking about?" he growled. "You're not the police."

"In the United States of America, a citizen can arrest someone," Mary said authoritatively.

I shot her a quick look, since I wasn't absolutely sure about this citizen's-arrest thing. I thought it used to be true, but maybe that was just the kind of police lore that we picked up from television shows.

However, it seemed to impress the hell out of Ivan. He looked genuinely terrified.

"Turn around," she ordered. "We're going to Miss Dora's apartment."

"Mary, why don't we just go downstairs?"

She hissed, "Because Michael's in on it, and maybe the doorman, too."

"You're a very smart woman," Ivan said as he turned so that his back was to us.

"What about me?" I piped up. Not one of my finer moments.

"Intelligent, in your way, but you have a little problem with sex."

"I beg your pardon?"

Mary poked Ivan in the small of his back. "Walk forward. I will not hesitate to fire this gun if you try anything at all."

"She means it," I said. Then, "What's my problem with sex?"

"You let your desire get in the way."

I snapped, "That's called *passion*."

"Can you guys have this discussion another time?" Mary said. "Jesus."

"If you would wait just a moment," Ivan said, "I would like to offer you a cut."

Mary said, "A cut of what?"

"A cut of the proceeds of the business we've got going."

We were walking slowly and carefully through the living room. "What kind of business?" I said.

He swung his head around to look at us, and Mary rammed the gun into his back. I could see from the expression on his face that he believed she would shoot it. "Are you truly interested? If so, you have to prove it by letting us all sit down, perhaps have a martini, and discuss the possibilities."

"Oh, right," Mary said sarcastically.

I put a hand on Mary's arm to stop her.

"I'm interested," I said. "Just spit it out, though."

"What the—" Mary said.

I whispered, "We need proof."

Luckily, Ivan didn't hear me.

Mary nodded, understanding, then mouthed, *Be quick.*

Ivan said, "I import uncut diamonds from Russia. Very lucrative."

"Did the red dots tell you when a delivery was due?"

He turned all the way around, clearly astonished. "You knew about that, too?" He grinned. "That voice of yours is impressive."

"You told *him* about the voice?" Mary said.

"The investigation was heating up," I explained.

She rolled her eyes at me. I knew she had a point, but it was too late to worry about now.

Ivan noticed Mary's impatience. He said, "Yeah, they told me when a delivery was scheduled."

"And you unloaded through the wardrobe in the laundry room?"

His eyes opened wider and then blinked.

"Where are the diamonds?" I demanded.

"Delivery in two days." He smiled suggestively and looked directly at Mary. "I could arrange for a payment to you of one hundred thousand dollars. What do you say?"

Her answer was a hard poke in his back with the revolver. "Let's go."

We reached the doorway to my apartment. After we passed through, I shut and locked the door behind me. Then I pushed the down button on the elevator. "What if someone's on it?" I said.

"Perfect," Mary said. "We tell them to go to their apartment and call nine-one-one."

"I'm not sure Miss Dora is going to be able to deal with this," I said.

The elevator doors opened to an empty cab. We stepped on and I pushed the button for the second floor.

Mary snorted. "Actually, I think she'll be terrific." To Ivan, she ordered, "Stand facing the back. Don't make a move."

The elevator began its creaking descent.

I said to Mary, in a low voice, "So what happened about Jerome?"

"I don't believe you're bringing that up now!" Mary said.

"I know." I sighed, truly meaning the sigh *and* the words that followed. "I'm hopeless."

Mary spoke quietly. "Nothing happened. You were a positive influence, even though I didn't want to admit it at the time."

That certainly made me feel good.

Ivan said, "Who's Jerome? Does this have something to do with your argument?"

The man was really impossible. A gun was jammed into his back, and in approximately five minutes we'd be calling the police, but still, he was trying to get in on the gossip.

Neither Mary nor I answered. I could tell the silent treatment was definitely right on, because the muscles in his back twitched, and his hands opened and closed into fists.

We stepped off the elevator on the fourth floor. Mary said, "Turn right, then left. She's number two-oh-five."

When we were in front of her apartment, I knocked loudly. No answer.

Mary said, "You'd better pound the shit out of that door—poor lamb can't hear much."

"Is this the old lady who had the flashing lights all over that walking thing?" Ivan's voice was incredulous.

"The very same," I said.

Miss Dora opened the door and stared at us.

I gave a little wave and said, "Hi."

Her mouth dropped open.

From behind me, Mary bellowed. "Can we come in? We have to call the police!"

Clutching her cane, she backed up enough to allow us to enter. We all trooped past her. It was obvious when she saw the gun, because she let out a small shriek, raised her cane, and crashed it down on Ivan's arm.

"Hey!" he yelped, grabbing the injured arm with its opposite.

"I knew you were no damn good!" She followed us into her living room.

Mary barked, "Call the police, Anne!"

"You can't call the police from here," Miss Dora yelled.

My eyes darted around the room, ignoring what Miss Dora said. I spied an old-fashioned telephone with a round dial face. I dashed over and picked it up.

"I'm trying to tell you," Miss Dora said, "it went kaput this afternoon."

"Probably has to be digital or something," Ivan said helpfully.

"It's fifty years old—it just gave up the ghost," she said.

"If only you had your cell!" I said, frustrated.

"I was feeling a little fragile," she said, opening her eyes wide at me. "*You* know. . . ."

"Oh, right."

"I've got my cell," Ivan said sweetly.

"Anne, get his cell out of his pocket," Mary said.

"It's not in my pocket," he said.

"Where is it?" Mary pointed the gun straight at his heart.

Miss Dora said, "Don't go near him—he's not safe!"

Exasperated, Mary said, "This is absurd."

"Give me a few minutes," Miss Dora said. "I'll go down to that nice Michael in the management office."

Mary and I yelled in unison, "No!"

"But . . ." Miss Dora began her tedious walk toward the door into her apartment.

"He's in on it," I explained.

"I don't believe that!" she said.

"Believe it, baby," Ivan said.

"You're talking like an idiot," I said to him.

He smiled. "I'm trying to be an American gangster type."

"Okay," I said to Mary, "I'll leave the building and call from a pay phone."

As I headed for the door, I said, "Will you be all right?"

Miss Dora screamed, "Take a quarter! There's a pile in a dish by the door!"

Good advice. I grabbed a handful. Just as I ran out the door, I heard Ivan say to Miss Dora, "That's a beautiful diamond ring you're wearing."

As I got on the elevator, it occurred to me that I should descend all the way to the parking garage and exit down there, since Ivan had implied that both Michael and the doorman could be part of whatever was going on. The elevator, even pokier than usual, allowed me time to think. I stepped off on the lower level and abruptly veered toward the laundry room instead of heading out the garage. I was sure that the diamonds *had* arrived, because otherwise Ivan wouldn't have kept me locked in his apartment, and without evidence, I knew the police wouldn't be able to prove any criminal activity.

I was leaving Mary in a rather delicate situation upstairs, and she'd have killed me if she'd known I wasn't hightailing it out to a pay phone, but I figured a five-minute search wasn't going to endanger their lives. Mary had the gun, and no one was going to get it away from her. Not Mary. No way.

I circled the laundry room and revisited the back wall behind the clothesline, where I plunged into the wardrobe, knelt, and quickly unlatched its back. It rose slowly, as usual, and I impatiently ducked under to emerge into the garage. Nothing at all unusual. I returned the way I'd come and saw that two dryers at the very end of one row had big signs posted: OUT OF ORDER!!!!

I could understand OUT OF ORDER, and even the capital letters, but the exclamation points, four of them, were overkill. I dashed to the dryers and pulled off the duct tape that sealed the doors shut. Inside, I found the entire dryer drum filled with brown burlap bags. After some tricky fiddling, I managed to untie one of the bags. I gasped.

Diamonds tumbled through my fingers. They were uncut and unpolished, quite different from how I usually imagined diamonds. I picked up a single diamond and stared at it for a moment. I harbored unwomanly feelings about diamonds. As I'd mentioned before, I kept my massive diamond ring in a safety-deposit box. I couldn't remember the last time I'd actually worn it. I knew I wasn't in good company on this one; most women loved diamonds. But for me, they were too crisp and sharp, like harsh words in an argument.

Obviously, Ivan had lied about expecting a delivery in two days. Perhaps the red dots meant two dryers. It seemed like a red herring at this point, but even so, I didn't know what to do. I was scared to leave them for fear Michael might come down and clear them out just while I was calling the police. So, I grabbed one of the bags, slammed the dryer door shut, and attempted to reseal the duct tape. It definitely looked like it had been tampered with, but I could only hope it didn't matter.

I started to trot through the parking garage, the burlap bag hanging from one hand.

"Hey, Ms. Johnson, what's happening?" shouted the parking attendant.

I'd forgotten there would be someone on duty. I swung the bag up to my chest and wrapped both arms around it, trying to conceal it as best I could.

"Hi, Danny!" I yelled. Then I broke into a run, heading up the ramp into the late-morning daylight.

"It's raining!" he shouted. "You need an umbrella and a coat!"

I heard his footsteps pounding after me.

They were all in on it, I thought. I wasn't surprised. If both dryers were filled with diamonds, that was going to be worth a lot of money.

I ran faster, trying not to let him catch up with me, though I knew Danny was young and probably much faster than me. I also knew that I couldn't let him stop me. We exploded out from the garage entrance, and the rain was like buckets of water suddenly crashing down on my head. I took a quick look behind and saw that Danny was right at my heels, waving the umbrella wildly. He was going to kill me; that was obvious. I released the bag from where I was clutching it next to my chest, allowed it one full swing, then whirled around and smashed the bag of diamonds into Danny's face.

He let out an unearthly scream, much louder and more dramatic than I expected. It made me a little queasy, actually. For a moment, I almost asked him whether he was all right. He'd doubled over and dropped the umbrella. I turned, still clutching the bag, and ran up the driveway, straight into the path of a huge SUV, its windshield wipers frantically swishing back and forth, and the headlights beaming so brightly into my eyes that I was momentarily blinded. I dashed like a scared rabbit to the side of the driveway, but there was very little space, and I realized that though I'd managed to just squeeze out of the way, I'd left Danny bent over double, injured and incapable of escaping. Even if Danny *was* a diamond smuggler, I didn't particularly relish the idea of his being run over and flattened by this huge black vehicle.

Needless to say, I wasn't thinking very clearly. No one else, given what had been happening over the last twenty-four hours, would have been in their right mind either, so I'm not going to apologize for what I did next.

I leaped toward the passenger side of the SUV and pounded on the window. Luckily, there was a passenger, a lovely child, who looked about six years old. She turned and stared at me in horror, her red mouth open and her tongue curling around perfect white teeth. It was amazing what you noticed when time stopped. I saw her mouth become a dark cavern, and I knew she was yelling.

The SUV screeched to a terrifying halt four feet beyond me. I closed my eyes briefly, trying not to fully visualize Danny's smashed body. I ran around to the front of the car and saw him standing upright, staring in shock at the SUV, which had stopped exactly one foot away from him. He was again holding the umbrella.

"Ms. Johnson," he whined plaintively. "Why'd you hit me like that?"

"I thought you were part of the gang hiding stolen diamonds in the laundry room," I said.

"What?"

"You're not?"

Suddenly his legs folded beneath him and he collapsed to the ground. The driver of the SUV got out and rushed around the front of the car.

Danny whispered, "I wondered if something fishy was going on, but Michael said not to worry about it."

"That's because he's in on it."

The driver held out his cell phone. "Are you all right? Should I call an ambulance?" He spoke English with a French accent.

"I'm fine," Danny said. "Just give me a second to stop shaking."

I literally grabbed the cell phone out of the man's hand. "I'm calling the police."

He said, "I wasn't speeding, and Danny says he's okay—"

I interrupted, "Something much more serious—I was on my way to a pay phone."

I hit 911, got the police, and explained as coherently as I could what was going on. They told me to stay in the parking garage, so I wouldn't alert Michael or the doorman. They'd send the police in unmarked cars. The SUV followed Danny and me as we trailed into the garage. I was so drenched that water poured down the tip of my nose like I was a faucet that couldn't be turned off.

"I'm sorry, Danny," I said for the tenth time.

The owner of the SUV parked and then walked over, holding the hand of the little girl. We introduced ourselves all around, which was when I found out that the girl's name was Annie. Since she still seemed frozen with an expression of terror, I tried to ease things. I bent over and shook her hand. "My name is Anne, too." Her eyes opened even wider, which I had trouble interpreting.

I glanced at the man, Paul, who had introduced himself minutes before. "I think she believes I'm some kind of monster."

"Annie is visiting me from France." He smiled. "She understands virtually no English."

Okay, so despite *everything* that had happened, and promised to happen in the future, having to do with police, guns, danger, and hot sex with a Russian diamond smuggler, I immediately wondered if he was her father (in which case he'd have to be divorced, since he'd used the pronoun *me*) or her grandfather (in which case he'd have to be divorced or widowed, since he'd used the pronoun *me*). He was gorgeous in that older-man-with-a-mane-of-gray-hair-and-powerful-physique way that made me immediately imagine being tossed around in bed. By him.

I wasn't at my best, obviously. I was soaking wet, which plastered my adorable short hair to my head and made me look like an old boy, a paradoxical concept that didn't end up making me adorable at all. Using the sleeve of my shirt, I swiped at my nose.

Paul held out a handkerchief. "Please," he said kindly.

It smelled like him.

Perhaps love couldn't happen like that. Perhaps love had nothing to do with the scent on his handkerchief, which, after all, might not *really* smell anything like its owner. Cotton had a distinctive smell in its own right, and the detergent in which the handkerchief was washed had a distinctive smell. All of this could mean that I'd fallen in love with a smell, not the owner of the smell.

Either way, I was filled with the horror of extreme desire. Not like Ivan, whose body was desired by my body. Of course, my body was certainly signaling complete interest in Paul, and my mind had registered his charming French accent, which made me jump to scenarios of his extraordinary wine collection, a summer home in Provence, and his charm, but this was somehow different. He smelled right.

I mopped at my face with the handkerchief, then debated returning it.

"It's yours," he said.

"Thank you." I peeked into his face. His eyes were kind and warm, but also deeply amused. "What's so funny?" I blurted out.

"You."

Danny chimed in, "You *do* look funny."

"Well, that doesn't make sense."

Paul said, "Why not?"

So I told them what had happened to me over the last twenty-four hours. When I got to the part where Mary and I were on the floor, laughing hysterically, Paul burst out with a loud guffaw that sounded more like the hoot of an owl than a normal human laugh. I stared at him (well, actually, I'd been staring at him pretty much nonstop, but I focused even more intensely on his face). "Wait'll you hear what happens next," I said.

He leaned forward, bending to get his face and upper body close to me. I wanted to step against his body, to be folded into the shape of him. I didn't, of course, but I bent closer to him, too. "We smashed his jewels to smithereens," I announced triumphantly.

He recoiled. I realized later that men instinctively took the side of a man whose jewels had been clobbered. They couldn't help it. Instantaneous horror eclipsed their ability to be rational. Women had nothing comparable, so they had to be especially understanding on this issue. Why had I sounded so gleeful as I told the story? Decidedly insensitive. Obviously, I often behaved as if I had a death wish. Or a murder wish, to be more apropos.

A murder will be committed in thirty days. Prevent it.

How many deaths does it take to be born, do you suppose? How about an even dozen? Would that do the trick?

"He was dangerous," I said in my defense.

"*Mais oui,*" he muttered, grasping Annie's hand even more tightly. "I wonder if we can go upstairs now."

"The police said to wait until they came down," I said. Then, as if it were all my fault, "I'm sorry to inconvenience you."

Distantly, he nodded.

"I could call up to Sally at the reception desk," Danny said.

"Yeah, go ahead," I said to Danny.

Suddenly, as I watched Paul walk away deliberately, I didn't care. I didn't care whether I should or shouldn't do this or that. And in the not caring I thought of something. I hadn't had time to really wonder *why* Mary had been so determined to find me. How had she known that I was in danger? I might have been out shopping, at the library, or doing any number of other activities.

I knew, suddenly, that she'd heard my voice calling to her. She heard me!

Spontaneously, in my mind, I said, *Paul, turn around and come back to me.*

I was astounded when he didn't turn around. I truly believed he would hear me and do as I demanded. Height of insanity, I knew that, yet the events of the last three weeks had convinced me of my own, well, *power.* The voice had spoken in my head. The voice had grabbed me by the scruff of my neck, as if it were the big mama cat and I a newborn kitten needing to be transported from one nest to another. The voice was my voice.

This time, my mind yelled. Not aggressively, I hasten to add.

Just a guttural yell. But the pièce de résistance was that I yelled, silently in my mind, in *French*.

Paul, viens ici.

Slowly, as if he didn't understand why, he turned. He walked toward me and he spoke. "*Quoi?*" he said.

"My name is Anne," I said even though we'd obviously already exchanged names.

We stared at each other. Then his unattached hand rose and moved through the air to land on my head. He tousled my hair hard. Back and forth, raking and smoothing, raking and smoothing, as if I were a child he was alternately punishing and rewarding, punishing and rewarding.

Finally, I ducked. "That's enough!"

"*Mignon,*" he said.

"That's what my fake French hairdresser said."

"I am not fake."

I said, "Do you have a significant other?"

He shook his head. "I do not."

"Would you like to come by my place tomorrow afternoon for tea?"

Paul said, "I have the pleasure of Annie for another three days."

"Please bring her—I'll make cookies."

"Thank you, that would be marvelous."

Only a Frenchman could say *marvelous* without sounding absurd.

Danny stuck his head out of the parking attendant's office. "They want you upstairs," he shouted.

As we marched to the elevator, I muttered, "I can't wait to try to explain why I kept returning to Ivan's apartment, despite all the warnings."

"Why *did* you?" Paul asked.

I gave him a look.

He grinned. "Oh—that."

"Yeah."

When we stepped off the elevator on the main floor, the entrance to the Kennedy swarmed with police. Paul, who was continuing on up to his eleventh-floor apartment (I wondered whether he had the penthouse, a truly exciting thought), said, "See you tomorrow afternoon, and *bon chance* with all of this."

I saw Ivan in handcuffs, with Michael next to him, also cuffed. I avoided looking them in the eye. Mary stood like a glorious statue about ten feet away from them, surrounded by three policemen, a man and two women. She waved, and in moments, I, too, was surrounded.

Eventually, we ended up in the leasing office of the Kennedy. The diamonds were emptied from the dryer drums. Michael and Ivan were carted off to jail, after which I returned the bag of diamonds and spent an hour giving my statement. I'd called Peter early on, and he came down as my attorney to sit through the interrogation with me, though obviously I'd done nothing wrong. When we were finally allowed to go, Mary was picked up by Jay.

She said, "I'm taking off tomorrow, but I'll call you first thing."

"I need to talk to you," I said.

Mary cocked her head, curious.

"I know what you should do when you grow up," I said.

"Cool." She grinned and headed for home.

Peter put an arm around me, urging me toward the elevator. "Are you feeling all right?" he asked solicitously.

I shrugged off the arm. "Never better," I said.

He looked hurt. "I'm pretty pissed off at you, and so are the kids."

"Uh-huh."

"We warned you about that guy."

"You did."

"You don't seem to care that your kids were frantic with worry."

We stepped off the elevator, and I opened the door to my apartment.

"How could they be worried when they didn't have any idea what was happening *when* it was happening?" I headed for the kitchen, where I opened the refrigerator and peered inside. "I need something to eat right away."

"How about I get some takeout?" Peter said.

I smiled. "That's a terrific suggestion. I'd like number fifty-one at Nam Viet."

"You always have that."

"That's because I love it."

Finally, we both smiled. When he was gone, I called Andrew and Laura to assure them that I was safe.

For some reason that I couldn't entirely fathom, I was euphorically happy. Though, really, I knew why. I'd saved my own life.

When Peter came back, I put the carryout containers directly on the dining room table, protected by thick hot pads. I'd set the table and given us both tall glasses of ice water. We were quiet as we ate, until I'd finally eaten enough for my mind and mouth to function.

"Phew—I think I was about to collapse with hunger," I said.

"Me, too, though you had more reason than I."

We gazed at each other, quiet.

"Tell me how your second session with Dr. Armstrong went," I said, hoping to deflect him from giving me more grief about Ivan.

"I may have been overreacting to that woman's death," Peter said.

I made a genuine effort not to give him the look I'd perfected during our twenty-five years of marriage, which said, *I told you so.*

"What about wanting to patch up our marriage?"

Peter grabbed the leftover trash from our takeout and headed into the kitchen. I gathered the remaining stuff and followed him.

"Okay, so I was overreacting on that issue, too." He opened the cabinet door under the sink and stuffed everything in, then stood aside so I could add my trash.

"You know what I think?" I said gently.

He cocked his head at me, the quintessential Peter gesture, the one I still enjoyed seeing. His never-ending curiosity.

"I believe you've fallen in love with that young woman you brought to my party."

His face flushed violently. "Why do you say that?"

"Because I really liked her, and I could just, I dunno, *imagine* you loving her."

I started rinsing the forks and plates, then loading them into the dishwasher.

"I'm terrified I'll hurt her the way I hurt you," Peter whispered.

And so the moment finally came. I leaned against the kitchen cabinets and took a deep breath. I said, "It wasn't all your fault."

"I hurt you," he repeated. "There's no excuse for that."

"You hurt me because I hurt you."

He stared at me.

"Have you ever wondered *why* you were unfaithful?"

"Yes." He shifted his weight, uncomfortable.

"Because I didn't love you enough."

He whispered, "Why didn't you?"

"Think."

A long silence; then he spoke tentatively. "Because you didn't love yourself enough?"

"You get first prize. It wasn't your fault. I didn't love you enough because I didn't think very highly of myself. I'm doing a lot better on that score." I grinned at him and shook my head, amazed at how good it felt to tell him the truth. "You won't hurt her—I don't know how I know it, but I do."

His eyes swam with tears. "Are you absolutely sure?"

"Yes, I am absolutely sure." I laughed. "The voice told me. It said, 'Just as you have changed and grown, so has he. He is capable of loving this woman with fidelity and passion both.' "

He looked excited. "Did you really hear a voice say that?"

I laughed harder. "That's for me to know."

Though it was only three o'clock in the afternoon after Peter left, I started to run a bath. I felt like I'd been hiking the Appalachian Trail for three months. I needed to get clean. When I sank into the steaming hot water, I let out a loud groan. I stared down at my body, partly obscured under the water, and I remembered making love with Ivan.

I had a choice. I could feel dirty and guilty about what I'd done. But it was hard, looking at myself, to get into that attitude. Wouldn't it, after all, take me backward, to when I hadn't loved myself enough? I splashed the water with the flat of my hands. *Slap, slap.* I grinned. I just couldn't do it. I'd enjoyed sex with Ivan, plain and simple. No guilt, thank you very much.

Restless, I kicked my legs. I wondered what to do when I got out of the bath. Nightgown? A waft around the apartment? My legs twitched and kicked so much that small waves rose over the sides of the porcelain bathtub and dribbled to the floor.

What should I do? I asked the voice in my head.

And the voice answered.

Manage the Kennedy.

"What?" I yelled, so thrilled at hearing the voice that I hadn't paid attention to the message.

You heard me.

I washed quickly, toweled off, and jumped into clean sweats. Then I ran to the computer. First, an e-mail to Peter.

> Dear Peter,
>
> I've had a great idea. Since Michael, the former manager of the Kennedy, is under arrest, they will need a new manager. I know your firm has done some work for the owners of the building, and I'd like to apply for the job. Can you put in a good word for me? Meanwhile, I'll write to them and make a formal application.
>
> Yours truly, Anne

Then I sent an e-mail to the owners. Ten minutes later, Peter called.

"You got it," he said.

"Really?"

"They want you to start next Monday. Can I negotiate the contract for you?"

"Sure."

"By the way, this was an inspired idea."

I thought, *Little do you know.*

We hung up and I dashed around the apartment, unable to contain my excitement. I tossed throw pillows into the air, switched on every light in the apartment, started both fires, turned the music up loud, and I danced.

25

The next day, I convinced Mary to meet me at an up-scale French restaurant in Bethesda, accessible by Metro. I wanted to treat her to lunch as a thank-you for coming to my rescue.

We both dressed up, and I'd never seen Mary look so glorious. She wore a bright red dress that clung to her curves, matched by red lips. She literally swept into the restaurant, and everyone stared with admiration. I felt a bit mouselike in comparison, though my bright, royal-blue dress really wasn't mouselike at all.

We ordered salads to start, then coq au vin.

I told her about becoming manager of the Kennedy.

She narrowed her eyes suspiciously. "How'd you get that idea?" she asked.

I grinned and danced my eyebrows up and down.

She exclaimed, "The Lord spoke to you!"

"Mary, it's *not* the Lord—how many times do I have to tell you?"

She huffed. "You believe what you want. Did the voice speak to you again?"

"You know it did."

Our iced teas and salads arrived. We took a break to sip the tea.

I said, "Did you talk to Jerome?"

She shook her head. "I've got to respect his wishes."

"So, are you going to give marriage counseling a chance?"

"Yeah, but don't gloat about it."

"I won't." Then I gloated, which involved a facial expression that made Mary laugh.

"Aren't you dying to know what I decided you should do when you grow up?" I said.

I speared a piece of lettuce and jammed it in my mouth. I'd never figured out how to eat salad in a ladylike fashion.

"Get my high school diploma," Mary said after she'd finished her first mouthful.

I pointed my fork at her. "I knew that's what you'd think! But, surprise, surprise, that's not it!"

Resigned, she shook her head. "I know I've got to do it."

"No, you don't—that is, not unless you really want to. I mean, if you're going to lie on your deathbed and lament the fact that you didn't get a high school diploma, then you should. But that's dumb—"

"Oh, thanks."

"You want me to express myself or not?"

"I guess."

"Seeing as how I've had the best idea *ever,* you're not being exactly *enthusiastic.*"

Mary straightened in her seat and said brightly, "What should I do when I grow up?"

"Be a detective."

She didn't react. Total blank.

I pointed my fork at her again. "Say something!"

"I can't think of anything to say." She ate more salad.

"You were fabulous with that gun and handling the situation with Ivan. Much better than I was."

She smiled politely. Finally, she said, "You need a high school diploma to become a detective."

"Nope—you can start at the bottom with a private investigating firm. I know something about this, because Peter's law firm uses their services all the time."

I saw the glimmer of interest. "I'd have to catch men and women doing what I was doing with Jacob." She laughed and shook her head.

"You have a huge advantage over other people, Mary."

She gave me a questioning look.

"You're intimidating—I told you that when we first started to get to know each other. You make people nervous, which is perfect."

Suddenly she pointed *her* fork at *me*. "This isn't a bad idea at all."

I was so excited that I pushed both hands through my hair, messing it up, though it was basically impossible to seriously mess up. "I think Peter could get your foot in the door."

"I've got big feet."

"Exactly, and anyway, you only need one foot, not both."

We spent the rest of the lunch reviewing the situation with Ivan, and I told her every last detail—few though they were—about Paul, the man coming to tea that afternoon.

When I got home, it was already three o'clock. I'd made chocolate-chip cookies in the morning, so I had time for a quick shower. I'd decided to get a little dressed up, since Paul had seen me only in my drowned-rat look. I wanted to do an absolutely-without-question-sexy look that afternoon. I chose a short black skirt, sheer black stockings, and high heels. On top, I wore a tiny cashmere sweater, the color of an emerald. I stood in front of the full-length mirror and messed up my hair aggressively. Not exactly teatime apparel, but I didn't care. This was the new Anne. *Watch out, world.*

Paul rang the doorbell promptly at six o'clock. He, too, had dressed up in a sport coat and tie. I gulped. Annie was bewitching in a beautiful dress that I immediately imagined to be Parisienne. I spoke to her in the little amount of French I knew, and she relaxed enough to let go of Paul's hand. Paul didn't say a word as I showed them around my apartment, and I started to get nervous by his silence.

Finally, when I'd poured the tea in the living room and given Annie a glass of milk and a plate of cookies, he spoke. "I am enchanted by your apartment."

I sat opposite him, aware of the slit in my black skirt and the length of my crossed legs. I felt so deliciously desirable. I felt as though I'd never been so marvelous. I felt like a Frenchwoman! Then I lifted the teacup to my lips and dumped the entire contents down the front of my sweater. "Oh, shit," I yelled, leaping up.

Paul burst out laughing. I ran to the kitchen, grabbed some dish towels, and began mopping myself. I looked up and saw Paul standing there. He was still laughing.

"This isn't funny!" I said, laughing myself. "I was trying to be sexy and debonair."

"I know." He took a step toward me.

"I was trying to be a *French*woman!"

He nodded. "Yes, yes."

Another step.

"But maybe you like American women?"

He took the dish towels from me and pulled me close.

"No," I said. "I'll get tea stains all over your beautiful jacket."

"Let's hope so," he murmured.

"Annie—"

"She's reading a storybook I brought along."

His face was close, but he wasn't kissing me yet. In a fit of anxiety, I blurted out, "I heard a voice in my head once. Actually, not that long ago. That's why I got into trouble with the Russian guy."

Paul kissed me, his mouth slightly open, two hands folded around my face. He said, "*Pas de problème*."

I knew enough French to understand.

Not a problem.

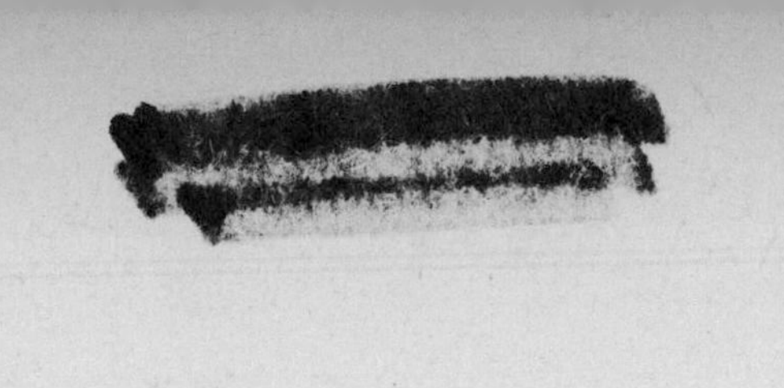